Bijapur

Tor Books by Kara Dalkey

BLOOD OF THE GODDESS
Goa
Bijapur

Bijapur

Blood of the Goddess
II

Kara Dalkey

TOR®

A Tom Doherty Associates Book
New York

BIJAPUR

Copyright © 1997 by Kara Dalkey

A Tor Book
Published by Tom Doherty Associates, Inc.
175 Fifth Avenue
New York, NY 10010

Tor Books on the World Wide Web:
http://www.tor.com

Tor® is a registered trademark of Tom Doherty Associates, Inc.

Library of Congress Cataloging-in-Publication Data

Dalkey, Kara
    Bijapur / Kara Dalkey.
        p.   cm. — (Blood of the goddess; v. 2)
    "A Tom Doherty Associates book."
    ISBN 0-312-86001-3
    I. Title.   II. Series: Dalkey, Kara Blood of
    the goddess; v. 2.
PS3554.A433B54   1997
813'.54—dc20   96-41695
                                                        CIP

First Edition: April 1997

Printed in the United States of America

0 9 8 7 6 5 4 3 2 1

Bijapur

PROLOGUE

What, you wish another story of me, traveller? Either you flatter my skill, or time weighs heavy on your hands.

Very well. Sit and I will tell you something of a Sufi tale. No, I myself am not a *sheykh*, nor count myself a wise man. I tell these tales to amuse. Yet, is it not wonderful if one gleans a grain of wisdom from a simple pastime? Rather like finding a ring of gold in the threadbare rug one has purchased cheaply in the bazaar.

So. Once there was a woman who had lost her family from misfortune and she found herself all alone in the world. But she was a woman of learning and intelligence and great curiosity. And she had heard of an amazing garden, in which grew a tree that bore the Golden Figs of Paradise. This tree, it was said, gave one who ate its fruit all the wisdom and knowledge one could ever want. Having no family, the woman could think of no better goal for her life than to seek out this marvelous tree.

She went to the wisest man she knew of, a dervish who lived in the forest. "O Great *Pir,*" she said to him, "I wish to find the tree that bears the Golden Figs of Paradise."

The sage nodded and said, "I know of this tree."

Joy filled the woman's heart. "Tell me, then, how I may find it!"

"Well," said the sage, "I could accept you as a disciple. But it would mean a long period of study before you would learn what you need to know."

The woman's hopes fell, for she knew her own restless nature. "Forgive me, wise one, but I do not think I am suited to such study."

The sage replied mildly, "No matter. If you wander the world with firm purpose of heart, you may find what you seek."

So the woman gave away what goods she had and became a pilgrim. She visited the tombs of saints and golden-domed mosques. She listened to many learned teachers. She spoke with rich and poor, suffered floods and drought, heat and cold, watched sunrises and sunsets, climbed mountains and crossed deserts. But she did not find the Golden Figs of Paradise.

Thirty years passed and, her hair now grey and her face weathered by sun and wind, the woman returned to her homeland. She went to the forest and found the wise man she had first spoken to . . . who seemed not to have aged at all.

"It must be that I am unworthy," she said to him, "for I never found what I sought. It is just as well that I did not become your student, for your time would have been wasted on me."

The sage only smiled and took her hands in his. "Come. Let me show you something."

He led her down a nearby slope to a hidden dell. There stood the tree, heavy with the Golden Figs of Paradise.

"What a fool I have been!" the woman cried. "To have wandered so many years when the tree was here all along. Why did you not tell me you were its Guardian?"

But the Sufi shook his head. "You would have thought I was boasting; you would not have accepted the gift without a difficult journey of mind or body. Besides, the tree only bears fruit every thirty-and-one years."

Therefore, traveller, have patience. Enlightenment will come at its proper time, in accordance with the journey you have made.

—Gandharva
Musician to the court
of Ibrahim 'Adilshah II
of Bijapur

I

ROSEMARY: This most beloved of herbs bears thick leaves that are dark above and fair below, and it brings forth blue flowers late in spring. Some say the rosemary gave shelter to the holy family as they fled into Egypt, and therefore the flower is become the blue of Mary's mantle. It was worn in wreaths by students in ancient Greece to aid their learning, and is oft seen at funerals as token of remembrance for that which has passed away. A sprig of rosemary beneath the bed brings deep slumber and protection from nightmare. Smelling rosemary preserves youth. Rosemary will flourish near a house where a woman or virtuous soul rules the home....

TOWN OF BICHOLIM, GOA PROVINCE,
EARLY OCTOBER, 1597

Thunder rolled across the black-clouded sky. Rain followed, grey and hard as iron nails. As Thomas Chinnery, apprentice apothecary and unwitting adventurer, dismounted from the saddle of his mule, the animal jumped and pranced sideways. His sore arms were tugged painfully hard and his foot was trod upon by a small, sharp hoof. " 'S'blood, devil take this blasted beast!"

A broad hand slapped him on the back. "Take care, lad. Summon not the horned one, lest he appear."

Thomas looked around into Andrew Lockheart's broad, black-browed face. "Methinks I've already seen 'im once or twice since coming to India."

A wide grin spread across the Scotsman's face. "More reason, then, for you to guard your tongue. And be kinder to your dumb friend here, lest he take unkindly to you. 'Twould be a shame to have come all this way for an ass to become thy executioner."

" 'Twould be but meet, given how strange events have turned withal," said Thomas. He bent down and gingerly tested the damage to his foot, finding it merely bruised. He stood and shook the water out of his eyes. "In this rain, I may drown first. I am glad it waited until after our caravan was ferried across the Mandovi River. What is this place?"

" 'Tis called Bicholim. A good place to trade for gemstones and minerals, I am told. But there is no caravanserai here, so we must find shelter wheresomever we may."

"A goodly thought, shelter. Let us find some quickly." The caravan's horseboy, naked but for a loincloth, appeared and took the reins of the mule, leading it to a stand of palms.

Thomas limped, Lockheart by his side, to the wall of a nearby house where wide, thatched eaves provided some cover.

Water poured down off the roof in a grey curtain, seeming to cut them off from the outer world. "Whence this downpour? Is not the monsoon season passed?" Wet and shivering, Thomas rubbed his aching shoulders, not yet fully healed from being hoist upon the strappado during his sojourn within the Goan Inquisition.

"Dame Nature does not adhere to man's timetable, lad. Mayhap Jove wished one last tossing of the bolts, or as the Hindoo would claim, Indra drives his chariot one last time through Heaven."

Thomas barked a laugh. "Surely some divinity frowns upon our journey. But you mix your metaphysicks, Andrew. Take care, lest you belie that Jesuit's robe you wear."

"But the robe is a lie, lad, as I have told you. What, think you I'd surrender my manhood to the Paulists for your rescue? This cloth is but borrowed. Anon, 'twill not matter who knows."

"Not matter? I'll remind you we are not to safety yet, though Goa be miles behind. If you be truly my sire-sent guardian angel, methinks you'd have more care for my safe-keeping."

"What, an this whining be my thanks? Tom, Tom, travel has made you o'erwrought with care."

"Experience has taught such care is wise. Minions of the Inquisition, I have learned with much pain, do not think as ordinary men. Were Padre Gonsção to learn of your deception, he would take it ill."

"What of it? He'll not turn us back. And what have you to fear now, O keeper of the secret of the resurrection powder? The Padre is not madman enough to harm the one who guides him to its source."

"I hope so." *But heaven help me,* thought Thomas, *should it be discovered that my "secret knowledge" is as much a lie as that robe you wear.*

"As for the good Padre," Lockheart went on, "I should seek him out to learn if he has found us better shelter than these eaves. Ah, here comes your other guardian, so I need not leave you solitary."

Bounding toward them through the rain was Joaquim Alvalanca, a small, wiry man wearing a padded cuirass and a peak-brimmed morion helmet, which shed the rain before and behind him in spouts.

Thomas was almost glad to see him, for although Joaquim was one of the Goan soldiers watching him, he was also nearly a friend. They had met in the noisome Aljouvar, the Governor's Keep in Goa, wherein, as tradition had it, all men are brothers, for all had sunk so low as to be equals.

"Alo, *inglês!*" Joaquim joined them beside the wall. "I am glad to see the mule did not make sausage of you," he said in Portuguese-accented Latin. "I would have been of more assistance, but I needed to help the carters make sure our food stays dry."

"I understand," said Thomas. "You are clearly a man who knows what is important."

"Of course. That is why I was chosen to go on this expedition for the Santa Casa."

"I thought it was because you would be hung for a thief if you did not."

Joaquim placed a hand on his sword hilt, still smiling. "Have I not warned you, Tomás, not to wound my tender pride? Good Brother Andrew," he said turning to Lockheart, "would you be so kind as to entreat to God to stop this rain?"

"Why should I do that, Senhor," said Lockheart, "when this weather is so beneficial to the ducks and fishes hereabout?"

"Because we are men, not ducks and fishes, Brother."

"Indeed we are, and therefore we should be able to withstand a little water, should we not? Take care, Tom, not to be cut by this one's sword or tongue while I am gone, eh?" Lockheart pulled up his hood and sauntered off into the rain.

Joaquim stared after him. "That one has not been a monk very long, has he?"

"No, I'd wager not," said Thomas. "Why think you so?"

"Monks are supposed to be meek and that one has no meekness in him. Why is he on this journey? The Santa Casa does not like Paulistas. He seems to know you well."

"We sailed on the same ship together from England."

"Ah. It must be he was coming to Goa on a pilgrimage to see the incorruptible body of Francis Xavier, yes?"

"No, actually we weren't headed to Goa at all—"

"There is a funny story about Xavier's body, you know. There was this woman pilgrim who, when she went to kiss the feet of the body, she bit off the little toe and carried it away with it in her mouth. I would call that extreme devotion, yes?"

Thomas winced. "Well, mummy powder is sometimes

used in the more expensive medicines my master makes, so I suppose it would not harm her. But you were asking about Brother Andrew—"

"She confessed later and they made her give it back. I hope I am not famous when I die. I should like there to be something left for them to bury. How will it be for poor Padre Francis when the Day of Judgment comes and he awakens to find bits of him missing?"

"I am sure he would be distressed but—"

"But why do you change the subject, Tomás? I was asking about your good Brother Andrew."

"Yes." Thomas sighed. *Perhaps they set you free so you would no longer bedevil the inmates of the Aljouvar.* "We were headed originally to Cathay. Our ships carried many traders, and a letter from my Queen to the Emperor. My master had sent me hoping I might set up a factory there. He had heard of the most marvelous Asian medicines; ginseng, and phoenix stone—"

"So why were you in Goa if that was not where you were going? Your tillermen had such poor sense of direction?"

"No." Thomas sighed again, watching the groaning camels of their caravan being led to the shelter of trees.

"They are not so bad in the rain," said Joaquim. "You cannot tell when they spit on you. But you have not answered my question, *inglês.*"

Because the answer wants delicacy, Thomas thought. "Our captain, I fear, wished to do battle with ships of your nation. We came upon a small galley and tried to take it—"

"Of course, Tomás. We know you *Inglês* are all pirates and thieves. But continue."

Alas, he is not far off the mark. "In any case, we were driven off by the largest carrack I have ever seen."

"That would be the *Santa Rosa*. A veritable mountain on the water, no? So she captured you?"

"Not quite. She damaged our ships badly. We took two

hostages and some goods from the small galley and found harbor on the Indian coast for repairs."

A shimmer of color crossed the sheet of rainwater in front of them and Thomas could make out the shape of a purple-curtained golden palanquin passing by, surrounded by women in skirts of vermillion, scarlet, and yellow-green. Thomas watched intently, hoping to catch a glimpse of the lovely Hindu woman who rode within the palanquin; the woman who had been one of the hostages from the Portuguese galley, who had tried to aid him in Goa, and who, he hoped, would be able to help him again.

He felt a nudge in his side from Joaquim's elbow. "They are beauties, no? Padre Gonsção has told us to keep away from the caravan mistress, but perhaps when he sleeps we can make friends with her ladies."

"That is a welcome thought."

"But go on with your tale, Tomás. How did you get to Goa?"

"I thought I had told you all this in the Aljouvar."

"So? I have forgotten. And we must pass the time until the Padre comes for us. What better way than to tell stories? Go on."

"One night we . . . were betrayed to a band of Oman coastal raiders." *Though it is best not to tell you that Lockheart was our Judas.* "I foolishly went aboard one of the pirate ships to see what I could do, and I became myself a hostage."

"That is justice. And Brother Andrew, he was a hostage also?"

"The raiders . . . took him with them as well. They brought us, and the two Goans we had captured, back to Goa, hoping to get ransom for us."

"So the Paulistas ransomed the brother?"

"I presume." *He ransomed himself.*

"And the Santa Casa took you from the Aljouvar. Why?"

"It was most strange. I was brought to Goa in the same

cart as one of the people from the galley. It happens he was a notorious sorcerer sought by the Inquisition. He was escaping Goa when we captured him. He . . . died in the cart, and so they questioned me, thinking I knew something of his sorcerous doings merely because I had been in his company."

"Ah, now I am remembering. This sorcerer is the one you murdered, yes?"

"No! That is, I was giving him a medicine, which he said would ease his pain. Instead, it killed him." *A medicine I had believed a great panacea. For had it not brought a dead boy back to life but days before?*

Joaquim shrugged. "But that is the way with you alquismistos, no? Medicines, poisons, it is all the same. You sell potions for too much money to people who think they are sick, or want others to be sick."

Thomas gritted his teeth. "I am an apothecary, not an alchemist, and my master never sells poisons. Even those who came to us simply believing they were sick were much aided by our tinctures and pastilles."

"Truly? Are you certain you are not yourself a sorcerer, Tomás?"

"Joaquim . . ."

"Ah, now I have wounded *your* tender pride. Forgive me, for here comes the Padre and we must not upset him with our quarreling."

Lightning flashed and Thomas saw, beyond the sheet of rain, Padre Antonio Gonsção trudging toward them, a hooded Lockheart beside him. The Padre's head was bowed, his arms hidden within the full sleeves of his blackfriar's robe. He walked with deliberate, unhurried steps, as if defying the wind and rain to sway him from his path.

"And so Brother Andrew and the Paulistas interceded for you to the Santa Casa?"

"He interceded for me, yes." *And the fool brought the resurrection powder to the Inquisition's attention.*

"And that is why they let you leave in one piece?"

"More or less."

"One thing I am wondering, though. What is it truly you and I are on this expedition to find?"

Thomas regarded him sharply. "They didn't tell you?"

"The Santa Casa tells no one anything."

But at that moment, the Padre stepped through the curtain of rainwater. In Latin, he said, "God grant you good evening Magister Chinnery, Joaquim."

Thomas nodded to him. "And to you, Padre."

"How do your arms feel, Magister?"

"Hm? Oh, it is but a slight ache. I had a difficult dismount when we arrived, that is all." Thomas felt discomfort whenever the blackfriar was solicitous of his health. He had to remind himself that Padre Gonsção was not the Inquisitor who had ordered him tortured, nor the one who took his forced confession. In fact, the Padre seemed no happier to be on this expedition than Thomas was.

"The good Padre," said Lockheart, "has managed to get us rooms for the night."

Padre Gonsção sighed. "It is not as I would have wished. There are no inns in this region, therefore we must be housed among the natives. The Domina Agnihotra has found for us a merchant, a Christian at least, who is willing to give some of us shelter in his home."

"Ah. And where will the Domina be lodging?" asked Thomas.

The Padre paused and frowned slightly.

Thomas mentally boxed himself. *Thou fool! Wherefore did I speak thus? I must not let him know I am acquainted with the caravan mistress.*

"Her clan, the Marathas, is widespread and she apparently has relatives here. Why do you ask?"

"I . . . only hoped that she would be comfortable, Padre. She . . . seemed old and frail and such persons can become ill in foul weather such as this." *Dear God, forgive my lame false-hoods, but he must not know who it is now travels under the name Agnihotra.*

The Padre's smile was not entirely trusting. "Of course. It is the concern of a professional healer, I assume." Padre Gonsção turned once more to Lockheart. "The Christian who will be host to us enjoys discussing scripture, I am told, so we will at least have some intellectual entertainment this evening, Brother."

Lockheart poorly concealed a wince. "I shall look forward to it, Padre."

"I had hoped you would. By the way, have you seen Brother Timóteo? It worries me how that boy dashes here and there with no concern for himself."

"Your pardon, Padre," said Thomas, "but Timóteo does speak the local languages, Goa-born as he is. This is not so strange and fearsome a place to him as it may be to a man fresh from Lisbon, as you are."

"Indeed," said Joaquim, "he is the most fortunate of all of us. By now he has no doubt found the best wine and the best food and the best lap in which to sleep."

The Padre scowled at the soldier. "It may be his very familiarity with this land that conceals the danger from his perception. He has spent little of his life outside of the Santa Casa, I was told, and is still an innocent in many ways. I would appreciate it, Joaquim, if you and your fellow *soldados* would not tease him or tempt him into fool-ishness."

"Padre! We are loyal servants to Governador da Gama, and the King and to God. We would never do such horrible things."

"I will trust your word on that, Joaquim. For tonight, I will have you room with Magister Chinnery, as you seem to find him companionable. But I will tolerate no embarrassing be-havior. We must show our host all grace and courtesy as becomes fellow Christians. I may have Brother Timóteo stay with you also, once he is found. I will see if he can make a balm for your shoulders, Senhor."

"I thank you, Padre."

"Ah, the rain appears to be easing. Follow me, if you please."

The Padre set off at a quick stride, Lockheart at his heels.

Thomas followed also, but fell back a few paces to speak with Joaquim. "What of the other *soldados?* Where are they staying?"

"My less fortunate compadres will be guarding the supply carts, at the other end of town from the caravaneers. The Hindu merchants will not permit us *soldados* to stay near their goods, for they fear we will steal or damage them. Their fears are correct, of course, but we must sleep somewhere. I shall be envied for being your friend, *inglês*—I will have a roof over my head tonight."

"I am glad to be of service," Thomas said with a wry smile.

The house of the jewel merchant turned out to be a three-story palace-in-miniature, with onion-domed towers at each corner. Thomas, Padre Gonsção, Lockheart, and Joaquim were fed supper on a colonnaded balcony overlooking a fountained garden. The scent of wet earth and jasmine blossoms wafted up from below.

"Our host does not join us?" said Thomas, as girl servants entered, bringing dishes on silver platters. He had seen only servants since they arrived at the house.

Padre Gonsção only shook his head.

Lockheart said, "Although our host is a Christian, he has kept many of his former Hindu ways, including that of eating in private."

"Perhaps you and I may persuade him to change his ways in our discussions this evening," said the Padre. "The breaking of bread in good fellowship is surely preferable to taking a meal in solitude."

"I shall have to remember that," said Joaquim softly to Thomas, as he ogled the serving girls in their diaphanous skirts. "It could make for good sport. If you find a Hindu about to eat his dinner, you could follow him from room to room and prevent him from ever getting a bite."

"Joaquim . . ."

"Ah, but do not scowl at me. I am only making the joke. Let us see what repast the lovely dark-eyed angels have brought for us."

The dishes held spiced rice with chicken and raisins, eggs in a butter sauce, puffy flatbread with onions. The serving girls poured a milky liquid into cups for them. Thomas tasted it, and found it much like white wine. "What is this?"

"That is called *tadi,*" said Joaquim. "They make it from the palm trees. *Arrak* is better, though. Same thing, but it is distilled with ganja root. Drives all the pains of the world from a man's mind. You must try it sometime, *inglês.*"

"I see I must." Thomas was feeling some need of pains-ease, as his shoulders ached and his arms and hands were having difficulty responding to his will. *Perhaps they are easily wearied by use, as they have not yet fully healed. But I had hoped for better recovery.*

After the repast was finished, Padre Gonsção and Lockheart were called away to meet their host, the jewel merchant. Thomas and Joaquim were shown to their room, at the top of the southwest tower. Except for the occasional small crucifix on the wall, Thomas could see little similarity to the Christian households with which he was familiar. The walls were painted with frescoes of peacocks and pheasants. The mattresses on the low beds were softer than those to which he was accustomed, and they were adorned with long, tubular pillows. The windows of their tower room filled much of the wall, and were topped by scalloped arches.

Thomas gazed out the east-facing window, noting that the skies were clearing. The light of the setting sun delineated a range of mountains far in the distance, just visible above the palm fronds.

"Clever of the Padre," muttered Joaquim behind him, "to give us this room. We cannot depart without being noticed."

"Hmmm?"

"To meet with the Hindu girls. What are you staring at, Tomás? Some pretty heathen catch your eye?"

"Those mountains there, Joaquim. Will we cross them?"

"Oh, those. Sebastião—one of the carters, the squint-eyed fellow—he has been on this road before. He says those are the Ghats. Terrible name. Sounds like a sick old man's cough. Ghat. But they are not really mountains, he says. That is where the land rises to a plateau called the Deccan. And yes, we must go there."

"What sort of land is this Deccan?"

"Oh, it is a horrible place, Sebastião says. First there are jungles, then there is desert. And the fevers—half of us Europeans will die before we reach Bijapur." Joaquim said this with no more care than if he were describing the weather.

Thomas felt his heart sink. The further from the sea they marched, the more difficult escape would become. He would be all the more at the mercy of foreigners and whatever God directed his fate, whether the Anglican deity he knew from birth, or the Catholic one to whom he had made forced confession in the Santa Casa. *Or perhaps more infernal forces in this God-forsaken land. I had been told I might make escape in Bijapur, but 'twould seem I've only half a hope of arriving there.*

"You were going to tell me, Tomás, before the Padre came for us, what it is our little expedition is searching for."

What do I dare tell him? I know the Padre would have me silent about the power of the rasa mahadevi. "We seek the source of a great medicine, Joaquim."

The *soldado* laughed. "A medicine! You cannot think I will believe you, Tomás. I cannot believe the Santa Casa would want to *heal* their prisoners."

"I do not know what the Inquisition wants it for. I only knew that they would release me from their dungeon if I agreed to lead them to it."

Joaquim nodded slowly. "I understand, Tomás, the wish to escape from a dungeon, no matter the cost."

Could it be, thought Thomas, *that I have an ally close to hand? That my guard might become my means to freedom?* "There is something I would ask, my friend."

Joaquim regarded Thomas a moment, clearly hearing the hint of something important. The *soldado* smiled and strolled over to lean against the wall beside Thomas. He pulled a dagger from his belt and began to idly clean his nails. "Ah, my friend. The *inglês* does me the honor of calling me his friend. Have we not been brothers in adversity? Ask what you will."

As Thomas opened his mouth to speak again, Brother Timóteo breathlessly ran through the doorway. His damp brown robe clung to his thin frame, making him look all of his awkward and gangly thirteen years. He was holding up the hem of his robe, carrying something in its fold.

"Tomás! Here you are!" Timóteo exclaimed. He sat at Thomas's feet and shook his black, bowl-cut hair like a dog who has come out from romping in a pond.

"Ay!" cried Joaquim, following it with a stream of epithets in Portuguese.

"Have we not enjoyed the rain enough, little brother," said Thomas, "that you must share more of it with us?"

"Your pardon, Senhor," said Timóteo to Joaquim. "But see, Tomás, what I have found!" He opened the fold in his robe, displaying a variety of leaves, twigs, flowers, and roots. "Here are sehund flowers which will prevent snakebite. This is bark from the chaulmugra tree—its oil is good for leprosy. And this is khus-khus root, and sumbul root. These are cotula leaves, which ease cholera and fevers. Malva flowers for the sore throat, and champa leaves—"

"Timóteo, please, enough!" said Thomas laughing. "Your

grandfather would be proud, but now is not the time for this lecture." Thomas thought it odd that he had become a friend of sorts with this boy who was a most devoted acolyte of the Santa Casa. Timóteo had been Thomas's "advocate" during his trial and torture, showing genuine deep concern for the state of Thomas's soul. Thomas had found he could not dislike the sweet-tempered acolyte, no matter what mad masters the boy served. Timóteo's grandfather, Garcia de Orta, had been one of the great herbalists of Europe, one of the first to describe herbal medicines of the East; a shared interest that could not be denied.

"But Tomás! Soon we will be up in the Deccan, where these plants do not grow."

"Save them for me, little brother. My arms are still weak and I can neither write nor draw right now."

"I will draw and write for you, Tomás!"

"Can it not be later, Timóteo? And have you spoken to the Padre? He has been terribly worried by your absence."

The boy looked away a moment, then said, "The Padre will make me do some form of penance. So I must tell you these things now, while I can. You will explain to the Padre this is important, yes?"

Thomas smiled at Joaquim with a helpless expression. The *soldado* took the hint. "Timóteo," Joaquim said, "are you still a virgin?"

Timóteo went rock-still as his brown cheeks flushed. "Senhor?"

"Have you gotten to know any, you know, girls?"

Timóteo swallowed, his eyes wide. "I . . . the Santa Casa forbid me to know any . . . girls."

Joaquim clicked his tongue. "Such a pity you are leaving Goa, then. You will miss coming to manhood amongst the lovely *senhoras* there. What a shame. You know, they have breasts like enormous ripe mangoes, topped by raisins hardened in the sun. Their thighs are smooth and brown as teak, and what they do with their tongues! Why, boy, they would make your little rod harder than the Rock of St. Peter, and you would spurt higher than the fountain in the Plaça do Santa Catarina."

Timóteo jumped up, spilling the leaves and twigs from his lap. "Your pardon, Senhores," he said quickly and he ran out the doorway, crossing himself.

Joaquim laughed. "Ah, that one will have soggy dreams tonight."

"No doubt. Thank you." Thomas felt his own cheeks had grown warm.

"So. What was it you wished to ask of me, friend Tomás?"

"Oh." He cleared his throat and checked to see that no one was near the doorway to overhear. He returned to Joaquim's side and said, softly, "First you must swear that you will reveal to no one what I ask of you."

Joaquim raised a brow. "I swear on the holy hem of the gown of the Blessed Virgin, Tomás. Ask."

"I did not intend to continue long with this expedition. My hope had been that, when the opportunity arose, to escape and find my way home to England. I had hoped to leave at Bijapur, but from what you say, the journey may prove too perilous. And my arms are not healing well. I will need help, and soon. You have no loyalty to the Santa Casa. Should an opportunity appear, may I rely on you for assistance?"

With a sad smile, Joaquim leaned close, pointing his dagger toward Thomas's neck. "Tomás, it is fortunate that you ask this of me, for I alone will not hurt you, or betray you for asking it. But know, Tomás, that I am the last man in this expedition who would help you."

"But . . . in the Aljouvar—"

"In the dark stink of the Aljouvar, all men are brothers, it is true. But we are no longer in the Aljouvar. We are now under the watchful eye of the Santa Casa. And the Santa Casa, she is everywhere; in Lisboa, Madrid, everywhere.

Should I help you to escape from here, there would be no escape for me. The Aljouvar was a pit, but it left me whole. The Santa Casa is not so kind, as your shoulders no doubt tell you each day. There would be no swift death if I betray her. I would be dealt my punishment piece by piece, understand?"

Thomas nodded.

"I, too, dream of escape from this pestilent place. But now I am given a chance to earn it, and return to Lisboa with a pension, and perhaps return to my studies. You will not take this dream from me, *inglês*. As we were once brothers in the Aljouvar, I will keep my oath and tell no one what you have asked. But the only escape I may offer is that which my little friend can deliver." Joaquim gently laid the edge of his dagger against Thomas's collarbone.

Thomas stood very still. "I hope such desperate escape will not be needed, Joaquim. Forgive me. I will not ask this of you again."

"Good." Joaquim returned the attention of his dagger to his fingernails. "You know, I feel for you, Tomás, truly. The Devil has surely taken a hand in your fate. For you have no friends on whom to rely in this company. None of us can be. The Santa Casa will see to that. We are all merely companions on the road to Hell."

II

POMEGRANATE: This tree grows in Persia and the East. It bears waxy, crimson flowers in summer, and has a many-seeded fruit which produces a tart juice. It is thought a symbol of wealth and fertility. Some have said it was the forbidden Fruit of Knowledge in the Garden of Eden. Its branches are oftimes used as seeking wands. In the East, bundles of pomegranate twigs are used to ward off demons and bewitchment. A tincture of the tree bark will drive out worms from the intestines, and is a curative for women's complaints....

FORT OF AHMADNAGAR, SULTANATE OF AHMADNAGAR
MONTH OF *ZILHIJ*, YEAR OF THE PROPHET 975

The Mirza Ali Akbarshah, Omrah of ten thousand men and trusted general to the court of the Padshah Emperor Akbar, watched his host in the manner of a well-fed tiger gazing upon a deer. But this deer had sharp horns and a swift mind. The Mirza knew he must use caution.

Across a table laden with extravagant refreshment, the Princess Chand Bibi, Sultana of Ahmadnagar, sat on a low, cushioned dais. She was dressed in the manner of the Hindus she ruled, wearing a short-sleeved *choli* bodice that left bare her midriff, and a *ghagra* skirt. Over these, she wore a long *peshwaz* jacket of the finest transparent *shabnam* muslin. An *orhni* mantle of blue silk draped over her head and shoulders.

The Mirza tried to imagine how she must have appeared in armor and helmet when she had rallied the defense of the fort only the year before. Akbar's son, Prince Daniyal, had described her as quite fearsome in aspect.

But she did not seem fearsome now. The Sultana was small, and in her early forties in age. Her lined face showed calm determination, and her long black braided hair was veined with iron grey. It was rumored that Chand Bibi had survived several poisonings and other assassination attempts attributed to sons impatient for their inheritance. No one understood how she endured, be it from strong faith, cleverness, or merely a healthy constitution. Neighboring sultans thought her a wise strategist. Others called her a sorceress. Whatever the source of her strength, Chand Bibi had held Ahmadnagar together for years through much adversity.

The Mirza Akbarshah rolled a stuffed date between his fingers and said, "You show much hospitality, Sultana, to one who comes unexpected and uninvited."

Chand Bibi tilted her shoulders and smiled coolly. "An emissary of His Imperial Majesty the Padshah is never unwelcome, nor entirely unexpected. For such a noble visitor, the inadequate hospitality this poor house can provide is nothing."

The Mirza gazed at the table, and the dishes of peeled mangoes in honey, lemons and pomegranates, spiced roti with onions, lamb in mustard curry, and steamed hearts of lotus. Cuts of fish swam in pepper-ginger sauce and game fowl roasted with garlic and walnuts. Beside these were humbler bowls of saffron rice and yogurt with mint. Tea spiced with cardamom and cloves was served in elegant porcelain cups. But the Mirza Akbarshah had known the great feasts of the Imperial court. The Sultana was right: this was nothing.

They had exchanged pleasant lies about their health and their families, decried the end of the life-giving season of monsoons while thanking Allah the Merciful for few floods and plagues this year. Servant girls cooled them with peacock feather fans to enhance the lotus-scented breezes that now and then wafted from the gardens.

"It is far more pleasant," said the Sultana, "to converse with a neighbor across a table than across a battlefield, don't you think?"

"I do, indeed," said the Mirza, "as would his Imperial Majesty."

"And how fares your supreme Emperor? We hear stories, you know, even in this distant kingdom, although many of them may simply be vile rumor."

"Stories?"

"It is said, for example, that the Shahinshah has . . . fallen away from the true faith."

The Mirza sighed. Such rumors were common in Agra and Lahore, and not without reason. "These stories are passed along by the ignorant who do not understand His Majesty's intellectual curiosity. He enjoys exploration and discussion of other's beliefs. But there should be no doubt that he remains, in his heart, a loyal follower of the Faith."

"I am most reassured, for we have heard terrible things: that he has formed his own cult, for example, and worships fire like a Parsi."

"These are false," the Mirza said firmly.

"Are they? What masterful liars travellers must be. We had heard that, not five months ago, His Imperial Majesty received a sign of divine disfavor. A lightning strike, was it not?"

"Ah. That. Yes, a bolt of lightning did strike the imperial palace in Lahore."

"And it burned for three days thereafter, we were told."

Her spies keep her well informed. "Yes. Some of the *ulama* who had felt ignored by the Emperor attributed the fire to Akbar's . . . unusual philosophies, and spread hateful rumors."

"So it is not true that the Padshah Emperor thereafter secluded himself, except to speak with mystics and soothsayers, particularly those he had felt he had wronged?"

"As I understand it, that is indeed the case. However, the Emperor emerged from his seclusion a humbler man and has now returned to the practices of a proper Muslim."

"This is most pleasing to hear, of course," said Chand Bibi. "It is good that he remains among the faithful. And his sons, how do they fare? The last I heard of Prince Murad, he was still suffering from his . . . chronic illness."

His drunkenness, she means. How fortunate for her rule that Murad is enthralled by wine; he cannot control his generals who fight among themselves too much to conquer Ahmadnagar. "I understand his Highness is . . . recovering, and obediently awaits the direction of his father."

"Ah, good. Sons should be obedient. I know the pain caused by troublesome offspring."

"The Padshah is a patient and forgiving sire."

"The Padshah is a brave man," said the Sultana, with a touch of irony.

"The most courageous of all men," said the Mirza. "And as we are speaking of kings, what do you hear of your nephew, the Sultan Ibrahim?"

Chand Bibi smiled. "Bijapur prospers under his guidance. He has built many new palaces and mosques, and brought many fine artisans to his kingdom. His poetry is much praised, his painting as well. His musicianship is so refined that, I understand, he is writing a book on *ragas*. Should you be passing through Bijapur, I am sure you will be much impressed with his talents."

I would be more impressed, thought Akbarshah, *if his talents were more applied to leadership and skill in war, as had been those of his redoubtable uncle, Ibrahim I.* "And what of the tales we hear in Agra, that your esteemed nephew has fallen away from the Faith?"

The Sultana's expression hardened. "They are no more true than those rumors concerning the Padshah Emperor."

"I am glad to hear it, for indeed I and my men will be passing that way. I had hoped the Sultan would be as kind and hospitable as you."

"Ibrahim welcomes all sorts to Bijapur, even strangers from faraway lands. If you come in peace, he should be no less welcoming of you. But, if I may be so bold, what is it you are seeking? I hardly think His Imperial Majesty would have sent you with only five hundred men, one hundred horse, and ten elephants in order to conquer a kingdom."

The Mirza smiled. "You are well-informed, Great Lady. No, I am not on a mission of conquest, but of exploration. I am ordered to go deep into the Deccan, perhaps as far as the Krishna River."

"South of Bijapur? That is a dry and dismal land, full of dark, barbaric people. What should the Emperor hope to find in such a place?"

"I am sent chasing a legend, Sultana."

Chand Bibi laughed. "I see your Emperor continues his eccentric ways. Has the Shahinshah so drained his kingdom of entertainment that he must send his generals in search of stories?"

"You misunderstand me. I seek to prove a legend, one which His Majesty heard while in seclusion."

The Sultana paused. "Tales of great treasure can do much to whet ambition."

So. Perhaps she does know something, as His Majesty suspected. "I said nothing of treasure, Sultana."

"Ah. But what else could bring the attention of the Shahinshah. Unless you are spying for him, learning which little kingdoms are ripe for plucking."

"It is no secret that His Majesty wishes to make all India his empire. Remember that he is descended from the great

Chinghiz Khan—ambition is in his blood. I am sure any information I gather on such matters will be useful. But that is not the purpose of my expedition."

"What, then, is this folktale that has the power to fascinate an Emperor?"

"It concerns a great *rani*, who may be descended from gods, who lives in an impregnable, hidden fortress."

"Is this meant to flatter me?"

The Mirza laughed gently. "Alas, Sultana, though you are a ruler to be reckoned with, the queen I seek is of powers more supernatural. Some say her palace is hidden within a mountain of stone. Some say she is the queen of djinn, or a wife of one of Shaitan's sons. It is said she may be immortal, she is centuries old, and is wiser than the angels. Her power comes from sorcery, not armies. It is this story I follow, and it is said this *rani* lives in the Deccan."

Chand Bibi had gone very still. "Of course. The Hindu tell many tales of gods and kings, and the Deccan is such an empty place that anything might be thought to inhabit it. I will tell a tale to match yours. Not far from here is a forest some think is sacred. Among the roots of its trees, there are soldiers of stone, wearing armor and bearing swords of a sort not seen since the days of the great emperor Ashoka. Every year, after the monsoon, more of their stone heads and bodies are revealed by the rains. Those who live near this forest fear it. They say it is the work of a vengeful demon. The Hindu know of many demons, such as the *nagas*, who are said to be part serpent, part man. Demons who can kill with only a glance."

Had they been seated in the wilderness beside a fire, the Mirza might have shivered a little at her words. Now, he was only irritated. "Do you mean to frighten me, Sultana? This forest, if it is real, merely covers some ancient ruin filled with statues and carvings. I have seen many such in my travels. Surely this land held wonders even before the time of the Prophet. But they are long dead, with only whispered tales to give them life. Your story has nothing to do with my search."

"Are you certain, great Mirza? How can you judge that one tale has more worth than another? Would not these legends die if there were no frame on which to hang the fabric? I hear even Crown Prince Salim is afraid to go into the Deccan."

The Mirza snorted in annoyance. "That is because His Highness Salim is a vain, pompous little coward. I fear he will be the death of his father someday."

Unexpected delight lit up the Sultana's face and she clapped her hands together. "Most worthy Mirza, is that not treason?"

"Salim is still a boy and not yet king and I need not give credit to his petty fears. I had been hoping, Sultana, that you, as an intelligent and perceptive woman, might be of more help than to ply me with superstitious nonsense."

"Now you do seek to flatter me. I worry for you, great Mirza. It is not a good sign when a king sends his best generals chasing legends. Disaster must surely come of this. Remember Fatepur Sikri."

"It was a great city. An architectural masterpiece."

"Yes, but your Emperor built it on a whim, to honor a Sufi mystic who told him he would have sons. Alas, he did not plan for an adequate water supply and the city had to be abandoned after only fourteen years."

"You cannot blame his Majesty for the mistakes of his workmen."

"If your endeavor fails," said the Sultana softly, "who is the workman who will receive the blame?"

"There is always the risk of a servant disappointing his master. Which is why I must strive all the more for success."

The Sultana sighed and reclined against her cushions. "You seem to value nothing I say, therefore I shall waste no more of your time. Ask any mud-hued child you encounter on the road for more stories of this demon queen. Now I am sure you have much to do to resupply your caravan. Our bazaar will happily take your Emperor's silver. I must see to many matters of my own. This is not an easy sultanate to govern, as you are doubtless aware."

She knows something but will not tell it, and wishes to discourage me from the search. These are encouraging signs. The Mirza stood. "I thank you, then, Sultana, for your most generous hospitality. I assure you I and my men will not remain long, nor drain the resources of your hard-pressed country."

"Sometimes I think it is a good thing that Ahmadnagar is not a land of wealth and abundance. It might stimulate greed among the neighbors and make them itch for conquest."

"Surely you need not fear conquest, Sultana. His Majesty is ready to welcome you into the family of provinces that do him homage. A good father does not smite his prospective daughter-in-law, even if her dowry is poor. I hope you will be as wise and generous when His Shining Majesty comes himself to welcome Ahmadnagar into his imperial family. May Allah, the Compassionate, the Merciful, give you guidance."

With a final bow, the Mirza allowed himself to be escorted from her audience chamber.

Chand Bibi watched him go, gripping her mantle in tightening fists. "Ukha!"

A stocky, muscular woman swiftly entered, her lance at the ready, the plates of her armor clattering. Once chief of the harem guard for a neighboring sultan, Ukha was now Chand Bibi's most trusted personal guard. "Sultana? What is your wish?"

"A crisis has arisen. I must prepare for a journey to Bijapur. I will want you to accompany me."

"Sultana? It will take days to prepare a caravan."

"I shall not be traveling in state but in stealth. Arrange for the fastest horses to be available in the stable."

"Even so, Sultana, Bijapur is a seven-day journey."

"I am aware of that, Ukha. But it will be a longer journey

for the Mirza Akbarshah and his army. And Ibrahim should be prepared for their arrival."

"Could you not send some other messenger, Sultana? A *pattamar*, perhaps? Such runners can travel even faster than horses. Things are so unsettled here. Is it wise for you to travel now?"

"How many should be told the secret of my survival, Ukha? How many can know it before the secret is spilled? No, I must deliver the news myself. Besides, Ibrahim is more likely to believe me and take what I say with due seriousness."

"But what of your sons?"

"Let Lady Meghaduta put out word that I am ill, and sequester herself, posing as me. She has successfully done this before. My sons will set to squabbling over who will inherit what, hoping I am, at last, near death. It will keep them amused until I return and stage yet another miraculous 'recovery.' Meet me at the stables at sunset. Akbarshah and his men will be at prayers then, and may not notice our departure."

Ukha bowed. "It shall be as you wish, Sultana." She swiftly departed. Chand Bibi left the audience chamber also, for her dressing rooms.

Ahmadnagar could not stand forever, Chand Bibi knew, against the might of the Mughal Empire to the north. But she owed a debt to the power that had helped her endure so long. *Akbar must not learn of the* rasa mahadevi, *and the sorceress queen who guards its source. Once he knows, he would let nothing stand in the way of conquest of Ahmadnagar, Bijapur, and all that lies beyond.*

III

MUGWORT: This plant has jagged leaves with downy stems, and bears flowers of a yellow-green in late summer. A tincture of this herb soothes the eyes, and prevents one from tiring. To sleep on a pillow stuffed with mugwort will bring visions of one's fate to come. It is said John the Baptist wore a girdle of mugwort to sustain him in the wilderness. For this reason, it is oft worn by travellers, tucked into the shoes or clothing. It is an herb of protection, and will guard against stinging insects, enchantment, lightning, misfortune, and wild beasts....

The jungle pressed in close around them, allowing little sunlight to reach the struggling Goan caravan. The air was hot, moist, and still. The road was choked with roots and low branches, at times seeming to disappear beneath the underbrush. The mule Thomas rode picked its way carefully, yet still stumbled now and then upon a hidden stone. The damp silence was only punctuated by the cries of strange birds or the whirring of insects. Thomas could not help peering into the dark tangle of trees, expecting to see the eyes of some great, ravenous beast staring back at him.

How different this land is from yesterday's travels, thought Thomas, wishing for a little breeze. For two days, since leaving Bicholim, the terrain had been pleasant: orchard-covered hills, watered by wide streams filled with ducks and elegant cranes, beside which lay prosperous villages. Brother Timóteo had happily pointed out to him the great hanging nests of bower birds and the tracks of fox and wild deer. It had helped to ease his dark mood, and resign him to suffer the journey until his strength returned or some opportunity to flee presented itself, or until they reached Bijapur.

But the dark jungle and stifling air weighed down his spirits once more. "How oppressive and dismal is this forest," he muttered.

"My exact thoughts," said Lockheart riding beside him. "Even our beasts have no love of this place."

Thomas noticed how Lockheart's horse pranced, anxious and wide-eyed. Thomas's mule was twitching its ears and whuffing the air. "True. I wonder what disturbs them."

"What they cannot see, no doubt. This jungle is too close, and might hide all manner of threat. I once thought on forests as places of healthful bounty, full of game and other wonders bestowed by divine favor. But this place hath a foul miasma, a forest twisted to suit a demon's dwelling."

It brought to Thomas's mind memories of the hold of the *Whelp*, after the attack on the carrack, where men lay sick and dying in noisome tropical air while he did his best to tend to them. "If what physicians say be true, this stifling air will bring the sickness and fevers that Joaquim said would plague us."

He turned in his saddle, noting that the *soldados* and the supply carts had fallen far behind, no longer visible amid the vines and twisted trees. The camels and palanquin of the caravan mistress were far ahead, equally invisible. Only Padre Gonsção and Timóteo were nearby.

'Twould be a good place for an ambush, although the rogues that would brave this tangle would be desperate indeed. Thomas wondered at the irony of it. Had his arms been strong and the for-

est more open, now might have been one of the better chances to run. He was still within five days of the coast and might seek a ship that needed extra hands, no matter whose. *But not with these shoulders still weak as a babe's. And to try to 'scape amid that morass—* He shuddered suddenly.

"What is the matter, Tom?"

"Hm?"

"You shivered and your face turned pale. You've not caught a fever so soon, have you?"

"No, no. I was remembering a nightmare I had last night."

"Ah. The nightmares continue?"

"They have not left since I set foot on India's coast."

Padre Gonsção, whom Thomas noted had been watching them for some while, turned his horse (with some difficulty for his steed was also disquieted) and rode back to join them.

"I do not suppose, Magister Chinnery," said the Padre in Latin as he flapped the collar of his robe, "that you learned from the sorcerer De Cartago any route more pleasant and passable than this?"

Thomas laughed without humor. "If I knew one, Padre, I would surely have chosen it over this."

"Wasn't there a map drawn by De Cartago?" said Lockheart. "Did the Grand Inquisitor not give it to you?"

The Padre paused and regarded the Scotsman a moment. "He did, Brother. But I have found it somewhat . . . lacking in detail. That is why we must be grateful for Magister Chinnery's assistance."

"Naturally," said Thomas, "Magister De Cartago did not want his secret ways so easily revealed."

"So our route becomes similar to the ways religious mystery is approached," said Lockheart. "Slow and by diverse paths, with hardships to overcome and riddles to solve."

"Magister De Cartago did say the source was in the keeping of a goddess," Thomas agreed.

"And I expect," said the Padre, "that it shall all prove to

be pagan nonsense. But tell me what it was that you were discussing that caused you to turn pale, Magister Chinnery. As you can understand, I have cause to be concerned about whatever might alarm you."

You mean we have been talking too long in a tongue you do not understand, thought Thomas. *The Padre has some suspicions, and therefore is no fool.*

"We were discussing Magister Chinnery's dreams, Padre."

"Dreams?" the Padre said, raising a brow. He pulled his horse alongside Thomas's mule. "What dreams are these?"

"I have been plagued by nightmares ever since childhood," Thomas explained. "When I set sail from England, they faded, but now that I am upon land again, they have returned."

"Some of my brethren," said the Padre, "say that nightmares are the torment of demons who wish to drive man to the sin of despair. Others have said that such dreams are torment man brings upon himself when he is battling his better nature."

Do my cares show so plainly upon my face? Thomas wondered.

"And some," said Lockheart, "say they are messages from the realms of angels."

"The first seems the most likely cause," said Thomas, "for mine are of a most singular, frightening nature. I am always pursued by three female creatures . . . hideous, horrible things who appear in different guises. Once they were hunters, and I a deer fleeing through the forest. Last night they appeared as woodsmen and I was an oak tree. They chopped at my boughs, crying 'Murderer! Murderer!' which is what they always say." Thomas rubbed his shoulders. "I fear these demons want my death and shall be satisfied with nothing less."

He turned to see Lockheart staring at him with a gaze that held awe and fear combined. "What is't, Andrew?"

"I believe I will let the good Padre do your interpretation," Lockheart said, with a smile that did not reach his dark eyes. "I have become concerned about our carters, whom we have not seen for some time. If you will excuse me, Padre, Thomas, I will go back and see if they require aid."

The Padre nodded. "A wise thought, Brother. Return and tell us if we should stop to wait for them."

"I will, Padre." Lockheart turned his horse on the narrow track, and kicked him into a trot as he departed.

What has affrighted him so? thought Thomas. *What sort of guardian is he who flees from nightmares not his own?*

"I wonder at the cry of 'Murderer' that you hear in these dreams," said the Padre. "I presume it cannot concern the *fidalgo* De Cartago, in whose death you were complicit, if the dreams have been with you since childhood. Is there some other death that weighs heavily upon your soul?"

Thomas shook his head. "There is only my mother, who died at my birth. My father, at times, when angry with me, would accuse me—" Thomas broke off and stared at the ground, suffused with the pain of half-buried memories.

"Of killing her?" the Padre finished for him. "Grief can bring a man to say grievous things, my son. Your father, in his pain, struck out at the cause, although the cause itself was innocent. The Lord took your mother at her time appointed and although you may have been His agent, you should not be blamed. Therefore the root of your dreams may be unjust self-torment after all. If there are other cares that trouble you, I will gladly hear confession from you. Now is not the proper time, of course."

Thomas drew in a deep breath to steady himself. "Yes. I thank you, Padre. I will think on these things."

The Padre smiled and laid a hand on Thomas's shoulder, causing him to wince. The Padre lifted his hand off at once. "Your pardon. How are your shoulders today?"

Thomas paused before admitting, "They are worse, I

fear." In fact, he was having difficulty holding up the reins of his mule and often let them rest on the animal's neck.

The Padre nodded. "It is not unusual, for one who has suffered the strappado. Brother Andrew may have reset your arms too soon."

"I had thought the resetting of the shoulders would bring a swifter healing."

"Eventually, it does. But your arms will become useless again, for a time, while they heal. I have seen this before. You must be patient and pray for recovery."

Ah, I had forgotten. How often, I wonder, have you seen victims of the strappado? How often have you sent men to such a fate by your own order? "Does the healing take a long time?"

"Several weeks, as I recall."

Fortunate for you, Thomas thought, dismayed. *It will be far longer before I may consider escape.*

"Padre, Tomás, look!" Timóteo was pointing up from where he sat on his burro, at a brightly colored bird flitting amid the jungle canopy.

Thomas chuckled. "At least one of us is still enjoying the journey."

"Ah, the curiosity of youth. He reminds me of when I was a boy. There was once a day, when I was ten, when I had accompanied my father as he delivered some lutes he had made to Huelva, in Spain. There was a Moorish trader in the town, and he had with him, wonder of wonders, a camel. I had never seen such a beast, and I ran to look at it. The Moor was offering rides to the children, and I begged my father to let me ride the camel too. But he dragged me away and cuffed me, saying he would sooner sell me to the Devil than let me ride the demon beast of a heretic. Now that I am grown, of course, I understand his anger, but . . . what is it, Magister Chinnery?"

Thomas could not help grinning. "Merely that it is easy to forget that other men have been children too."

"Yes. So it is, my son." His smile was awkward.

"So. Your father was a lutemaker. You did not continue in the family craft, then?"

"My father discouraged me from it."

"How did you find yourself serving the Santa Casa?"

It was as if a wall fell suddenly between them. "I will not discuss that matter."

"Your pardon, Padre. I meant no disrespect."

But the Padre did not reply, and in the heavy silence, Thomas tried to think of something simple and untroubling to discuss, for the pleasant conversation had made the journey almost bearable.

As the Padre shifted with discomfort on his saddle, Thomas said, "If I may be so bold, Padre, why is it you do not ride in a palanquin, as the Domina Agnihotra does? Would it not allow you to travel in greater comfort?"

The Padre scowled. "Palanquins are for women."

"And for worthy men of note. As leader of this expedition, in the name of the Santa Casa, wouldn't a palanquin have give you more respect in the eyes of those caravaneers who accompany us?"

"Perhaps. But I prefer to see where I am going, and to only be at the mercy of a horse, not native bearers. If the camel drivers think less of me for this, then so be it."

"Ah." In fact, Thomas admired the Padre somewhat more for refusing to travel in ostentation. "And if I may ask, what has brought a simple lutemaker's son to these distant shores?"

Timóteo looked over his shoulder and called back, "He was sent by the Cardinal and the Pope!"

"Timóteo!" barked the Padre.

The boy murmured apologies and fell into embarrassed silence.

Sighing, Padre Gonsção added, "It is the business of the Santa Casa and we may not speak of it. The Rule of Silence, Magister, applies to me and Timóteo as well as to you."

"Ah, the Rule of Silence. I had forgotten." Thomas had

sworn to it at his tribunal, and saw it as part of the madness of the Inquisition. But, of course, this madness had its purpose—if never spoken of, no one would know the horrors that the Santa Casa committed upon its "guests."

Thomas wondered at Timóteo's words. *The Pope? For what great cause would such a feared and venerated figure send an emissary to India?* Again, Thomas had the curious feeling of having two minds; his former self would have considered the Padre the servant of the Devil. Now, if he were the new-found Catholic his confession had declared him, he should feel the Padre had been commanded by Heaven itself. Unable to reconcile these, and aware that the Padre would say nothing more, Thomas returned his attention to the jungle and the treacherous road.

Padre Antonio Gonsção regretted having been short with the young *inglês*. And Timóteo had meant no harm—the boy was simply being enthusiastic. But he had to take care, in these wild, alien surroundings, not to lose sight of those strictures that guided him. Without them, Gonsção felt he might lose all sense and sanity, in this land where nothing was familiar.

Goa had been unsettling enough, on the surface so much like Lisboa, but beneath decayed and corrupted by foreign influence. But compared to this wilderness, Goa now seemed a haven of civilization.

It would have been unthinkable to explain to Magister Chinnery that he had been sent as a Special Envoy by Cardinal Albrecht (not really the Pope—that had been a slight exaggeration to secure Timóteo's cooperation) to investigate why first a governor and then a viceroy of Goa had been deposed and recalled to Lisboa on charges of heresy and sorcery. How this could have happened in a colony where an outpost of the Inquisition had been established for the purpose of keeping watch on such things merited grave concern.

When Gonsção had arrived in Goa, he quickly learned the rumors about the Goan Santa Casa had been true; it had fallen into corruption, interested mainly in persecuting those who had wealth to confiscate. But as it happened, there was more to the case of the unfortunate governor and viceroy than this.

At first, Domine Sadrinho, Inquisitor Major of the Santa Casa, had seemed cooperative, offering the information that the ex-governor had been seduced by a cabal of sorcerers, led by Senhor De Cartago and a mysterious woman named Aditi. Then, as Gonsção was trying to learn more about this cabal, events turned very strange indeed.

The sorcerer De Cartago had escaped from Goa, and was then returned to the city by pirates, betrayed by one of the very English who had rescued him from his Portuguese pursuers. However, he was returned dead. The only person with any link to the sorcerer was Magister Thomas Chinnery.

Domine Sadrinho had behaved in a bizarre manner during the questioning of the young *inglês*, withholding information from Gonsção, and trying to exclude Gonsção from the hearing. That is, until the fortuitous meeting with the Jesuit monks Padre Estevão and Brother Andrew Lockheart. In an effort to convince the Santa Casa to release Magister Chinnery, the monks claimed the sorcerer was not dead, only feigning death, and they would prove it.

At the trial of Magister Chinnery, the corpse of the sorcerer De Cartago was brought to the Audience Hall, and the monks applied a brown powder to its mouth. And Gonsção learned it was this powder that had fascinated Domine Sadrinho, and was his primary interest in the case. For this strange brown powder brought the decayed sorcerer's corpse back to life.

Seeking out the source of the powerful, dangerous brown powder was the purpose of the Padre's expedition. The sorcerer would not reveal the secret and died once more. But the young *inglês* had had a map. And the young *inglês* was hung on the strappado until he confessed. And the young *inglês* offered to guide the expedition to the source of the miraculous powder.

Gonsção was not sure how much he trusted Magister Chinnery. The young man seemed cooperative and earnest. Certainly, with his arms injured, he was no threat. But it was clear he had not taken to his new faith with a full heart. That was not so unusual for the newly confessed, but it bore watching.

And there was more between the young *inglês* and the Jesuit Brother Andrew than just one European aiding another. They had known each other a while, it seemed.

Brother Andrew was another cipher; knowledgeable in foreign ways and languages, even worldly. His learning had proved helpful to the expedition, so far. Brother Andrew acted as though concerned about Magister Chinnery's welfare, but Gonsção wondered at the monk's motivations.

The young *inglês* claimed to be an apothecary and might have mercantile reasons for seeking the source of the *pulvis mirificus*. Gonsção had agreed to lead the search for one purpose only; not to return a supply of the powder for the Santa Casa's use, as Domine Sadrinho hoped, but to destroy it.

His horse suddenly stopped and uttered a deep-throated neigh, bringing Gonsção's attention back to where he was. "Idiot beast," Gonsção muttered, "this is no place to stop." He shook the reins. The horse's ears flattened and it began to back up. Gonsção looked around, but saw no reason for the animal's stubbornness. "Get on with you!" He kicked the horse in the flanks.

In the blink of an eye, the horse screamed and reared. Gonsção tumbled to the ground, landing hard on his hip and elbow. "Maria e Jesu, I shall whip that beast," he growled. He heard a cry of pain behind him.

Gonsção rolled over and saw that Timóteo and Magister Chinnery had also been thrown from their mounts, which were galloping madly back down the road. The *inglês* lay on the ground, clutching one shoulder, grimacing with pain. Gonsção began to stand to give aid, when Timóteo leaped to his feet and pointed up the road.

"Padre, watch out!"

Gonsção turned his head. Before him on the road, three arms-lengths away, was a tiger.

Gonsção stared, open-mouthed, having never seen such a magnificent, fearsome beast. The tiger crouched, bared its teeth and snarled at him.

Gonsção had no pistol, no crossbow. He had no experience in fighting, and had brought only a dagger for protection. He tugged at the knife hilt as the enormous cat crept toward him.

"Ai, ai, ai, ai, ai!" Brother Timóteo cried behind him, and rocks began to fall between the Padre and the tiger.

The tiger looked up, startled, and took a step back.

"No, Timóteo!" said Gonsção. "Look to Magister Chinnery and get to safety! Go!"

But Timóteo continued to yell words Gonsção could not understand, and threw stones at the tiger. The great cat's eyes widened and it snarled again, slashing the air with its paw. Timóteo managed to fling one rock right onto the tiger's nose. The tiger jumped back, shook its head, and with an offended glare at Timóteo, loped off into the cover of the jungle. Timóteo ran to the spot where the animal left the road, still shouting strange words and hurling pebbles.

"Enough, Timóteo!" called the Padre. "Come back!"

After a minute, Brother Timóteo left off his attack and returned, his face flushed and hands shaking. "The tiger is gone, Padre."

"Thanks be to God." Padre Gonsção groaned as Timóteo helped him to stand. "That was either very brave or very foolish, my son."

Timóteo shrugged. "It is what my cousins said to do when meeting a tiger. They said it would either fight back or run away, but it makes the tiger as afraid of you as you are of it. To throw rocks is better than being eaten, no?"

"So it is," said Gonsção, dusting off his robe. "What is it you were yelling at the creature?"

"I was telling him to go away and find his dinner elsewhere, in Marathi."

"How fortunate for us that the tiger understands Marathi. Well. I seem only to be bruised. Let us see to poor Magister Chinnery."

As they walked back to the *inglês*, who knelt huddled on the road, Gonsção said, "We owe you a great debt, Timóteo."

"It is nothing, Padre. I am happy to have helped."

As they came up to him, Magister Chinnery said through gritted teeth, "I am ashamed. I should have come to your aid, but—"

"Do not blame yourself, my son," Gonsção said, shaking his head. "What could you have done, but become a meal with me?" He helped the *inglês* to stand and felt gently the area around his left shoulder. "You have not dislocated again, so, with luck, you are no more damaged than before."

"I fear that is of little comfort at the moment," groaned the *inglês*.

"I don't have any more betel leaves," Timóteo said apologetically. "Maybe I can get you some later."

"I thank you, little brother," said the *inglês*, "or perhaps I will beg some *arrak* off the soldiers when we meet up with them again."

"Alas, that may be some time," said Gonsção, looking back down the road. "Our animals have disappeared. If we are fortunate, the carters may catch them before they run all the way back to Goa."

"We may as well walk back to meet them," said Magister Chinnery. "Brother Andrew will be worried when he sees our mounts have returned without us."

"No doubt. Can you walk, my son?"

"It is my arms that hurt, not my legs. I will manage. But, slowly, if you please."

"Very well. Lean upon me should you need to."

As they carefully walked back along the rugged track, Timoteo asked, "Padre, are tigers evil?"

"Evil, my son?"

"Tigers are creatures of God, are they not? But they are made to hunt and eat meat. Does this mean they are monsters?"

"But they are not to hunt Man, Timóteo. Remember, of all creations of God, Man is favored, for only we are made in God's image. It is our place to dominate and subdue Nature, not to submit to it."

"Oh. It was a beautiful animal, no? I hope I didn't hurt him too much. Is something evil just because it is dangerous?"

Gonsção laughed. "Enough questions, Timóteo. I am too unnerved to discuss philosophy at the moment. You have a good heart, but you have so much to learn."

"Yes, you are right, Padre," said Timóteo. "I have much to think about."

There are different sorts of danger, Timóteo, Gonsção thought. *Dangers to the body, and dangers to the soul. And it is the danger to the soul that is most often masked by beauty. Someday you must come to understand this.*

IV

TURQUOISE: This blue stone is found in Persia, and is said
to protect against contagion. The Hindoo believe that to look
on a turquoise during the new moon will bring great wealth.
The Mughuls wear it to protect against serpents and ailments of
the skin. When given as a gift, it will make a friend of an enemy.
It is said to protect against falls, in particular those from
horseback. An amulet of turquoise has the power to warn its
wearer of danger to come....

The Fort of Ahmadnagar could no longer be seen behind
the dust of the Mirza's army. Sunlight glinted, blindingly
bright, on the lanceheads and shields of the Mughul horsemen. Their steeds tossed their heads and snorted, jingling
their bridles and trappings.

The Mirza Ali Akbarshah wished he were astride his own
spirited horse, Niyazik, instead of the ungainly behemoth beneath him. It was galling to one descended from Tatar blood.
The two hundred cavalry were his own men, fine Mughul
warriors all. But the five hundred infantry who walked behind in a scarcely controlled mob were Hindu and other *harbis*, chosen from the available and the expendable. This

rabble required clear symbols of leadership, and Hindu *rajas* led their armies from elephants.

His back ached from the rolling gait of the beast, the painted and gilded *howdah* creaking with each step. The Mirza was all too aware what a prominent target he would be for a skillful bowman.

The only advantage his perch provided was a better view. Yet he found little in the Deccan landscape worth viewing. Red sandstone boulders littered a plain of red sandstone mud, which, drying in the sun, produced red sandstone dust. The monotony was broken only by the occasional hillock of rock topped by a fortress, or small, scrubby village hidden behind small, scrubby trees. *This sameness of scene is one hazard Chand Bibi failed to mention.*

A shout from beside his elephant provided him distraction. The Mirza looked down from his *howdah* and saw his lieutenant, Jaimal, riding alongside. "Some words with you, Lord Mirza?" shouted the lieutenant.

"Of course," said the Mirza, glad for the company. He leaned forward and spoke to the *mahout*. With a few deft taps of his guide-stick, the *mahout* brought the elephant lumbering to a halt. Jaimal gave his horse's reins to another rider and clambered up the harness ropes to the *howdah*.

The *mahout* tapped with his stick again and the elephant lurched forward, causing Jaimal to collide with the Mirza. They both had to grab the *howdah* seats to keep from falling over.

"My apologies, Lord Mirza," said Jaimal, readjusting his turban.

"None are required," said Akbarshah with a rueful smile. "I cannot fathom how maharajas manage to be comfortable on these beasts."

"Perhaps they have wider posteriors, my Lord, from sitting on cushioned thrones."

"Perhaps. It is warm this morning."

"It will be scorching this afternoon," agreed Jaimal.

"I hope a shaded place may be found for our midday prayers."

"Yes, although our comfort should not come before our duty in our thoughts."

The Mirza paused. "Of course. You are right, Jaimal. It shall not." Although the Mirza was Sunni, Jaimal was Shi'a. Jaimal had served Akbarshah well for many years, but still the Mirza exercised caution when discussing matters of faith with his lieutenant. "Nonetheless, it is a foolish general who never thinks of the comfort of his men."

"I am pleased to hear you say so," said Jaimal. There was an odd tone to his voice that the Mirza had come to recognize.

"But you fear I may have forgotten this truth?"

"My Lord, never would I think so ill of you."

"But the subject has been worrying you?"

"Worry? Worry, my Lord, is a thief begging by the door. Let him in out of sympathy and he steals all your courage."

The Mirza Akbarshah sighed. "Then we have nothing to discuss on the matter of comfort?"

Jaimal seemed to be studying the patterns on the rug beneath him. "Perhaps, my Lord."

"Then speak. Have my ears ever been closed to you?"

"Not to me, my Lord. But some of the men have . . . concerns."

"I shall hear them as though they were my own."

"Very well. It has been observed, Lord Mirza, that we left Ahmadnagar with unsociable haste."

"Unsociable?"

"His Shining Highness, Prince Murad, had offered to share food and women from his supply, as well as the aid of his men in finding what we seek. Your warriors wonder why you have disdained his generosity."

"Do they? You are no fool, Jaimal. Can you not see some purpose hidden within Prince Murad's 'generosity'?"

After a moment, Jaimal replied, "He had hopes we would

reciprocate by adding more men to his troops and to help him provoke Ahmadnagar to rebellion. Perhaps to take the province at last."

"And bring long-sought glory to his name. Just so. But would this not mean an indefinite delay to our expedition. Perhaps an end to it?"

Softly, Jaimal replied, "Some might prefer a swift battle for a prize they can see, than a long march toward one they cannot."

"Ah. Do they not know that, if we are successful, the power we will capture for the Shahinshah will make Ahmadnagar seem trivial?"

"I have told them, Lord Mirza. But they fear we are chasing phantoms."

"I see. What do you think would reassure them?"

"If my Lord could promise that there will be great treasure awaiting them at our destination, and that each man will have his share—"

"Would you have me lie to them, Jaimal? There is but one treasure the Padshah ordered me to find, and that will be for his possession alone. What would become of us if the men felt we had unjustly tricked them? In a distant land, it is easy for commanders to be lost to 'ravenous tigers' or other unforeseen disasters."

Jaimal sighed. "I understand, my Lord."

"I will not goad the men with tales of great treasure. Duty to the Shahinshah and glory to come should be sufficient."

"For our people, perhaps, but for the *harbis*—"

"Fear of punishment should serve for them."

Another shout came from ahead of them down the road. The elephant lurched to a halt again and horsemen rode past. The Mirza peered around the *mahout*'s shoulder. "What is happening?"

"There is a man standing in the road, Sri Mirza." The *mahout* pointed with his stick.

Some yards ahead, a lone figure in a dusty robe of white wool and an unkempt beard, stood, arms upraised. "The fool," said Akbarshah. "What could he possibly want?"

"It may be a trick, my Lord," said Jaimal. "This area is infested with brigands. He may have stopped us to distract us from an attack."

The Mirza looked around. "An army of brigands would have difficulty hiding in this region. Go and see what he wants. And tell the men to be alert in case it is a trick."

"Very well, my Lord." Jaimal slipped over the side of the *howdah*. At his orders the elephant was quickly surrounded by horsemen, swords at ready.

Some minutes later, Jaimal returned alongside the elephant, the strange-looking man with him. "My Lord. This man would speak with you."

"What is he?"

"He is a Sufi, my Lord. Come from Bijapur."

"From Bijapur. News of our approach moves quickly. I have heard Sufis are capable of miracles. Send him up." In truth, the mystic Way of the Sufis was baffling to the Mirza, and he could understand why some of the Faith claimed it to be heresy. Yet princes throughout the Empire, and the Islamic world beyond, sought the counsel of Sufi *sheykhs*.

Akbarshah lowered a rope ladder and the odd man climbed up swift as a monkey. Jaimal climbed warily behind. The Sufi smiled broadly as he entered the *howdah* and knelt on the rug.

He appeared to be past thirty years of age. Long, unkempt hair stuck out from under his turban and his long, unkempt beard splayed over his tunic of white wool. Yet there was an eager intensity in this man's eyes that showed his ill grooming was not from poverty, but that his attention was directed elsewhere.

"The Lord Mirza is gracious to receive this humble follower of the Path," said the Sufi.

"You do me honor to accept my invitation," said the Mirza. "Will you accept some water from me?" Akbarshah poured some water from a stoppered ewer into a silver cup. This he handed to the Sufi.

The mystic took the cup in both hands and drank it down in one swallow. He then held out the cup for more. "If the Lord pleases . . ."

The Mirza poured another cupful and again the Sufi drank it all at once. The Mirza frowned. "You have much thirst. Will you partake of some dried fruit and almonds?" He opened a cloth sack to serve a portion.

"The Lord Mirza is most generous!" said the Sufi, and he reached a hand into the sack. Pulling out a fistful, the mystic eagerly gobbled it down.

The Mirza shared a glance with Jaimal, but said nothing concerning their guest's horrid manners. "You have great hunger as well, I see. Have you refreshed yourself at all since leaving Bijapur?"

"Very little, Lord Mirza," said the Sufi around a mouthful of dates. "So great was my wish to find you."

"To find me?"

Jaimal scowled. "What is your name, man? Who sent you?"

The Sufi ducked his head in a quick bow. "My name is Masum al-Wadud. I come from the Chisti compound on Shahpur Hillock, outside of Bijapur. I am sent by the will of the Compassionate One Who Sees All Things. It is our way to be unconcerned for the body, if it prepares the way for meeting the Divine."

"I have heard of these Chisti Sufi. They are poets," Jaimal said with disapproval, "and artisans. Who is your teacher, your *pir?*"

Masum smiled gently and shook his head. "That I may not tell you. My *pir* has forbidden it."

"You see, My Lord, the rumored arrogance of these peo-

ple is true," said Jaimal. "They disdain the company of noblemen."

"No, no," said Masum. "It is not from arrogance. We are
merely aware of the temptations of court life. Should a *pir*
offer himself to the company of princes, he becomes inca-
pable of the solitary contemplation that brings wisdom. My
pir only wishes to spare himself from contamination—"

"There, you see?" said Jaimal. "As if we were the lowest
of Hindu castes. Is it not taught that all men are equal in the
sight of the Merciful?"

"Jaimal, please," said Akbarshah, raising a hand. "Tell us,
Masum, why you felt it was so important to find us."

"I have had dreams, Lord Mirza."

"Ah. Dreams."

"Powerful dreams, Lord Mirza. I dreamed I saw a great
general who journeyed from north to south in search of the
Fountain of Life. In the dream, he found what he sought, yet
it was surrounded by serpents, and the fountain contained
not water, but blood."

The Mirza rubbed his beard. "Such a dream could have
many meanings."

"Perhaps. But this dream occurred on many nights. I told
it to my *pir* and he said surely it is a message from the angels.
He said I must follow the dream until I am led to that which
it signifies."

"And you believe I am the general in your dream?"

"Is it not apparent? I have encountered you here on a road
heading south." Masum turned to Jaimal. "I dreamed of you
as well."

"Me?"

"Indeed, there was a man with the general in my dream
who looked much as you do. In one hand he held gold, but
this turned into dust. In the other hand he held dust that
turned into gold."

Jaimal laughed. "If that dream were true, I should fill my bags with the dust of the road."

"It would serve you as well as if they were filled with gold."

Jaimal's smile faded into a frown of confusion.

"So, Masum," said the Mirza, "now that you have told us your dream, I will tell you the truth. We are indeed on a quest on behalf of the Shahinshah Emperor Akbar. We seek a queen who lives in a hidden fortress in a mountain, who may be immortal, and has powers of life and death."

The Sufi raised his eyes to heaven and murmured a soft prayer. "Truly I am rightly guided," he said.

"So," said the Mirza, "now that you have found the truth behind your dream, what will you do? Have you come to warn us? Will you try to dissuade us from our journey?"

"Dissuade? No, Lord Mirza. I believe I am . . . to witness. And to give counsel where I may. I believe what you seek is of great importance, greater than the ambitions of sultans or emperors. I offer what little strength and wisdom I possess to your service."

"My Lord," said Jaimal, "we do not need a beggar to be another drain on our resources."

"But I will not be as the guest who stays too long," said Masum. "I have been a soldier. And although I am now a man of peace, I still remember what an army requires—the many lowly tasks, the grooming of horses, the carrying of water, the polishing of swords, and so forth."

"And a holy man such as yourself," said Jaimal, "is willing to stoop to such 'lowly tasks'?"

"My *pir* teaches that by submitting oneself to the daily work required by life, one learns the meaning of duty and the steadfastness that paves the path to the Divine."

"You will find much to guide you to enlightenment among us, then," said the Mirza with a wry smile. "But now that you know our goal, have you heard any folklore near Bijapur concerning the great *rani* we seek?"

"Ah, as to your goal. I do know a story that is pertinent."

Jaimal held up a hand. "My Lord, he is only going to tell us some infernal Sufi tale."

"If it is pertinent as he says, Jaimal, then I will hear it. Continue, Masum."

"As you will, Lord Mirza. Once, long ago, three men, a Scholar, a Merchant, and a Beggar, all went to the same teacher, all on the same day, at the same hour, each demanding that the *pir* show them Something Wonderful. The *pir* told all of them that if they walked for one entire day due east from the town, they would, indeed, discover Something Wonderful.

"So the following day, these three men walked together, from sunrise to sunset down the road leading east from town. As the sun was setting behind them, they came to a small, shaded spring. The keeper of the well gave each of the thirsty travelers a cup of water.

"The Scholar, who had hoped to come upon a School of Great Learning, gulped the water down and looked around. 'I see nothing special here,' he complained. 'Do you, friend?'

"The Merchant, who had hoped to come upon a Treasure of Great Value, said, 'No, not at all.' After downing his cup of water, he added, 'I think we may have been tricked.'

"But the Beggar, who knew only that he was hot and weary after their long journey, sat in the shade and sipped the cool, pure water of the spring and sighed, 'Ah. This is wonderful.' " Masum bowed, to show his story was finished.

"I hope," grumbled Jaimal, "that we will come upon more than a cup of water at the end of our journey."

The Sufi looked at him sadly. "You will find what your journey prepares you to find. If you accept the lessons given you, what you find at the end of your Path will, indeed, be wondrous."

"Ah-hmmm," said the Mirza. "I had hoped for a story that said more about our journey across the Deccan, not the spiritual journey of life."

"I was speaking of them both," said Masum.

The Mirza Akbarshah was spared a reply by the sound of the call to prayer. "Well, Masum, it would seem you have chosen our prayer-site for us. Jaimal, when prayers are finished, see that our new servant is assigned tasks appropriate for him. I will take to heart all you have said regarding the concerns of the men."

Jaimal nodded once and escorted the Sufi down out of the *howdah*. The Mirza was about to follow when his hand fell on the silver cup from which the Sufi had been drinking. He picked it up and looked into it. *Something wonderful . . .* he mused. But he saw only his own distorted reflection at the bottom of the cup.

V

CALENDULA: Also called pot-marigold, this plant has furred leaves and golden flowers that bloom much of the year. 'Tis said the Holy Virgin favored this flower and wore it upon her garments. An infusion of the leaves will ease pains of the heart, while a paste of petals and leaves will heal all manner of wounds. Some say it can bring visions of a thief who has stolen from you. The flower is oft used to determine if one is loved and whether that love is true. Though some say the marigold brings ill-luck to love, for it sprang from a Greek maid who pined from desire for the Sun god, Apollo....

"E *mpura! Ho!*" Lockheart shouted and the *soldados* and carters pushed as one, while the oxen strained to pull the cart up the rutted road.

This horrid track scarce deserves the title of "road," thought Thomas, watching from his mule. Though now out of the jungle, the way up the Western Ghats had become even worse than before; it was narrow and cut by rivulets, blocked by boulders, and at times disappeared entirely beneath mud and rockfalls. It did not improve matters that there was a sheer drop on one side down a stony mountainside into thorny brush and scrub. It was worse than any road Thomas had seen in England.

"Ai! Cuidado! Cuidado!" The cart was rolling but sliding perilously close to the mountainside's steep slope. There came a spray of rocks and the cart slewed sideways, its right rear wheel going over the edge. The cart tilted and bundles came loose from their ropes and tumbled away down the mountainside. Two carters went sliding down to retrieve them, while others braved the slopeside to brace the cart up.

Dear God, if the cart tumbles, 'twill take men, ox, and all with it. Thomas slid off his mule and ran to aid them. He pushed his back up against the right rear corner of the cart, ignoring the pain that lanced through his shoulders. He turned and pushed with his legs, crying out as the weight of the cart bore down on him. The ox bellowed as it strained against its yoke, as its flanks were desperately whipped by its driver.

More men joined Thomas beneath the cart, even Padre Gonsção. Together they gave a mighty shove and the cart slid forward, all wheels again coming to rest on the road. A cheer rose up from the *soldados* and carters, and Thomas sighed with relief.

He turned to walk back to his mule and his left foot slid out from under him. Thomas's right knee buckled and that leg slid down as well. Thomas flung out his arms with a shout, but the only purchase his hands could find were more rocks and pebbles that pulled loose at his grasp. Inexorably, he slid faster and faster down the gravelly slope.

"Magister Chinnery!" In moments, Padre Gonsção was at his side, scrabbling at the hillside with him. Together, they slid into a large bush. A grouse, disturbed by their impact, burbled and took off in an explosion of feathers.

"Are you well, Magister?"

"I seem to be," Thomas gasped, although his shoulders burned with pain. He looked back up the slope where concerned faces peered down at them.

"Ho, Tom!" called Lockheart. "How fare you?"

"Alive, methinks."

"And the Padre?"

"The same."

"Have you a rope?" Padre Gonsção yelled up at them.

"I believe we can salvage one."

"Then do so, if you will."

"Padre," Thomas said as he sat up, his back against the bush, "a rope will be no use to me. I have done more hurt to my arms and can grasp nothing."

As one end of a hemp rope came tumbling down the hillside, the Padre said, "Do not be foolish, my son. I will tie the rope to you and those above will haul you up."

"And how will you ascend?"

"I will pray that you do not break the rope, so that it may be thrown down again."

As the Padre tied the rope around his chest, Thomas said, "This is much kindness you show to a former heretic."

"We must take good care of you, my son. Without you, we are all lost, are we not?"

You are lost with me as well, though you know it not, thought Thomas.

"However," the Padre went on, "as Timóteo has rescued me, and I have helped rescue you, next time it is your turn do to the rescuing, eh?"

Thomas responded with only a weak smile as the men above hauled him up.

"You've no hurt, then?" said Lockheart, as he helped Thomas to stand.

"Only my shoulders and arms, as ever. And my pride."

"Ah. That must be why you fell, as your pride went before. Rest here a moment."

Thomas was propped up against a cart as the *soldados* pulled the Padre up the slope. For a moment he wondered, *What if the Padre had died, in the fall or by the claws of the tiger? What would become of our expedition? Might we disband and thereby might I find my freedom?* Thomas shook his head, deciding the thought unworthy. *Freedom may come, but may it not be through any man's death.*

Thomas glanced up the road and saw, far ahead, the camel drivers waiting. Their sure-footed beasts better suited to such uncertain paths, they had had no trouble ascending the hill. But none of Sri Agnihotra's merchants had come back down the road to give the Goans aid.

"Why do they not help us?" said Thomas.

"Mayhap you should ask the Padre, lad. Ah, here he is. I shall leave you in his care, for I spy another cart in danger of a prideful fall."

As Lockheart departed, Thomas turned to see Padre Gonsção dusting off his once-white robe. "I am glad to see the rope held, Padre. But tell me, do you know why the Hindu merchants watch us struggle with no offer of assistance?"

"It is their heathen stubbornness," the Padre growled with a dark glare up the road.

Thomas wondered if there was a specific incident that had led to the Padre's distrust of the caravaneers, or if Gonsção merely trusted no one who was not Portuguese, or at least European. "Perhaps," he said, "someone might diplomatically suggest that we will reach our mutual goal faster if they add their strength to ours."

The Padre regarded Thomas for some moments. "You are right, Magister Chinnery. Someone should go to them. And, as it seems that more harm may come to you here among the carts than the good you might do, you are clearly the proper emissary."

"Me? But wouldn't Brother Andrew be more suitable, as he speaks their language?"

"At this time, the good Brother's brawny arms are more useful than his knowledge. And Domina Agnihotra, you remember, has some interest in you. She asks about you nearly every day."

Though his heart raced, Thomas attempted to keep his

countenance calm. "Has she? Well, she finds my yellow hair and light-blue eyes unusual. She thinks me an amusing freak."

"Perhaps you can charm her, then, into sending us aid. Take Timóteo with you. The boy can speak for you to the camel drivers, and it will keep him out of our troubles down here."

"As you wish, Padre." *Surely he cannot suspect there is aught between the Lady and me if he sends me to her very side. Although mayhap the little brother's company is meant to be a check upon my behavior. No matter. At last I may speak again to the woman in whom all my hope lies.*

"Good. Let me help you onto your mule."

Thomas winced as, with a shove from the Padre, he flopped, belly down, onto the saddle and swung a leg over. "Should Joaquim come with me, do you think?" The *soldado* had been helpful at keeping Timóteo at bay before and might do so again.

The Padre eyed Thomas with a slight smile. "We need his strength here as well. Magister Chinnery, I do not think you are so foolish as to abandon us in the midst of nothing, with your arms as they are. I have found that if you treat a man as if his word were good, he often proves it so. Go on with you." He slapped the rump of Thomas's mule to start it walking.

Thomas carefully negotiated his beast around the oxcarts and milling men, wondering if Joaquim had broken his vow, or if the Padre was simply a keen observer of humanity. He hoped it was the latter.

He found Brother Timóteo sitting on his burro at the front of the line of carts. "Padre Gonsção says you are to come with me."

The boy's somber face brightened and he clicked at his burro to bring it alongside Thomas's mule. "Where are we going, Tomás?"

"Up the road to Sri Agnihotra's people, to see if we can convince them to give us assistance with the carts."

"Oh. I do not think they will."

"Why not?"

"I do not think they like us." Timóteo then fell silent.

Thomas let the conversation lapse, and let his mule pick its way up the road as he looked out at the vistas to the west. Below, a trace of mist clung to the forest and rolling hills, and far beyond lay the grey-blue expanse of the sea. To the southwest, he could just barely see the tallest buildings of Goa. Here and there, exotic domes and pyramidal temple roofs jutted above the jungle canopy. The view would have been beautiful, did it not show him how far he was from things familiar, and the ocean route home.

Thomas became concerned at Timóteo's uncharacteristic quiet. "Is something wrong, Timóteo? Have you become homesick?"

"Hmm? Oh, no, Tomás. Well, a little maybe. But . . . well . . . the . . . Padre, he is not happy with me. He lectured me about braving the tiger. And about running around and looking at things when we have stopped for the night. He told me it was wrong to make him worry about me when he has so many other things to worry about. I am important to him and our quest and I must take better care for my own safety. He is right. I have been foolish."

Thomas laughed gently. "That does not mean you should be harsh with yourself. You are young and this is your first long journey. Naturally everything interests you. Should one not be as forgiving to oneself as one is to others?"

"But I have an important duty," Timóteo said. "God has sent me on this journey for a purpose. I must remember that." He nervously toyed with the string ties to a jute bag that hung from his saddle.

Thomas wondered at the boy's odd, prideful words. *Yet see how he frowns with care. Perhaps pride is not the cause.*

At last they reached the top of the switchback, where the road widened onto a broad ledge, shaded by a cluster of evergreen trees. Camels kneeling in the shade raised their long necks to stare at the new arrivals. The Lady Aditi's gold-and-purple palanquin was ensconced in the deepest shade, surrounded by her waiting girls who sat fanning themselves.

As Thomas and Timóteo approached, the girls pointed and chattered excitedly. One of them jumped up and spoke into the curtains of the palanquin.

Thomas was surprised by the warm anticipation he felt as he saw the palanquin. Before Goa, his more tender thoughts had always been filled with Anna Coulter, his Master's daughter. Thomas had assumed that, upon his return from the East with greater wealth and experience, that the mild and patient Anna would become his wife. But since meeting the exotic Aditi, Anna's face had become hard to recall, and her name caused no more stirring in him.

Casually, Thomas said, "Do you speak Greek, Timóteo?"

"No, Tomás. Though I would like very much to learn it."

"Hm. Perhaps I will teach you some one day." *But at least you will have no understanding of what I say to Aditi now.*

"Would you? I would like that very much, Tomás. My grandfather told me all the old Greek stories, about the gods and monsters and all. That is why—" Timóteo suddenly stopped and looked down at his saddle. "That is why I would like to learn," he finished at last.

Something strange has come over the boy. I suppose the Padre does not approve of Timóteo's love of pagan stories. Well, I shall not concern myself with that now.

As they rode up, the girl who had spoken to the palanquin ran up to Thomas, taking the reins of his mule.

"Do you understand what she is saying, Timóteo?"

"She says you are to speak with her lady at once, Tomás."

"Then I suppose I must do so. It would be helpful if you would go talk with some of the camel drivers. Tell them we can all move faster if they would help us with the carts. See if there is anything they require, or if they have recommendations about the road ahead."

Timóteo pursed his mouth, his eyes fearful.

"The Padre said it is important that we keep good relations with Ad—Agnihotra's people. You can speak their language, yes?"

"Perhaps. I think so. They may not speak to me because I am a Christian."

"Ah. Well. If that is a problem, I suppose you will have to go sit and talk with the serving girls, then. Perhaps you can charm them into persuading the camel drivers."

Timóteo's eyes widened. Clearly that was a more terrifying prospect. "I will try to talk to the merchants, Tomás."

"Good. The Padre will again be pleased by your courage, Timóteo. Do the best you can."

"I will, Tomás," Timóteo murmured, and he rode off into the midst of the blinking, grass-chewing camels.

Thomas let his mule be led up to the palanquin. He paused before attempting to dismount, and then realized he would seem a fool no matter what. He grit his teeth and braced his hands against the mule's withers and swung his leg over. To his relief, the mule did not shift and he slid down beside it without falling. He rested against the neck of the mule for a moment while the pain in his arms subsided. Then he went to kneel beside the purple curtains.

The woman within said, in Greek, "Ah, Tamas. How wonderful that you should be sent to visit me. It has been a long time since we talked." Her voice was smooth and sweet as warm honey. Thomas was both amazed and frightened by such bewitchment.

Softly he replied, "And I am pleased to speak with you again, Despoina Aditi. I trust the journey has not been a trial to you thus far?"

"I have traveled a great deal in my life, Tamas. I was born

to a family of caravaneers. I am used to it. And you, Tamas, how do you fare?"

"Well enough, Despoina, though with difficulty. My arms, I fear, do not serve me well, and the Padre says my recovery will be slow."

"Poor Tamas! Does the priest of the Orlem Gor still torment you?"

"No, Despoina, no, the Padre treats me with all courtesy. Just this morning, he risked his life to aid me when I fell down a hillside. I am watched and guarded, but no harm has been done me since we left Goa."

"A priest of the Orlem Gor saved your life? I can hardly believe it."

"Nor I. But Padre Gonsção is from Portugal, not Goa. Perhaps the . . . Orlem Gor is different there."

"That is not what Bernardo told me. Poor Bernardo. At least he left this world before the Orlem Gor could get their claws into him."

Thomas paused and decided that it would only bring her pain to know that Bernardo De Cartago had, indeed, been taken into the Santa Casa, and his rotting corpse revived with the *rasa mahadevi*. Still, the sorcerer had his vengeance—his resurrected body could feel none of the Santa Casa's torments and he soon died once more, revealing no secrets.

"Why do you not speak, Tamas?"

"I was remembering Despos De Cartago. I still feel some guilt for his death."

"Do not. It was best for him. But let us talk of pleasanter things. Why has the Priest Gonsção been so kind as to let you speak to me?"

"I am sent because there is little I can do to move our oxcarts any faster, with my arms useless as they are. The Padre hoped that I could persuade you to send some of your camel drivers down the road to aid our men."

Aditi clicked her tongue. "My people tried to dissuade

the priests of the Orlem Gor from hiring oxcarts. They told them the road would be too difficult, but the priests would not listen. The Orlem Gor does not trust our merchants, and would not allow their goods to be loaded upon our camels. It is their own stubborn pride that has brought this trouble. I would not think of insulting my caravaneers by making them help such ingrates."

Thomas laughed. "How curious, Despoina. The Padre believes it is your people who are prideful. Shall I inform the Padre that you are offended?"

"If you think he would listen. You say you are guarded. Who watches you now?"

"The boy monk, Timóteo, rode here with me. But I sent him to speak to your camel drivers, so he is not near."

"Then we are alone?" A slender arm, adorned with a silver bracelet in the shape of a serpent biting its tail, slipped out from between the curtains. The long fingers lightly brushed against the skin of his forearm, causing the sun-bronzed hairs to stand on end.

Thomas sucked in his breath and shivered. "But for your handmaids, Despoina."

"They are my eyes and ears, Tamas. They are loyal to me. Ah, if only you could slip inside my palanquin and talk to me. It has been so long since we gazed at one another's faces."

Thomas's eyes widened and his pulse raced at what she might be suggesting. "Despoina, that would not be . . . seemly. Neither your people nor mine would think well of it. It would not be wise." *Nor have my arms the strength to bear my weight nor hold you, desirable as that may be.*

"Wisdom flees," she said gently, "when beauty beckons."

"When we first met, Despoina, you were not so . . . taken with my beauty."

"When we first met, Tamas, I was a prisoner on your ship and you were helping your captain arrange my ransom."

"When I begged your aid in Goa, you said I had less dignity than the lowest Hindu caste."

"Well, to disguise yourself by rolling in mud, Tamas, was a foolish thing. But you have since proved yourself brave and clever. Few escape the Orlem Gor as you have."

"It is questionable whether I have yet escaped."

"But you will, Tamas."

"I . . . will you aid me?"

"Have I not said that I joined this caravan for that very purpose?"

Thomas leaned his head back against the frame of the palanquin and breathed a sigh of joy. "I have told the Padre only that Bijapur is our next destination and that our route will be determined from there. Will you speak to the Sultan of Bijapur on my behalf so that he might grant me refuge in his service?"

"If that is what you wish. But I had thought you wanted to follow a more spiritual path, to seek the Mahadevi and learn her ways."

With a shock, Thomas realized he had entrapped himself. He had first gained Aditi's help in Goa by claiming that the sorcerer Bernardo De Cartago had convinced him to seek out the mysterious goddess, she "whose name is Strength," and to learn the secrets of the *rasa mahadevi*, the "blood of the goddess," as the miraculous powder was called.

"Ah," said Thomas. "Nai, so I intend. But first we must be rid of the Padre and his men, mustn't we? In Bijapur, the Sultan will have the power to send them away. Once free of them, I will be able to continue my intended journey." *Which tends now more toward home than spiritual quests.*

There was a long pause behind the curtains of the palanquin. "Of course. It would be impossible for the priest to find the *rasa mahadevi* without you, nai?"

"I believe so."

"There is some doubt?"

"He has in his possession De Cartago's map."

"He has a map?" Aditi's arm shot back inside the palanquin as if it had been burned.

Damned fool! Wherefore did I tell her that? "Calm yourself, Despoina. It is only paper with symbols upon it. The Padre cannot himself interpret it. That is why I was brought on this expedition."

"How did he get this map?"

Thomas sighed, wondering at this turn of conversation—speaking less of love and more of intrigue. "De Cartago had given it to me for safekeeping when we were held together as prisoners of the Arab sea raiders. Alas, when I was captured and taken to the Santa Casa, my clothing was taken from me and searched, and the map therein was found."

"You have seen this map and know that it is unreadable?"

"No. I was only told so by De Cartago, who explained some of the symbols to me."

There came a soft torrent of foreign words that might have been vociferous cursing.

"Forgive me. Have I distressed you, Despoina?" Thomas was suddenly distracted as he saw Lockheart approaching on horseback.

"Distressed me? Tamas, it must be that you do not understand."

"Your pardon, Despoina. Another comes who speaks this tongue. I may no longer be free with you."

"Ah."

"Ho, Thomas!" The burly Scot gave Thomas a knowing grin as he dismounted. "If you've plans on close diplomacy with our lady, lad, best be quick. The Padre has come to his senses and has called for redistribution of the goods to horse and muleback, to speed our progress. Which brings me to my purpose. I've come for your mule."

" 'Tis not my mule," said Thomas. "Take him as you will. You may have Timóteo's ass, as well."

"My appetites do not run to young boys, Tom."

Thomas felt himself blush and he scowled. "You know well my meaning, Andrew. You would scandalize the Padre, if he heard you. What manner of monk speaks thus?"

Lockheart sighed as he dismounted. "I grow more aweary of this guise each passing day. A man may not be a man in't."

"What funny-speak I hear is this?" came Aditi's voice in strange, high-pitched broken Latin. "I do not understand funny-yellow-hair. Amused not me. Be kind to old woman you."

Lockheart smirked at Thomas and said, "Forgive us, Domina Agnihotra. We speak the tongue of our homeland. No doubt it sounds strange to you."

"Like the hissing of belching snakes, it sounds."

"A very . . . picturesque description, Domina."

Thomas heard the rapid pounding of feet, and Brother Timóteo rounded the palanquin.

"Frater Andrew, are the carts coming?"

"In time, little brother. But we require your burro and Thomas's mule."

"Let me come back and help you. I can do nothing here. The drivers shoo me away and the camels spit at me."

Lockheart chuckled. "I am sorry, Frater Timóteo, but Padre Gonsção insists that you remain. He says you should not often dare the intercession of angels, or one day they will tire of you and let disaster strike. Take care of Magister Chinnery for us and we will return soon."

With a frustrated sigh, Timóteo sat in the dirt beside Thomas. Lockheart walked to where Aditi's handmaidens had tied the mule and burro. Taking their reins in hand, Lockheart remounted his own steed and, with a cheery wave, returned down the hill.

"Who is out there?" said Aditi in her strange Latin.

"It is only I and young Brother Timóteo, Domina Agnihotra," said Thomas.

"Hmp. Leave me now. I wish rest."

Thomas felt his spirits sink. "As you will, Domina. Well, Timóteo, where shall we go? Have you noticed any interesting herbs nearby?"

"No, but I will help you look, Tomás."

"Then let us go." Thomas let Timóteo help him up and lead him away.

Aditi wrapped her arms around her knees, her thoughts churning as Vishnu had churned the sea to bring the immortal-drink *amrita. It is all more complicated than I had planned. More dangerous. Must I kill the priest of the Orlem Gor too?* She fingered the hilt of the knife in her skirtband. *It is unfortunate enough that I must kill such a pretty one as Tamas.*

It surprised Aditi how much she had hoped the Englishman had truly wanted to learn of the Mahadevi. *Is it loneliness? I have felt alone since Bernardo's death. I did not love him, but he was a good companion. He understood me, I think. Was it wrong to choose my dharma over a life with him? He might have lived, had I done so. But could I have left all I had ever known, all that I was meant to do, for a man I did not love? Would that have been so different from the rest of my life?*

After all, she had been born a wanderer, to a family of caravaneers in Rajasthan. By the age of six, she could ride a camel, spoke four languages, and had seen more of Sind than many a prince and conqueror. And at age seven, her family took a caravan south toward Calicut, across the Deccan. They were set upon by bandits who slew them all, save for Aditi who had hidden in a crevice in some rocks.

She had wandered, alone, the next day, following the one remaining camel, as her father had often advised her to do if lost. It led her to a village beside a broad, brown river. The villagers were so amazed to see a girl-child come out of the wilderness alone, a child with grey-blue eyes (not so rare in Rajasthan, but unknown in the Deccan) that they assumed she was a gift from the gods. They named her Aditi, after the goddess of the sky, and took her to their holy mountain, Bhagavati, where the Mahadevi dwelled.

Thus Aditi grew up the ward of a goddess, a woman she only saw in shadows on a screen—for to look upon the face of the Mahadevi brought death. Her *ayas* were two old women who claimed they had been ancient forever. She was taught their language, Hellenica, and how to read and write, and many other things no Hindu girl had the privilege to learn. And when she was old enough, Aditi was again sent out into the world, to serve as the Mahadevi's eyes and ears, and Her messenger.

Since then, Aditi had traveled throughout western Sind, revered and respected by some who received her, feared and shunned by others. But always a stranger, in a land where the bonds of family and caste affected all things.

Great Mother, what shall I do? If only Tamas had not followed me into Goa and begged my aid. If only I had turned him away. If only I did not feel that somehow his life and mine are joined in some greater purpose.

But he is lying to me. I hear it in his voice. He is an herbalist and healer, he says. Perhaps he seeks the rasa mahadevi *for his own knowledge. If it were him alone—I could take him to the Mahadevi, and She would teach him if his intentions were honorable, destroy him if they were not. But I cannot let the priests of the Orlem Gor find Her—the destruction She would cause if Her wrath were awakened would be terrible.*

Perhaps Tamas only wishes to escape Sind, to go home. Yet, even so, he might tell those of his nation of the rasa mahadevi *and armies would come in search of it. Bernardo told me all Englishmen were barbarians, liars, and thieves. Perhaps he was right.*

VI

CARNELIAN: This clear, red stone has held importance since the ancients, who used it for their seals and would place it upon the throats of their dead. It was thought to dispel witchcraft, and to keep at bay nightmares and ghosts. It protects the wearer from collapsing houses. It cures ailments of the lungs and teeth. It is said that the Prophet of the Mohammedans wore a ring of this stone, and to those of that faith it brings peace amid disorder, tempers anger, enhances dignity, and bestows courage in battle....

The Mirza Akbarshah stared up at the starry night sky, seeking a sign from Heaven. *Ras al Ghul*, the Demon Star, glared redly down at him. *Merciful One, may that not be what influences our deeds.*

Beyond a line of rocky hills ahead of them lay a village. Scouts had returned, reporting that the villagers refused to speak or offer hospitality to the Mirza's men. *So. The Shahinshah wishes his might to become known in the Deccan. And my men have become restive, like the horses beneath them. So. It is time to let them have their head. May Allah, the All-Forgiving, judge that I have done right.*

Drawing his long *talwar* saber from its sheath, the Mirza

held it up outside of the *howdah*, where every man could see it. Torchlight glimmered on the steel, illuminating the inscription on the blade: "He that heeds not the warnings of the Merciful shall have the Devil for his companion." There was an eager stillness in the men assembled below him.

"Allah Akbar!" the Mirza shouted, and he pointed the saber forward.

He was answered with an eerie howl as though a horde of djinn had been released from bondage. The horsemen swirled past the Mirza's elephant, as though it were a boulder in a rushing stream, horse manes flowing like sprays of water. The Mirza sighed, wishing he were riding with them.

Instead, his elephant lumbered, trumpeting, into the village behind the horsemen as they crashed through the flimsy stockade, a surging flood of flesh and steel. Small dark-skinned villagers ran screaming from their hovels. The horsemen rode to every hut, jabbing the mud and straw walls with their lances. "Come out, worthless *harbis!*" they cried. "Come forth and meet your masters! Behold the might of Allah and tremble!"

The footsoldiers entered every hut and rousted out what residents remained, whether hiding or sleeping, and herded them into the center of the village. Some of the soldiers built a bonfire there, out of the broken fence and bits of houses. The villagers huddled anxiously together, their skins and gold jewelry glistening in the firelight. They stared at the Mirza on his elephant as he urged the beast toward them, their eyes wide and distrustful.

The elephant stopped and the Mirza regarded them a while, wondering what might unlock the secrets behind their eyes. *Were I a true Soldier of the Faith, I should seize each pagan by the neck and lay my sword against it, crying "Accept Allah as God or die!"* But this was not a jihad, much as his men might wish it so. Other things were needed from these people. Their souls would have to wait.

He leaned out of the *howdah* and shouted down, "In the name of Allah, the All-Seeing and the Merciful, and his servant the Shahinshah Allahu Akbar the Magnificent, Khalifah and Ruler of all Sind, we bring you greeting." One of the footmen translated his words into the barbaric tongue of the villagers.

These words were met with silence. The Mirza heard only the crackling of the fire and the tired whining of an infant.

"You seem amazed at our arrival," Akbarshah went on, "yet we sent messengers to tell you of our coming. But they were not welcomed. Perhaps you did not believe them when they described our power. But now you see us. Now you must believe in the might of Akbar.

"But you need not fear us. We come as bringers of Truth, and seekers of Truth. We bring to you the Law of the One Pure Faith and the Word of the Shining Prophet. We seek from you knowledge of a great *rani* who lives somewhere in this region. A queen who may be immortal, and has the power of life and death."

The villagers looked at one another, but still no one spoke. Jaimal stepped forward and jabbed at some of the villagers with his lance. "Speak! Our Mirza commands you!"

The Mirza held up his hand and ordered Jaimal back. "Any who will tell us of this fabled queen will earn our favor, and come to know the generosity of the Shahinshah Akbar. We will give twenty bars of silver to anyone who will tell us what we wish to know."

The villagers began to murmur among themselves. Akbarshah noted how, even in calamity, they had sorted themselves into small clusters, the better dressed apart from those in rags. *How they cling to their castes, unaware that in the sight of the One, they are all equal.* Some of the poorer ones seemed inclined to speak up, except that their neighbors held them back.

"Very well. I have told you of the mercy and generosity of His Imperial Majesty Akbar. Now I give you warning of his anger. If you tell me nothing, your village will be burned, and your people sent in chains north to his Empire. Any who resist shall die."

Wails of protest and pleas for mercy erupted from the villagers. They raised their arms to him, and some fell to their knees, imploring.

"Silence!" the Mirza roared. "Let no one speak unless he tells me what I wish to know." But their wailing did not cease and no one came forward.

"My Lord General," came a voice beside his elephant. "I beg a word."

The Mirza glanced over the side of the *howdah* and saw the Sufi, Masum, clinging to the elephant's harness. "What would you? Be brief."

"My Lord, trouble these people no more, I beg you. I have found one who will speak of the thing you wish."

"That was well done, Masum. Bring this person to us."

"I cannot, Lord Mirza."

"You cannot?"

"No, Lord Mirza. We must go where she is."

"What nonsense is this?"

"She is not of this village, Lord, and her caste is such that she cannot enter this part of the village. We must go to her."

The Mirza sighed. *Would that my valiant ancestors had found a more sensible people to conquer.* He opened the door of the *howdah* and tossed down a rope ladder. *At least I have a reason to get off this inelegant beast.*

As the Mirza's feet touched the ground, Jaimal approached, concern on his face. "My Lord, why do you descend?"

"Our good Suf believes he has found one of these stubborn donkeys who will bray for us. But we must go somewhere else to hear its song. You and Fasim begin teaching the word of the Prophet to these people. Perhaps some new souls may be brought to the light while I am gone."

Jaimal frowned. "My Lord, send me to hear this ass."

"I wish to hear the story myself."

"Then let me come with you, my Lord."

"You fear a trap? As you wish. Fasim will say prayers for us both then, and have the other men see that these people stay where they are." The Mirza adjusted his swordbelt as Jaimal shouted out his orders. Jaimal took a burning brand from the bonfire to light their way and rejoined them. The Mirza gestured for Masum to lead on.

The Sufi did not take them down the main road through the village, but instead guided the Mirza and Jaimal along the perimeter. As they walked, Masum said, "My Lord, I should like to commend you on your restraint. Peace is a worthy but difficult goal for a man of war."

"My father taught me that one should not waste lives needlessly. Even unbelievers may unknowingly serve the purpose of the Great Reckoner."

"Just so. Your father was very wise. I have cast the bones on your behalf this evening, and my meditations upon them have yielded this; through the Gateway of Reflection, in Search of the Sanctuary of Joy, one will find the Door called Devotion."

"Ah." The Mirza turned his face to hide his annoyed bafflement. "Words to think upon, indeed, Masum. Where is the one we have come to hear?"

They had arrived at the village well. Beside it sat a woman in a tattered sari and *shal*, a wooden begging bowl before her. "This is the one I spoke of, Lord."

"A beggar?" said the Mirza.

"A woman?" said Jaimal.

"She is of the Erkala caste," said Masum. "Their men are hunters. Their women wander, telling stories and fortunes. She has set foot in many places beyond this village while those who live here have not."

"The Erkala keep pigs," said Jaimal in disgust.

"And weave excellent baskets," said Masum.

"Hold the torch higher, Jaimal," said the Mirza, "so that I may see her."

The woman's face was as dour as a camel's, and as handsome. She raised her thin arms to shield her face from the torchlight, but not before the Mirza noticed that her eyes were discolored and pale.

"Is she blind?"

"I see all I need to see," said the woman in halting Persian.

"How does a beggar come to learn the tongue of nobility?"

"I speak to many people, from many places. All wish to hear stories, and know their fate. You wish a story too, I am told."

"Be warned, woman," said Jaimal, "we seek a true tale, not falsehoods."

The Erkala ignored him. "I have had a vision of you, Prince of the North."

The Mirza crouched before her and held up a coin so that it glinted in the light. "I have a piece of gold for your bowl if you will tell me your vision."

"You seek a *rani* who has power over life and death." She reached out and touched the coin, but did not take it.

"That is no secret," said the Mirza. "Tell me more."

"Her city is hidden in a mountain of rock to the south and west."

"Ah. That is of more substance."

"Some say she is a genii of the Yoonan clan, some say she is a descendent of the great Iskandr. Some worship her as the earthly avatar of Sarasvati, or Lakshmi."

"Continue."

"If you would learn more, seek the tomb of the forgotten *shahid*, in the town that has lost its name. It lies upon the banks of the Sina River."

"How can we find a town with no name?" sneered Jaimal. "How do we find a tomb that is forgotten?"

"A shrine always calls to those who are pure of heart," said Masum.

"Sufis seek shrines like monkeys seek mangoes," said Jaimal.

"Yes!" Masum nodded, eyes bright. "Both are nourishment."

Ignoring their argument, the Mirza said to the beggar, "You are not of the Faith, yet you direct us to the tomb of one of our holy men?"

"Because the *shahid* was of your faith," said the beggar, "you may understand better what you see there. But remember, O Prince of the North, even foreign faiths can teach those who listen."

"So says our Emperor Akbar."

"I hear much of the wisdom of the Great Raja Akbar," said the woman. "I hope he has lent some of this wisdom to you. For beware, mighty Mirza. If you find the *rani* of Life and Death, you will find more and less than what you seek." She interlaced her fingers and wriggled them in front of his face, as though her hands were filled with a nest of small, brown snakes. Then she curled her hands once more onto her lap.

The coin in the Mirza's hand was gone. He fished another from the bag on his belt and let it fall into her wooden bowl with a loud clack. "Now tell us how you come by this knowledge."

The woman pulled her *shal* over her face and withdrew into herself, like a caterpillar that has been disturbed. "I have nothing more to tell you."

"How are we to believe you?" Jaimal said, but the Mirza gently pulled him away.

"There are times it is wise not to make enemies," the Mirza said. He turned again to the Erkala woman. "May Allah, the Compassionate, the Merciful, bless you and guide you to his path."

"May Ganesha the Wise bless you with understanding and success, O Prince of the North."

The Mirza walked back toward the village, stroking his beard pensively.

"My Lord," said Jaimal, "you do not intend to follow her advice, do you?"

"I don't know. Perhaps. What do you think?"

"What if the woman is possessed by the spirit of *Sheykh* Saddu, who is trying to make you stray from your goal?"

The Mirza chuckled. "*Sheykh* Saddu is a folktale, Jaimal, used to explain the strange whims of women and children."

"This *rani* we seek is also a folktale."

"No, I believe there is some truth to this queen. Too many people are fearful when we ask about her. What is it, Masum?"

The mystic had been dogging the Mirza's heels, humbly trying to get his attention. "I think we should do as the Erkala says, my Lord."

"And why is that?"

"Because she advised us to seek the tomb of a *shahid*. To a Sufi, this path always leads to wisdom."

"The woman was not a Sufi," said Jaimal.

"Allah may speak through unlikely tongues."

"So can devils."

"Enough!" said the Mirza. "Someone approaches."

A soldier carrying a burning brand came running up to them. "Lord General, the brahmin of the village refuses to allow us to preach to the villagers. He is organizing them in prayer to their heathen gods. He claims their gods will bring forth a miracle and destroy us."

The Mirza sighed. "They defy us. So be it. Bring this stubborn Brahmin to me." The Mirza strode toward the bonfire.

The soldier bowed and ran ahead of him.

"Shall we slay them all now, my Lord?" said Jaimal.

"Great Mirza, forebear," said Masum.

"They have rejected the Word of the Prophet!"

"As the wise Mirza himself said, no life should be carelessly spent. If these people are slaughtered, they are sent without hope to Shaitan. The more days they may live on this earth, the more chance their hearts may find the way to the Path."

Again, the Mirza ignored their argument as he stood before the fire. The Brahmin was brought before the Mirza and forced to his knees in full view of the other villagers.

The Brahmin's eyes, when he looked up at the Mirza, were full of quiet defiance.

"You refuse to accept the One True Faith?"

The Brahmin growled a long statement. This was translated to the Mirza thus: "We do not accept that your way is Truth. You are *mlecch*, unclean. We should accept nothing from you. Who are you to say that the *Mahadeva* has but one face and only you can see it? Your pride will bring the wrath of *Devadurga* down upon you."

The Mirza drew his *talwar* from its scabbard and lay the blade against the Brahmin's neck. His left hand he held out, palm up. "Masum, give me a handful of dirt."

The Sufi bent down and scooped up a handful of sand, which he poured onto the Mirza's palm.

The Mirza then held his hand higher and called out, "Behold the mercy of Shahinshah Akbar and the One True God he serves. It would be nothing for me to take this man's head from his shoulders, yet I will not." He lifted the blade away. He heard a sigh of disappointment behind him.

"Jaimal, pry open this *harbi*'s mouth."

As two soldiers restrained the Brahmin, Jaimal grabbed his jaws and forced his mouth open. The Mirza pressed the handful of dirt into the Brahmin's mouth.

"I give you earth to eat, for you have spoken only dirt, and in the eyes of the One, the Compassionate and Merciful, you are nothing but dirt. Under the law of Akbar, you and your people shall live as *dhimmi*. We will leave you to follow your heathen faith, but you will be taxed heavily for it. For you have shown yourselves beneath the respect and regard of the Faithful. Jaimal, have our men take half the gold of these people, and burn their shrines to the ground. Let them see no miracles will save them."

Jaimal bowed, smiling. "As you will, my Lord." He called out the Mirza's orders with great joy.

As the soldiers began to move among the villagers to take their possessions, the Mirza added, "Take only half of what they own. But should any refuse to pay, kill them." Then the Mirza stepped away from the bonfire, wanting distance between himself and the screams of women and children.

VII

RUBY: This precious gem, crimson in color, is credited with many healing properties. Powdered and mixed in wine, it will stop bleeding and clarify the blood, as well as ease swelling fevers. The Hindoos believe to wear it brings courage and strength, and enhances resolve. It will also guard the house of the wearer from storms, and permit one to be at ease in the midst of enemies. A clear cabochon ruby will darken and become cloudy to warn of danger to come....

The Sultana Chand Bibi ignored the aches in her hips, thighs, and back. She had taken cold satisfaction in astonishing the servants in the *Anand Mahal*, Ibrahim's Palace of Delight, with her sudden arrival, presenting herself to the old palace steward, who had served when her husband ruled Bijapur, and knew her by sight. She had greeted him brusquely, then demanded to be taken to her esteemed nephew at once, with no announcement.

She now stood behind a latticework screen that overlooked a balcony luxuriously appointed with pillows and plush carpets, on which sat trays of sugared fruits and sweetmeats. The Sultan Ibrahim 'Adilshah II sat cross-legged on the floor, dressed informally in a blue *jama* embroidered with gold-and-silver thread, and *shalwar* trousers of purple silk. He was tapping on a small tabla drum on his lap, eyes closed in bliss.

Beside him sat a blind musician plucking a *raga* on a *vina*, the gourd at one end of the fretboard in his lap, the gourd at the other end of the fretboard hooked over his shoulder.

Ukha looked at the Sultana as if to say, "This is how the wise Ibrahim rules his kingdom?"

"Truly," Chand Bibi said with a smile, "he must not have been a washerman in a previous life, as he claims, but a musician."

The *raga* finished, and Ibrahim sighed. "That is marvelous, Gandharva. You must teach me that one. I may include a description of it in my next book."

"You honor me too much, Majesty," said the blind man, inclining his head.

"Yes," said Chand Bibi, striding out from behind the screen. "He does."

"Auntie!" cried Ibrahim, and the drum tumbled away from his knees. Though a handsome, portly man of twenty-seven, at that moment the Sultan resembled a toddler caught in a naughty prank.

"My nephew," said Chand Bibi, bowing, "it is good to see you again after so long a time. Greetings to you, Gandharva."

The musician bowed over his *vina*. "A delight to hear your voice again, Great Sultana."

Ibrahim recovered himself quickly. "And I delight in again seeing you, although I hardly recognized you in your warrior's garb. Let me guess; your army surrounds Bijapur's walls, and you have come to take back my late uncle's kingdom."

Chand Bibi laughed. "No, dear Ibrahim, I find one sultanate quite enough to manage. More than enough." With a sigh and a grunt, she knelt facing him and motioned for Ukha to do the same.

"I sympathize, truly, Auntie. Why, do you know, I spent all day yesterday giving audience to the most petty petitions; merchants arguing over blanket space in the bazaar, men-of-arms claiming that the poor are building houses against the city halls, the poor petitioning to build more of them, an *alim* complaining that a rival school is permitted more students. Heaven have mercy."

"My poor Ibrahim," said Chand Bibi with gentle irony, "what trials you face."

"Which makes the distraction of your unexpected visit all the more welcome. Though I am brought to wonder if there is purpose in it, or do you just wish to ensure that I am not dishonoring our family through dissolute living?"

"I regret there is purpose, my nephew. I bring an urgent message that I felt I alone should deliver."

Ibrahim rubbed his well-trimmed beard. "This must be a message of import indeed, that you risk not having a kingdom upon your return, in order to deliver it."

"If what I fear comes to pass, we may both of us lose our kingdoms. And many more in the Deccan will, as well."

Ibrahim's manner became instantly serious. "Then, pray, be as clear to me as the water in the well that bears your name. Gandharva, perhaps you should leave us."

"No," said Chand Bibi. "He may stay. I remember those days that Gandharva graced my court. I am indebted to him for his gifts of wisdom and talent. And those of his Protectress."

Gandharva sat up, very attentive.

"And what of your servant?" said Ibrahim, looking at Ukha.

"She is aware of all matters concerned, and is worthy of our trust."

Ukha bowed her head. "I serve Your Majesties in all things."

"Very well," said Ibrahim. "Then tell me, dear aunt, this fearsome news."

"The Shahinshah Akbar has sent an army into the Deccan. This army has passed Ahmadnagar and is now headed here, to Bijapur. They are but days behind me."

Ibrahim nodded solemnly. "We have been expecting this. How strong a force?"

"Not strong. Only one hundred horse and five hundred men."

"Only that? What foolishness! Or is it a diversionary tactic, meant to draw our forces when the main thrust will come from elsewhere?"

"I see your uncle managed to teach you something of warcraft. But, no, this smaller force is not attacking us. The duty given to its general, the Mirza Ali Akbarshah, is peaceful yet threatening in its implications."

"My esteemed aunt, you are speaking in riddles."

"Hear me out. This general comes chasing legends."

Ibrahim raised his brows.

Chand Bibi went on. "He seeks an immortal *rani*, who lives in an impregnable, hidden city. A *rani* with powers of life and death."

"I see," Ibrahim breathed, wide-eyed. Gandharva sucked in his breath between his teeth.

"He knows She is somewhere in the Deccan, and he is asking any and all he comes across for knowledge of Her."

"Hah!" barked Ibrahim. "Let him find Her, then. She will make quick work of him and his men, will She not, Gandharva?"

"If you please, Majesty," said Gandharva, "daring the Mahadevi's wrath may only bring greater disaster. Great Sultana, can you tell me how the Shahinshah has learned of this . . . legend?"

"If the Mirza can be believed," said Chand Bibi, "Akbar has had a crisis of conscience, during which he talked to many mystics. Apparently one of them knew of Her."

"Or has heard stories second or third hand," said Ibrahim.

"Perhaps," said Chand Bibi. "But here is what I fear.

What if the Mirza beguiles Her into an alliance with the Pad-shah Emperor Akbar, promising Her more influence than our petty kingdoms can offer? What if She offers her gift to him? Can you imagine an immortal Emperor of Sind with an undying army?"

"No Deccan kingdom would be safe," whispered Ibrahim.

"Gandharva, is this possible?"

The blind musician sighed. "I cannot say what would be the will of the Mahadevi. But I do not think She would abandon those loyal to Her."

"This is not a time to be obscure."

"Forgive me, Majesties." Gandharva set his *vina* aside and pressed his forehead to the floor. "There is a matter of which I have knowledge that I now must make known to you."

"You have withheld something from us?" said Ibrahim.

"Only because I believed it would never become a matter for your concern. But the Emperor's Mirza is not the only one who comes toward Bijapur seeking the Mahadevi."

Ibrahim frowned. "Explain."

"A caravan is coming from Goa, bringing Portuguese priests of the Orlem Gor."

"What is this Orlem Gor?" said Chand Bibi.

"From what I have heard," said Gandharva, "it is thought a sacred house, but the Goans fear it. It is like a temple of Kali—people are taken there who never return, or are released crippled or mad, forbidden to speak of what they have seen. Perhaps it is where they make human sacrifice to their god Christos—but no one will say what happens there for fear they, themselves, will be taken and tormented. It would seem a worshipper was taken into the Orlem Gor and tortured until Her secret was revealed."

"Indeed?" said Chand Bibi. "I had heard dreadful stories of the Portuguese, but this amazes me."

"What do you expect?" said Ibrahim. "Their holiest symbol is their prophet nailed to two pieces of wood, with thorns on his head and a wound in his side. Their priests even speak of his 'sacrifice.' I have always suspected them of barbaric rituals, though the few such priests I have spoken to loudly deny it."

"And these barbarians are coming to Bijapur?" said Chand Bibi.

"Why haven't you told me this?" demanded Ibrahim.

"Because it is probable they will never arrive, and I did not wish to distress you unneedfully."

"You mean they will be a target for brigands on the road."

"Perhaps. And they are accompanied by another who serves the Mahadevi as I do. I believe you have met Sri Aditi."

"Ah," said Ibrahim, and he smiled.

"Who is this Aditi?" asked Chand Bibi.

"I met her only once, many years ago," said Ibrahim. "She had the most amazing eyes. I was but a young prince then, and I thought her dazzling. I would have asked her to join my hareem, if I dared. Lovely as a jewel snake, and perhaps as deadly. When she was here, there was a young Shi'a cleric who was threatening to cause trouble over my building of a temple to the Mahadevi's avatar, Sarasvati. Aditi invited him to visit her, ostensibly to be converted. The cleric was never seen or heard from again. Since then, I have on occasion wondered if . . . but no matter."

"And we must hope this creature disrupts the Goans?" said Chand Bibi. "If she fails, my nephew, you will have both barbarians and Mughals to contend with."

"True. I must prepare for that possibility." Ibrahim rubbed his cheeks and stared at the patterns in the rug. "It is as my former *alim*, Shah Sigbat Allah, had warned me. He said my love of pagan ways would lead me into trouble. Perhaps I should not have thrown him out of Bijapur. But he did start that riot with the Shi'a—"

"My nephew," said Chand Bibi coldly, "now is not a time for idle musings. You are called, in your kingdom, *Abale Bali*, the Defender of Women. You must now prove yourself again worthy of that name, as a defender of a goddess."

"Indeed." Ibrahim stood, clasping his hands together. "Indeed, it is a sign. A test. The time has come to repay Her generosity."

"What will you do, Majesty?" said Gandharva.

"If they come, I will receive them, of course. I will find out what they know, discourage them if I can." He paused. "Destroy them, if I must."

"You will receive the priests from Goa?" said Chand Bibi. "I thought you disliked the Portuguese."

"I do. But some of our merchants keep a lively trade with them—in horses, particularly. I will not overtly offend the emissary, unless I must. Although, I will tell you, if I am gifted with one more of their jewel-encrusted holy books, I shall chop it into shreds and scatter it to the winds."

"The Mirza may be offended by your courtesy to the heretics," said Chand Bibi.

"I have many palaces. One group need not even be aware of the other. Although," he paused and steepled his hands before his face, "it might bring amusement, if they are."

"Majesty, beware," said Gandharva, "the hatred and distrust of these priests of Christos toward the faithful of Islam can be without limit."

"Exactly," said Ibrahim. "And in so wise, the hate of the Faithful for Christians. And this," a sly smile grew on his face, "may be the very key to the legend-seeker's ruin. Auntie, will you stay to watch and give advice? Your wisdom would be most welcome."

Chand Bibi sighed and stood, bringing new discomfort to her aching joints. "Alas, Ibrahim, I cannot. Ahmadnagar may have been stolen from me even as we are speaking, and I must return. I can only hope none of my acquisitive sons has discovered my disappearance, and that Prince Murad has remained in his drunken stupor. You must face this situation on your own. If you apply as much cleverness to this as you do to your music and poetry, you surely cannot fail."

Thomas gazed out from the ornate little pavilion, to the tops of the clouds below, imagining himself as a Hindu godling in his own private paradise. He sipped from a small, porcelain cup a drink called *char-bakhra;* warmed palm wine mixed with sugar and lime juice. It was a spirit most soothing to Thomas's spirits, and the pain in his arms seemed nearly as distant as home.

Here at the top of the Ramghat Pass, some thoughtful, wealthy Hindu had built a travelers' rest. The Goan caravan had stopped for a couple of days to repair the oxcarts and give themselves and their animals a much-needed respite from the rigors of the journey.

Beside him, Padre Gonsção sat huddled under a blanket, his eyes dull and face pale. A fever had come upon him the day before. He sipped not wine, but *conjee,* a broth from rice and water. It was all he could keep down. Thomas hoped the cool, dry mountain air, so refreshing after the damp miasma of the jungles below, would ease the Padre's ailment. As yet, it had not.

"Base illusion," the Padre muttered in Latin. "False temptation begone."

"Padre?"

Gonsção blinked and looked up at Thomas. "Forgive me. I thought I saw a white-winged creature beckoning me out onto the clouds, as if welcoming me to Heaven."

"It is but a dream of your fever, Padre."

"Or an omen."

"You must not think thus. Has Timóteo been able to find herbs for you? He knows more of that which grows here than I."

The Padre waved a hand dismissively. "I shall take no

sickening or mind-numbing herbs, Magister Chinnery. Prayer alone must bring me to health. If it does not, then . . . it is God's will."

"God has permitted Man some knowledge of means to restore health. Will you accept no mortal help? Remember the importance of your mission, Padre. Surely our Lord would wish you to employ any reasonable way to speed your recovery."

"Mmm." Padre Gonsção pulled the blanket tighter around him. "Perhaps a bleeding, if it comes to that. Are you skilled with the lance, Magister Chinnery?"

Thomas sighed. "I have used it. But I do not believe it to be efficacious." During his final days aboard *The Bear's Whelp*, after the death of the ship's surgeon, Thomas had administered bleedings when asked to. Although, in one or two cases, it had brought recovery, for the rest it only seemed to hasten their death.

The Padre's eyes took on a faraway stare. "There is something else I must ask of you, Magister Chinnery. As I have said, if a man is given trust, he often proves himself worthy of it. Brother Timóteo, I have noticed, trusts you a great deal. He is perceptive, but so very innocent."

Thomas did not know what to say to this, and so he waited.

"If I should . . . not be able to continue with our quest," the Padre went on, "Timóteo will naturally turn to you for guidance. He feels less comfortable with Brother Andrew, who is of a different order than us and is more worldly. Therefore, Magister, I ask you to be a guardian for the boy. Protect him from the soldiers' rough ways. Let your good sense guide him, as you should let his purity of spirit guide you."

"You must not speak thus, Padre. Surely God will see that you return to health."

The Padre did not hear, or ignored, his words. "And there is, in my belongings, a gift for the Sultan of Bijapur. You must see that it is delivered to him, that it is not stolen. It is a beau-

tiful bible—the bindings are the work of the finest silver-
smith in Lisboa, the gemstones were selected by the jeweler
of King Phillip himself. The illuminations are the work of the
best Dominican scribes. You must ensure that the Sultan re-
ceives it."

"I am sure he will accept it with great joy, Padre, when
you give it to him from your own hands. Speak no more of
death, I pray you, lest it feel invited to your door. As what
passes for a physician among us, I advise you so." Thomas
turned away to again stare out over the clouds.

*What care I whether the Inquisitor lives or dies? Might it not be
to my advantage if the fever takes him hence? Nay, not here, not now.
There are still the soldiers to fear, and I have no wish to become
Timóteo's nursemaid, or leader of this doomed expedition. Better
the Padre should live 'til Bijapur, where my chance of escape is better. And he is a man, for all he may have done. I have not yet become so callous of soul as to wish a man dead.*

Thomas felt a tugging on his sleeve and turned to find
the Padre staring at him with an intensity that was unsettling.

"There is more, my son. I confess I do not know what
your intentions have been regarding our search—but I feel
you are a man of good heart, whatever else. Therefore, I will
tell you this. If God should call me to Heaven, I beg of you,
continue the search for the source of the *pulvis mirificus*, this
rasa mahadevi. Find it. And when you do, I beg you, for the
sake of all our souls, destroy it. It must not find its way back
into the hands of the Santa Casa."

"Padre?" Thomas blinked, open-mouthed.

"Ah," the Padre managed the ghost of a sardonic smile.
"I see you are amazed that I would betray the institution to
which I have devoted my life. But it is not betrayal, truly.
The Inquisition is a mighty weapon that can be used for
good or ill. In good, it can unite men under one faith, de-
stroying wrong-headed heresy as a good gardener must pull
those weeds that would choke the garden. But in the hands

of avaricious men, the Santa Casa can become terrifying in its evil.

"Domine Sadrinho, the Inquisitor Major in Goa, is one such. He dreams of using the powder to further his reputation, to plumb the depths of knowledge of the afterlife that God Himself withholds from living Man. You saw the horror created when Senhor De Cartago was resurrected."

Thomas nodded. He could not forget the sight of the grey, bloated, three-days-dead body of the sorcerer sitting up in his coffin, unable to speak for the rot in his mouth.

"There would be many more such horrors," the Padre went on, "if Sadrinho gets the powder. You must see to it that this does not happen! Will you do this?"

"If I can, Padre," Thomas heard himself say.

Padre Gonsção patted his shoulder and Thomas tried not to wince with the pain. "Listen to Timóteo. The boy has read the confessions of those who were in the sorcerer's cabal. He says the goddess we seek is, in truth, a monster."

Footsteps approaching made Thomas look up. "Padre, someone comes."

A stocky, black-bearded man wearing a long, high-necked, pale-green jacket and loose silk trousers was striding toward the pavillion. His turban sported a large gem with a peacock's feather and a dagger-hilt gleamed from the scarlet cummerbund around his waist.

It was not until this man bounded up onto the pavillion platform that Thomas recognized him to be Andrew Lockheart. "Andrew, you look splendid! Like a very Tamburlaine. Whence comes these clothes?"

"My thanks. I traded with Agnihotra's men for 'em, lad."

"Where is your cassock, Frater?" growled Padre Gonsção, who had become, if possible, more pale than before.

"Well hidden," Lockheart responded in Latin, "where yours should be also, Padre, if you were wise. Goa is far away, and we've but a dozen soldiers to protect us. There's many a pagan and heretic in the lands ahead with no love for the Portuguese or the Church. The camel drivers advised this guise to spare them trouble down the road."

"It is a man of little faith," breathed the Padre, "who will deny it for the sake of heretics and pagans. I would never disguise what I am, or what I believe. But I have noticed you, Magister Lockheart, keep much hidden about you."

"I have found it in my interest. It is clear you have not traveled much, Padre."

"I travel only when duty demands it of me."

"There we are alike, Padre. But I think my duties have been more demanding than yours."

The Padre's eyes widened and he seemed about to argue, when a fit of coughing seized him.

Thomas leaned over and placed his hand against the Padre's temple. "His skin is like fire. We must get him to bed rest, Andrew."

"My fault," muttered Lockheart. "I should not have encouraged more choler in him."

Thomas wondered if Lockheart were merely making a play on words or if he had some knowledge of Galen's medicinal theories. According to those, a fever such as the Padre's was produced by an excess of the hot, dry humour: yellow bile. Those herbs thought of as "cooling" were required to treat it. But those Thomas knew of—comfrey, borage, or barley—did not grow nearby. And Timóteo did not classify the local herbs in such a manner. *'Tis a wonder how so much wisdom can be of so little use.* "You must assist the Padre to walk, Andrew," said Thomas. "I cannot."

With a grunt of assent, Lockheart helped the Padre to stand and guided him back to the main guest house. Thomas followed, disquieted, his thoughts whirring like bees around a broken hive.

VIII

🌿 SESAME: This plant is also called gingilly or Turkish millet. It has long, narrow leaves and bears flowers of white or pale rose. Its seeds produce a sweet oil, which is good for the bowels, and a tisane of sesame seed powder in wine eases a troubled stomach. In the East, the plant has power to open hidden places where treasure may be found. The Hindoos offer it to their god of Wisdom, and give it as offering to the dead, believing that a new body may be made from a paste of sesame and rice....

The Mirza Ali Akbarshah walked into the shade of a wilting tamarack tree. Midday prayers completed, his men had spread out in a small, desiccated valley of the Sina River, to find what respite they could from the hot sun. The air had the stillness that precedes a storm, yet there was no cloud in the sky. *If this is an omen*, thought the Mirza, *I cannot read it.*

He noticed the Sufi, Masum, tending to the arm of a dark-skinned infantryman in the shade of some bushes nearby, and the Mirza went over to them.

The soldier nodded deferentially to him, saying, "May the Prophet and the angels protect you, Lord Mirza."

"And you," said the Mirza. "What is this man's injury, Masum? Did he fall from a horse?"

"He stood too close to a temple set afire at the village," said the Sufi. "I have been tending his burns these last two days."

"I have witnessed the power of Allah, the Great and Merciful," said the soldier through gritted teeth. "Now I follow only the Word and Law of the Prophet."

"He is of Hindu family," Masum explained, "but he converted after the attack. Several of the *harbi* soldiers have."

"You do not seem pleased."

The Sufi tied off the bandage on the soldier's arm. "It brings me great joy that he has found his way to The Path. But I have found that the entrance a man chooses may determine how far the path will lead him."

What does it matter? thought the Mirza, *so long as he honors the Word and upholds the Law?* But not wishing to argue philosophy with the Sufi, the Mirza said, "I did not know you practiced the healing arts, Masum."

"I have learned that to heal a man's body frees his mind for higher thoughts. I have studied the work of Ibn Sina, and *Unani Tibb*, the Greek medicine. I have covered this man's burns with a *surma* of honey and ashes. This will ease his pain until his humors come again into balance."

"Hm." The Mirza was suspicious of doctors and herbalists. He had seen too many of them arguing nonsense in Akbar's court. A warrior should be content to clean and bandage a wound and let divine will do the rest. "Why is so much made of Greek knowledge, Masum? All of their greatness is in the past. Iskandr is long dead."

"Much has been lost since Iskandr's time," said Masum, putting lids on little pots and placing them in a leather sack. "So many secrets and wonders. I confess, I am hoping this *rani* we seek will possess some of the ancient knowledge."

"I thought the way of the Suf' was to desire no earthly thing," said the Mirza.

Masum smiled, abashed. "You have discovered my Jinni of Temptation. My *pir* has said my curiosity would be the greatest barrier to my soul's progress."

A soldier with sweat running down from his turban came up to them. "My lord Mirza, the scouts have returned with news of the road ahead."

"Very good. I will see them at once."

The soldier motioned to two horsemen who waited at a distance. As they rode up, the Mirza again envied them their fine steeds and opportunity to ride. The men dismounted and bowed to the Mirza.

"So, what news do you bring?"

"Great Lord, some five *kos* from here, there is a town that is all but abandoned. There was a great famine in this region three years ago, and the inhabitants perished or fled. The few who now live there are squatters come from elsewhere. They do not even know what the town had been called."

"A town with no name," said Masum softly.

The Mirza glanced at the Sufi before asking the scout, "Will these squatters be a danger to us?"

"I believe not, Great Lord. They were afraid of us and it took much coaxing and some coin to speak to them at all."

"Was there a tomb nearby?" asked Masum.

"Indeed, one of the squatters mentioned a tomb to the south of town. Of course no one knew or cared who was buried there."

"My Lord," said Masum, "this must be the place the Erkala woman meant!"

The Mirza smiled patiently. "Well, then, I presume we must see it. May I borrow your horse, good scout?"

Two hours later, the Mirza, Masum, and Jaimal rode into the ruins of the village with no name. The air shimmered in the heat rising from the dusty road. The distant red sandstone cliffs wavered as if seen under water. Gaunt cattle with hides pale as bleached bones ambled across the road. Dirty children and women in plain, threadbare *shals* watched them from dark doorways.

We must be a sight to their eyes. I wonder what they make of us.

Masum went to one of the houses and coaxed the inhabitants into speaking with him. He returned, saying, "The *ziarat* we seek is just past the town, beyond that broken wall and behind the next hillock."

They followed the directions, rounding the bouldered hill to discover a small, square building of whitewashed brick surmounted by a low dome. A lone, bare tree stood beside it. Beneath the tree sat an old man, playing a flute.

As the three rode up to him, the old man looked up and his mouth and eyes opened wide with amazement. He slowly stood, leaning on a wood staff, polished by long use. His white turban and long kaftan were frayed and much mended but clean.

"It is true," the old man said. "You have truly come. Allah be praised!"

The Mirza dismounted, saying, "You knew we would be here? Has someone warned you of our arrival?"

The old man sunk to his knees and bowed. "Only the angels in an old man's dreams. Welcome, O mighty Mirza."

Reaching down, the Mirza gently coaxed the ancient to stand again. "Come, such honor is due only to the Emperor or to Allah, long may his many names be praised. Are you the guardian of this *ziarat?*"

"It has been the joyous duty of my family for generation upon generation, Great Lord."

"In that case, please accept our offering. We have come a long way to hear the story of your *shahid.*"

Jaimal placed a bag containing fifty gold *tumans* in the old man's hands. Tears formed in the ancient guardian's eyes as he accepted it. "It has been so very long since someone has come to hear of our saint. Pilgrims who have stopped here usually have mistaken it for some other shrine, or because it is a place to rest. But come inside, my lords, and I will tell you of the one whose remains lie within."

The guardian led them to the other side of the tomb to a wooden gate that was locked across a lancet archway. He pulled from around his neck a large wooden key on a leather strap. With a shaking hand, he put the key into the lock and pulled the bolt aside. He pushed open the gate and, removing his sandals, stepped inside. Just within the entry, a bucket hung from a hook on the wall. The old man took down the bucket, which contained a ladle and a small amount of water.

The Mirza put forth his cupped hands and the old man ladled some water into them. The Mirza ritually cleansed his hands and face with the water and then, removing his shoes, stepped into the shrine.

The old man poured water for Jaimal and Masum, and then himself, before returning the bucket to its hook and closing the gate behind them.

The interior of the shrine was a pleasantly cool, domed space, perhaps large enough to hold fifteen men. The walls and ceiling were whitewashed and covered with elegant *Taliq* calligraphy in black and vermillion. Where the paint had cracked or flaked away, it had been carefully restored.

"How old is this *ziarat?*" asked the Mirza.

"My family has tended it for twelve generations, Great Lord."

At the east side of the room was a set of stairs leading down into a small, dark chamber. "If my lords will please follow me," said the old man as he descended. The Mirza, Jaimal, and Masum crowded down the steps behind him.

With a flint, the old man lit an oil lamp and held it up. Its faint light revealed a massive block of black basalt that filled most of the chamber. Atop the stone sat a simple wood box the height and width of the Mirza's forearm.

The ancient guardian cleared his throat and began, "You behold before you, mighty Mirza, the vessel of the remains of a nameless martyr to the Faith. His story is this. It is said he was a disciple of the great Saiy'd Muhammad Gesudaraz, who came to this land three centuries ago from Persia to spread the word of the Prophet. Our *shahid* learned well from his master and wandered far, winning many converts. Many *rajahs* heeded his teachings and submitted themselves to The One, as did many of the poor.

"And then, one day, our *shahid* learned of a mighty queen who scorned the True Faith. She claimed herself to be a goddess, immortal, and said she had no use for the word of the Prophet. Our *shahid* traveled to her hidden city, high on a mountaintop, and there tried to teach her as he had so many others. But she laughed at him and tried to seduce him from the Path, using tricks and magic. But our *shahid* would not be swayed.

"At last, the wicked, proud queen was forced to reveal herself, by the power of our *shahid*'s faith. She showed herself to be a demon, the wife of the third son of Shaitan, Awan, the Companion of Kings, may the Compassionate forgive me for breathing that foul name. The wicked queen then attempted to drag our *shahid* down into Hell with her. But he prayed loud and Allah, the All-Merciful, heard him and turned our *shahid* into stone, so that he could no longer hear the queen's honeyed words, nor see her evil beauty. And thus our *shahid*'s soul passed into Paradise, leaving only a stone shell behind as an example to the faithful." The old man smiled and bowed his head.

"Truly," said the Mirza, "the life of your *shahid* was filled with wonders. How long ago did this happen?"

"Over two hundred years, Great Mirza."

"And this story has been told by your family for all these generations?"

"From father to son, Great Mirza, as my son will tell the story after I have passed on from this world."

"How is it your family has been given this honor?"

"It is said that my ancestor, Ali Ahmad, was a merchant who lived nearby and owned this land. He was host to the *shahid* before the *shahid* went to encounter the wicked queen. Two of the *shahid*'s disciples had remained behind with Ahmad. Then, one night, a tall, old woman came to my ancestor's door, along with the one disciple who had accompanied the *shahid*. The disciple had blinded himself to avoid the evil queen's terrible magic, and told Ahmad the story I have just told you. The old woman was a servant in the evil queen's palace, and had guided the disciple back to safety, bringing a remnant of the *shahid* back with them. In honor of the martyr's sacrifice, my ancestor built this *ziarat*. He felt it was a calling from Heaven. Ever since that time, the family of Ali Ahmad has faithfully tended this tomb."

"But surely," said the Mirza, "the disciples would have wanted their *sheykh*'s name to live in memory. Why has your *shahid* remained nameless?"

"The old servant of the queen, it is said, advised that it be so, lest the evil queen and the denizens of Hell learn of the *ziarat* and come to defile it."

"Tell me," said Jaimal, "how is it you and your family managed to survive the drought that ravaged this region not long ago?"

"Allah has truly provided for us," said the old man, "as there is a tiny spring behind our house. Though it is but a trickle, it has never dried up."

"I have a question that may sound strange to you," said the Mirza, "but have there been stories since the death of your *shahid* that imply that this immortal queen still exists?"

The old man tilted his head and frowned. "The sons of Shaitan are with us always, as are their wives and minions, demons and djinn. But the tales always say they are to be avoided, so that one may remain unsullied by their temptations."

The Mirza smiled politely. "Yes, of course. But your story

implies that this daughter-in-law of Shaitan lived not far from here. Do the stories in your family ever name a mountain in particular as her dwelling place?"

The guardian sighed. "My father once said the mountain was somewhere to the south and east of Bijapur, a place called the Serpent's Nest. But if Heaven is just, there is no such place, or it no longer exists."

"Then how can we know the truth of your story?" said Jaimal.

The old man brightened. "If you will permit me, my Lords, I will bestow upon you an honor that few are given. I should like to show you the remnant of our *shahid.*"

"You honor us too much," said the Mirza.

"No, no," said the old man, waving a hand. "What little I can do is insufficient. Nonetheless . . ." He lifted the lid of the wooden box and set it aside on the basalt block. He reached in and pulled out another box, this one made of silver and studded with cabochons of black stone. Calligraphic prayers were inlaid upon it in black lacquer. "I keep this in the plain box," said the old man knowingly, "to discourage thieves." With all possible care, he set the box down.

"Was this magnificent reliquary," asked Jaimal, his eyes wide, "provided by your merchant ancestor? Is that why your family is now so poor?"

"No one who serves a martyr of the Faith is poor," said the elderly guardian. "But the story of the box is this. Remember I told you of the old woman who brought the remnant of our *shahid* back from the palace of the evil queen? The family stories say she was a pagan, but with the paler skin of a northerner. But it is believed she did not approve of the wickedness of the queen she served. Along with the remnant, she gifted Ali Ahmad with a bundle wrapped in white wool."

"Ah," said Masum, as if this were significant.

"After the strange woman had departed, Ali Ahmad opened the bundle and saw it contained seven bars of silver.

He had three of them melted down to make this box. Two of them paid for the construction of this *ziarat*. The rest have sustained my family for these many years. Now . . ." The old man took a string from around his neck on which hung a tiny key. With this, he opened the silver reliquary, and stood back. "If you please, my Lords, see for yourselves."

The Mirza looked into the box. On a bed of white silk was a hand, clutching a roll of paper. The brown hand seemed excellently preserved, every pore, wrinkle, scar, and vein just as it must have been in life. The termination of the hand at the wrist was capped in silver. The rolled-up paper appeared to be a page from the Qu'ran, frayed along the upper edges. Very gently, the Mirza ran his finger along the paper from the edge to where the hand grasped it. Near the hand, the page was like delicately carved jade. Halfway along, however, the material became clearly paper. So gradual was the change that the Mirza could not tell at what precise point the paper became stone. "It is as though he was indeed transformed," he murmured.

Jaimal looked at the remnant also, but frowned and did not speak. Masum hummed prayers, swaying from side to side.

"This is truly a great mystery," said the Mirza. "I know of no sculptor who could do this."

"None but Allah," said the old man, nodding.

As they left the *ziarat*, and remounted their horses, the Mirza said, "It seems the Erkala woman you found, Masum, has pointed us in the right direction. There was such a queen as that we seek in this region, although centuries ago. Perhaps if we are dealing with a dynasty, or one who is truly immortal, we may find such a queen still. Jaimal, you have been silent. What do you make of what we have just seen?"

Scowling, the lieutenant replied, "I believe, Lord, we should be wary of trickery and treachery. I think that is what this pilgrimage should teach us."

"You do not believe the guardian's stories?"

Jaimal's eyes held restrained fury. "What good follower of the Faith would devote his shrine to idolatry? He venerates a piece of a statue and claims it is the hand of an ancient *sheykh*. At best, the old man is a fool, as are all his family, for believing the tales. At worst, he is a thief and an enemy of the Faith, taking the money of pilgrims and twisting their minds with lies."

The Mirza was taken aback with Jaimal's vehemence. "I do not think the worst, Jaimal. The old man clearly believed what he told us. Do you not think so, Masum?"

Masum looked at Jaimal. "I think the lesson of this shrine is that there are yet great wonders and miracles in the world. Darkness is but the mystery created by the light. But the man who sees only darkness will miss the light that permeates it."

"If a man is blinded by light, it is as if he has stumbled into darkness. You have strayed so far from your Path," said Jaimal, "that you are willing to worship a stone hand?"

"I venerate the Hand of the Creator," said Masum, mildly, "who might bring about the transformation of living flesh to stone."

"Enough!" said the Mirza. "I shall think on both of your wise counsels. I shall keep one eye watching for wonders, and one eye watching for treachery." *And pray I do not become cross-eyed in the process.*

IX

🍃 BASIL: This aromatic plant has toothed leaves of purple hue and blossoms that may be white or red. A tincture of basil is healthful to the stomach and eases coughs and the headache. It is sacred to the Hindoos and grows in every home there, to protect health and prosperity. The ancient Greeks, howsomever, believed it poisonous, and it is said to grow in boneyards. Some say it is an herb of lovers, others say of enemies. If a girl gives a handful of the flowers to a passing youth, it is said he will fall in love with her....

Aditi brushed out her long, black hair, which she had scented with rosewater, and let it drape over her shoulders and breasts. She wore only a diaphanous *peshwaz* gown of the lightest-weave silk, with a thin scarlet underskirt beneath. She looked out from the entrance to her tent at the moonlight rippling on the river Nesri. They were past the jungles of the eastern slope of the Ghats, past the town of Chandgala, and the air was now warmer and dryer, the breeze a comfort on the skin. By day, this area was a dreary wilderness of dry hills and sluggish brown streams. But on a warm night, with only the moon and stars to lend a silver light, it was magical.

"So, Sashi," Aditi said playfully to the Hare-in-the-Moon, "lend me your gift of hospitality, that I may charm my guest who is soon to arrive."

She stood and draped a silk mantle edged with silver thread over her head and shoulders. Impatient, Aditi walked toward the riverbank and gazed toward where her serving girls stood with raised lamps at the entrance to her campsite.

Ah, I am timely. Three men approached; two Goan soldiers with Tamas between them, answering her summons. The serving girls did their duty, cajoling and enticing the soldiers, so that they allowed Tamas to continue alone into the campsite.

Aditi tilted her head, allowing the moonlight to show her face to its advantage, and watched Tamas walk toward her. His pale hair glistened, and his eyes, a paler blue than hers, almost seemed to glow. *How wonderfully strange he is, almost as if a demon or divine avatar. A pity he is just a man. Would the Mahadevi forgive me if I brought him as a gift to her? Perhaps I could keep him as my own plaything. Ai, I must stop these unwise thoughts.*

"Sri Aditi," said Tamas, and he bowed in Hindu fashion.

"Ah, Tamas, I see you are learning our ways."

"We have a saying in the west, Despoina. If you are in Rome, live in the manner of the Romans."

Aditi laughed. The Mahadevi had told her about Rome. "But this is Sind, Tamas, and you may find our manners are more difficult to adopt."

"You may have the right of it, Despoina. May I ask why you summoned me?"

From the way he gazed upon her, Aditi could tell she had successfully caught his interest. "I only wished to share your company, Tamas. Come, let us admire the stars together and talk." She went up to him and gently took his arm, pressing her breast against it.

He blinked and seemed dumbfounded, yet there was

pleasure in his eyes. "Um. Out here in the open where we can be seen? Is this wise, Despoina?"

"I understand the priest of the Orlem Gor has taken ill, and sees and hears nothing. And his men," Aditi looked back to where the serving girls had taken the soldiers into their tent, "seem to have their interest elsewhere. Who is there to care what we do?"

Tamas smiled. "You are right again. Very well. Lead and I cannot help but follow."

Aditi returned his smile, feeling the beginning of a warm glow within.

As they strolled along the riverbank, watching night birds flitter among the reeds, Tamas said, "I have been thinking about your Mahadevi, and how to reconcile Her existence with all I have been taught. According to our English philosophers, your gods are merely fallen angels, ruled by Beelzebub to confuse and lead souls astray."

"What is an angel?" asked Aditi.

"An awe-inspiring being of light and beauty who is a servant of God. A messenger or guardian who does His bidding." His hand tightened on hers. "Perhaps you are one, for you are a servant of your Deity, and have been a guardian for me, nai?"

Aditi laughed and allowed herself to blush. "You flatter me, but I do not think so. Perhaps you are one, for your hair is light, nai?"

Tamas chuckled. "I do not think so either, Despoina. But how did you come to learn of the Mahadevi, or has your family always worshipped Her?"

Aditi tilted one shoulder. "I only learned of Her after She adopted me. I was taken into Her palace after my family was killed by brigands. She and Her two old *ayas* raised me."

Tamas stopped and stared at her. "You mean she is a woman of flesh and blood?"

"I do not know what She is made of, Tamas, but She is no ordinary woman. I was never allowed to look at Her, for to do so brings death. I know this is true, for I have seen what happens to those so foolish as to look upon Her. I only saw Her shadow on a screen, or heard Her voice in the darkness, but She taught me much."

Tamas turned his gaze toward the river, and remained silent.

Aditi went on. "You think I may have been duped by a fraud. But you have not seen what I have seen, nor learned what I know. I do not expect you to understand. No one does who has not experienced Her power. Perhaps, someday, you will know of it."

Gradually, Aditi led him toward a place along the river-bank where she had placed a rug and pillows. "Here. Let us sit and be comfortable." She gracefully knelt on the rug.

Tamas awkwardly sat beside her, wincing as he used his arms for balance.

"Poor Tamas. I have some scented oil I have warmed for you. I will rub it on your shoulders." She slid around behind him and slowly raised the tail of his shirt to his neck. Taking the pot of oil from under a pillow, she poured some onto her hands and spread it upon his pale back, kneading it into his muscles. His soft moans were encouraging.

Aditi nestled closer, her chin nearly on his right shoulder. "Look there, Tamas. *Rohihi* is very bright tonight, is it not?"

"Mmm? Oh. That star I know as Aldebaran. You have been taught astronomy?"

"My father taught me the stars and the movements of the moon when I was a little girl. He said that way, if we were lost in the wilderness at night, we could recover our direction. To the east there, in that dark place between the hills? That is the Head of Rahu, the Moon-Eater."

Tamas laughed. "I can see nothing."

"Of course not. One only knows he is there when the Moon disappears, and sometimes the Sun. Rahu, you see, was a demon, who dared to mingle with the gods and drink their *soma,* the wine of immortality. But he was caught and they cut off his head and flung it into the sky. Perhaps you should find a lesson in that, Tamas. It is not healthy to steal a gift of the gods."

"I have no intention of stealing anything."

"Ah. I knew you were wiser than the others." Aditi kissed his ear, and then his neck. "This is in the way," she said, tugging at his shirt. She crept out from behind him and pulled the shirt over his head, swiftly so as not to give his arms much pain. Then she placed a hand on his chest and pressed him back against the pillows. She ran her fingers over his warm skin and felt his pulse quicken.

"Aditi," he breathed, "I am unable, that is, with my arms thus I cannot hold you—"

Aditi laughed. "You westerners have such strange ideas about lovemaking, as if there were but one way it is done. Arms are nice, but they are not necessary."

As she kissed his chest, she slid her leg over to straddle his loins. She wondered idly what would be the best way to kill him. It would have been easiest had she kept some of the *rasa mahadevi,* but it had all been given to the Scotsman Lakart as price for her return passage to Goa. Cutting a major vein would be simple, but how to explain the blood? A lion attack, perhaps? There were poisons she could procure in the area, but how to make him drink it?

As he became stiff beneath her thighs and her desire grew, she thought, *There are many miles before Bijapur. I need not decide now. Yama can wait for this one a little longer. He need not die just yet.*

Timóteo jumped, looking up from his prayers as there came a pounding on the farmhouse door.

"What is it, Timóteo?" groaned Padre Gonsção from his pallet on the floor.

"I do not know, Padre. I will go and see." He stood and

ran across the dirt floor to the front room, where the Kummari caste farmer bowed low to the man in the doorway. Timóteo recognized the long-bearded, turbaned visitor as one of Sri Agnihotra's merchants.

"Master Timóteo," said the Kummari farmer in heavily accented Kannadan, "this worthy demands to speak to your Lord Gonsown."

"Your pardon," said Timóteo to the merchant in his best Marathi, "but my master is very ill and should speak to no one."

"Then you will have to speak for him," said the merchant. "Come with me."

"But . . . but I cannot leave him. What is the matter?"

"We have entered a new governor's domain and must pay a passage tax. The tax collector is demanding one *tuman* of silver per animal and two *tumans* per cart. This is your master's expedition, therefore he must pay."

Timóteo added up on his fingers the amount. "But that is impossible, sir! We do not have that much silver, or hardly any, in fact. We were not told to bring any for the journey."

"Then you will have to tell the tax collector this. Hurry, for he claims to have an army waiting in the hills who will take the tax from us by force if we do not give it willingly." The merchant grabbed Timóteo by the shoulder and pulled him outside, then pushed him forward until they reached the road.

There stood a tall man with scars on both cheeks and a sword on each hip. He glared down at Timóteo. "Have you brought the money?"

"P-please, sir tax collector," said Timóteo. "My master is only a traveling holy man. He carries no money, nor do I. We cannot pay your tax."

The tax collector scowled first at the merchant then back at Timóteo. "Well, someone must or you go no further on this road."

Shaking, Timóteo said, "I will see what I can do, sir."

He turned and ran, needing to find someone to help. He dashed into the *soldados'* encampment, tripping over a recumbent body.

"Ai! Little brother, must you wake me so rudely?"

"Senhor Alvalanca," said Timóteo, "you must help me. Where is Tomás?"

"He went to dally with Senhora Agnihotra. I do not think he wants to be disturbed. What is wrong?"

"A tax collector has come and is demanding that we pay twenty-three *tumans* of silver to pass on this road!"

The *soldado* blinked and then began to laugh.

"Senhor, this is a serious matter!"

"Little brother, don't you see? This tax collector is a thief, hoping to steal from us. We hear stories about it all the time in Goa. Didn't you know?"

"I never heard such stories in the Santa Casa."

"No, I suppose you would not." The *soldado* struggled out of his bedroll to stand, and Timóteo could tell he was drunk. "Let us have a look at this tax collector, Little Brother," he said, clumsily strapping on his sword. "I and my compadres will take his measure, eh?" He nodded to two other *soldados* sitting by the campfire, who stood with wide grins.

"You must be careful, Senhor. He says he has an army waiting in the hills to attack us if we do not pay."

"They always say that. Sometimes they do, sometimes they don't."

But as they stepped toward the road, they were intercepted by the long-beard merchant and three others. "Where are you going?" the merchant said. "Have you the silver?"

Timóteo translated to Senhor Alvalanca, who replied, weaving from side to side, "Tell him we are going to cut up the thief to ribbons. He doesn't look like much from here."

Timóteo dutifully translated this and the merchant exploded. "You fools! You would bring his governor's army down to massacre us all? We will not allow it. You must pay!"

"Tell the camel-kissing asses that if they fear so much for their lives, let them give some of their goods for the tax."

"Impossible! We will not give up our livelihood when Goans should pay. Tell this dirt-eating westerner they must give the taxman their horses."

"Our horses! Never!" The *soldados'* hands went to their sword hilts and the merchants reached for knives in their *kammerbands*.

"Please stop! Do not fight!" Timóteo ran between the groups of men.

"Out of the way, little brother," growled Senhor Alvalanca. "Let us teach these arrogant weasels a lesson about respect."

Then Timóteo noticed Brother Andrew in his Hindu garb come out from behind the merchants. "Frater Andrew, you must help! Stop them!"

"*Pare! Basta!*" Brother Andrew shouted at the *soldados*. He crouched down and said to Timóteo, "I have a possible solution, Brother. I overhead the Padre mention to Thomas a silver-bound bible. Perhaps the taxman or thief will accept that as a sufficient bribe and go away."

Timóteo backed away from Brother Andrew. "No! That is a gift for the Sultan."

"It will do him little good," said Brother Andrew, "if we do not live to deliver it to him."

"No! We must not!" Feeling trapped within a nightmare, Timóteo turned and ran toward Sri Agnihotra's encampment. He came to the outermost tent and shouted in Latin "Tomás! Tomás! Hurry! Help!"

Two serving girls came bustling out of the tent, hastily wrapping thin garments around themselves. Timóteo looked away.

"What is the matter, what is happening, what is wrong with you?" chattered the girls in Marathi.

"I must speak to Sri Tamas Chinri," said Timóteo. "We are in danger. It is most important."

"Tamas is sleeping," said a woman behind the tent, her voice low and firm. "I will not disturb him. Tell me what you want."

"Sri Agnihotra?" She did not sound old to Timóteo, but he knew it must be her. "Please, a tax collector, or he may be a thief, has come and is demanding money. Your merchants say we Goans must pay it, but we do not have it. The taxman says we will all be killed by his army if we do not pay it. The merchants and the soldiers are going to fight over it. I do not know what to do."

There was a long silence behind the tent.

"Sri Agnihotra?"

There came a string of soft cursing in Urdu. Then Timóteo heard her call out for her bearers and palanquin. In a minute, the purple palanquin appeared from around the tent, its bearers at the run.

Timóteo followed, as the palanquin came to a halt in the road in front of the tax collector. From within the purple curtains there issued a long, horrible series of threats and curses in a voice high and shrill that set skin crawling and hair rising. She spoke in a dialect of Kannadan that Timóteo could only somewhat understand and, from what little he did comprehend, he was glad of it. Sri Agnihotra, in high Brahminic tone, was citing close connection to the Sultan of Bijapur, and Governor so-and-so, and other powerful Brahmins and Marathis and powerful clans, listing what horrible things they might all do to the sorry taxman and his family. And how some goddess or other with great and fearsome powers who would wither the fruit of his loins for generations to come.

The tax collector visibly blanched under the torchlight, and he began to step back, eyes growing wider and wider.

A slender hand emerged from the curtains and flung a small bag, which jingled as it fell at the feet of the tax collector.

"Be happy with this," Sri Agnihotra clearly said, "or else."

The visibly shaking taxman, or thief, bent down and picked up the bag. After glancing to the left and right, he swiftly spun around and ran back down the road as fast as his feet could take him.

The *soldados* laughed and whistled rudely after the thief. "Ay, what a spineless bandit," said Senhor Alvalanca, "driven off by a woman's sharp tongue! I hope his wife doesn't scold him tonight, or he will shrivel away to nothing!"

The slender hand again emerged and beckoned to the three merchants. Timóteo could not hear what words she said to them as they came near, but from the angry tone of her voice and the frowns on their faces, she was clearly displeased with them as well.

Bowing to the palanquin, the merchants returned to their tents and camels, muttering to each other. Brother Andrew went with them, turning now and then to give the palanquin a speculative glance.

As the bearers picked up the poles again and bore the palanquin toward Timóteo, he ran over to it and walked alongside. "Many thanks, Sri Agnihotra. You have saved us. I am sorry to have disturbed you, but with the Padre sick, there was nothing I could do. Holy Maria and all the angels bless you. Again, I thank you."

"Do not thank me," growled the woman inside. "Thank Tamas the next time you see him. Begone, child, and trouble me no more."

"Yes, Sri Agnihotra. I will not." Timóteo stopped and turned back toward the farmhouse where the Padre lay. *But what if there is a fight again?* he thought, distressed almost to tears. *It is clear I cannot command this expedition. They will not listen to me. And how can I trust Brother Andrew when he would have me give up our precious gift to the Sultan? And Tomás . . . I suppose they wouldn't listen to him either.*

Timóteo pushed open the farmhouse door and walked straight to the pallet where the Padre lay.

"Brother Timóteo?" moaned Padre Gonsção. "What is it? I heard angry voices."

"There was a disagreement between the merchants and the *soldados*. But it is all right now. Do not be concerned. You must rest and recover."

The Padre weakly patted Timóteo's arm. "You are a good boy, my son. I knew you could see to . . ." His voice trailed off into a mumble and his head turned aside in sleep.

Timóteo knelt beside his pallet. *Please get well. Dear God, let him get well. No one else can lead us. Without him, our holy quest will surely fail.*

X

BAY TREE: This tree is evergreen and hath narrow,
aromatic leaves. In spring, it brings forth white flowers, which
become black berries in summer. Oil pressed from the leaves and
berries makes good salve for the rheumatics. A decoction of
the berry juice with honey is good against consumption and
pestilence. Wearing a wolf's tooth wrapped in a bay leaf will
ward off words of anger, and bay boughs are thought to be
proof against lightning and witchcraft. If a bay withers, it is an
omen of death, but it will revive from the root and thus is also a
symbol of resurrection....

Thomas sat in the shade beneath a colonnade, along the
village main street, grateful to be out of the sun. Few natives or travellers ventured out onto the dusty road in front
of him. Even the dogs and cattle hardly moved, if they could
manage it.

The village was called Hukeri, and it was the first place
of any pleasantness the caravan had come to since leaving
Chandgala, two days before. The road had taken them
through a desert wilderness of red rock and sand, broken
only by hills that seemed great heaps of boulders, some
topped by ancient ruined forts. The valley Hukeri sat in was
better watered, supporting large groves of fruit trees. That

bit of green was such a welcome sight after two days' travel through desert that even though the sun was still high, the caravan stopped for rest.

Thomas was still trying to reconcile the various stories he had heard about the incident with the thief posing as a toll collector. To hear Timóteo tell it, Aditi had worked some form of magic with curses that drove the thief off. Joaquim had claimed fear of the *soldados'* prowess had sent the would-be toll collector running. Lockheart had said that "Sri Agnihotra" had simply paid the man, after chastising him soundly. Aditi herself would tell Thomas nothing, showing great irritation when he even inquired of it.

And no one would explain to his satisfaction why such a dark mood had settled over the caravan as a whole. *Can it be the Padre's fever has cast this pall upon us?* Padre Gonsção had become so ill that he now had to be transported on a litter. *'Tis well he knows not his surroundings for it spares him shame.*

Under the colonnade where Thomas sat were deep, room-sized alcoves where travelers could rest. The one beside him, the largest in the row, had been claimed for the ailing Inquisitor. Thomas stood and walked slowly into the alcove. The Padre lay on the floor beside the far wall. Thomas had hoped the coolness of the stone would bring the fevered man comfort. There was little else he could do. Aditi had sent one of her pillows for his head. Brother Timóteo kept his vigil as ever, kneeling beside the Padre in silent prayer.

Thomas crouched beside Timóteo. "How fares he?"

Timóteo looked up with a start as if his mind were returning from a distance. "Ah? I cannot say, Tomás. He lives but . . ." The boy finished the sentence with a heavy sigh.

Thomas placed his hand against the Padre's forehead. *Not so heated as before, but damp.* The Padre was still very pale and his breath faint and shallow. Those fever victims Thomas had seen with such symptoms would either soon be on the way toward recovery, or dead. "Has he eaten?"

Timóteo shook his head. "Are you going to bleed him, Tomás?"

"No. I do not think it wise."

"So," said Joachim casually behind them, "does our Padre yet walk with the angels?"

Under his breath, Thomas cursed the *soldado*'s callousness. Patting the boy's shoulder, Thomas said, "Continue your prayers, Timóteo. That is all we can do for now."

Timóteo nodded and again bowed his head.

Thomas stood and motioned to Joaquim to follow him outside the alcove.

"You do not answer, Tomás," said Joaquim, joining him under the colonnade. "Is this a good omen or bad?"

"If you please, Joaquim, have a care for the boy. The Padre still lives and, God willing, we shall keep him so."

"Oh. A pity."

"What are you saying, man? Surely you do not wish him dead?"

"Oh, no, Madre Maria defend me, I do not wish him dead, Tomás. Such a curse would surely fall back upon my head. But, also, I do not wish to see a man suffer. And I will tell you a thing, Tomás. Our *sargento* has said that if the Padre dies, we all return to Goa. That is a thing to be wished for, yes?"

Thomas stared at the soldier. "If the Padre dies, the leadership of this expedition passes to Brother Timóteo. That is what the Padre wishes."

Joaquim laughed. "You think we will follow that boy further into this land of thieves and pestilence? You should have seen him when the merchants would come to blows with us. 'Oh, do not fight, Madre Maria, be peaceful!' " the soldier mocked Timóteo in a piping voice. In a more serious tone, he went on. "The Padre may be moved by his faith to ask foolishness, but we are sensible men. Already four of my compadres are sick with the fever. And when he dies, the

Padre's body must be returned to be buried in holy ground, no? It will, of course, be unfortunate for you, as it means we will have to return you to the gentle hands of the Santa Casa. I expect the Inquisitor Major will not be pleased with your failure."

Thomas clenched his hands and growled, "I will not go back into the Santa Casa. If you must return, leave me and tell them I am dead."

Joaquim shook his head. "They will want your body as proof, Tomás. Or, I suppose, we could chop off one of your limbs as evidence, if you feel there is one you could live without."

The heat, fear, and anger made Thomas's head spin. He advanced on Joaquim, backing the small, wiry man against the wall. "I—will—*never*—go—back—to—the—Santa Casa! Do you understand this? No matter what occurs, I will not go back to Goa!"

The *soldado*'s eyes went wide with surprise. "Of course I understand, *amigo meu*, that you wish not to return. I am only telling you what my *sargento* has said."

"Senhores?"

Thomas turned his head and saw Timóteo staring at them. Thomas took a step back from Joaquim. "Forgive us, Timóteo. We are having a . . . disagreement."

"Please do not have it here. You may be disturbing the Padre."

"Of course," said Joaquim. "We must be sure to let the good Padre rest in peace." To Thomas, he said softly, "I am sorry for you, my friend. But you cannot stop us from going back. Not unless you can work miracles." Tugging on the rumpled sleeves of his shirt, he strolled away as if nothing untoward had happened.

Thomas leaned against a pillar and moaned softly at his predicament, wishing for the hundredth time that his arms were not so weak and useless.

Timóteo came up beside him. "Tomás? What were you fighting about? I heard Senhor Alvalanca making fun of me. And I heard you saying you would never go back."

There is no point in deceiving the boy. "Joaquim was informing me that if the Padre dies, he and the other soldiers intend to return to Goa."

Timóteo's mouth dropped open. "They would abandon us?"

"No. They presume that we would return with them. But I told him I would not."

Timóteo smiled. "Of course, Tomás. You are not a coward, as they are. You know the importance of what we do. The Padre said so. You will not give up the sacred quest."

Thomas smiled tightly back. "Fear not. I will not return to Goa with them. But with good fortune, the Padre will recover, and this possibility need never concern us."

Timóteo looked back into the alcove. "He is in God's hands."

"Indeed." *And a miracle we sorely need. If I but had some of the* rasa mahadevi—*I could pull a miracle from a bottle.* And then Thomas realized there was one, perhaps two, among their party who might.

Aditi surely must, thought Thomas. *Yet, if I ask her, she may think I ask from greed. Tender though she may be, methinks she still is wary of me. And I must have her goodwill so that she will speak to the Sultan on my behalf. The good "Brother" Andrew, now, may yet have some. He has claimed to have given all to the Santa Casa, and yet I know him for a rogue and he may well have lied.*

Thomas looked around to ensure no one was near enough to hear. "Timóteo, might you have some of the drug called *datura* with you?"

Timóteo tilted his head. "No, Tomás."

"Can you find the plant and prepare it, or perhaps purchase some here in Hukeri?"

"It is a common drug. There is probably an herbalist in

the village from whom I can get some. But why? The Padre already sleeps and *datura* might do him harm."

"It is not for the Padre."

"No? Then for whom? Be careful, Tomás. There are some who say that to use *datura* leads to other evil deeds."

"Never fear, Timóteo. I wish it for a greater good. Can you keep a secret?"

Hours later, Thomas sat, leaning against the wall, beside the unconscious Padre. He tried to take comfort in the cooler evening air. Carefully hiding the cup containing the datura Timóteo had procured for him, he calmed himself for what he must do.

Timóteo appeared in the entrance to the alcove, Andrew Lockheart beside him.

"You sent for me, lad?"

"Aye, Andrew. 'Tis been too long since we have last spoken, and I have news of some import."

"Then I must hear it." Lockheart lowered his bulk to sit down beside Thomas.

Thomas looked at Timóteo, and said in Latin, "Thank you. I will keep watch on the Padre. You should get some rest."

Timóteo glanced dubiously at Lockheart, then bowed and went away.

Lockheart nodded toward the recumbent Gonsção. "Can he hear us, think you?"

"If so, we will be but part of his fever dream. And I doubt that, in his dreams, he understands English."

Lockheart smiled. "A point, but it is no sin to be wary. Much may be told by tone of voice. Will he live?"

"I surely know not."

"Mm. He seems still as a corpse, e'en now. Howsomever, this may fall out to our benefit."

"I think not," said Thomas. "Joaquim has told me that if the Padre dies, the soldiers plan to return forthwith to Goa."

"Ah. I thought I smelled something on the wind. But

this is good news, lad. I have been talking to Dame Agnihotra's merchantmen. They have no love for the Portuguese
and would gladly let them go home. For the price of a few
favors, they will transport you and I with them to Bijapur.
The Dame Agnihotra, 'twould seem, has been charmed
by you."

"I meet with some favor in her eyes, 'tis true. But hear
me out, Andrew, for there is more to my news. If the soldiers
decide to return to Goa, they will insist I go with them."

"Hm. There are but eight soldiers still in health. It is possible we could slip away in the night."

"I believe their horses are faster than camels. They could
catch up to us."

"Many of the merchants are armed, Tom. And we know,
for all their bluster, the Goan soldiers have little stomach for
fight. With the merchants' weapons we could keep the soldiers at bay, mayhap enough to convince 'em we are not
worth the battle."

"Wherefore should the merchantmen risk themselves for
our sake?"

"Because their lady asks it of them? Because they would
like a chance to slay some Portuguese? Surely we can find
reason enough."

The thought of seeing Joaquim, poor friend though he
might be, slain before his eyes was not appealing to Thomas.
"Let us hope it does not come to that," he said softly. In a
heartier tone, he added, "Will you drink with me, Andrew?
I find I have become quite fond of this *arrack*." With care, at
his side away from Lockheart, Thomas poured from a clay
pot into two wooden cups. He made sure to hand to Lockheart the cup that also contained the *datura*.

Lockheart grinned at him knowingly as he took the cup.
"Take care, lad. The seductive fruits of the East can lure a
man unknowingly to his doom."

"I shall remember," said Thomas with as blank a face as

he could manage. He clicked his cup against Lockheart's. "To our eventual success."

"To the end of our journey," said Lockheart. He saluted with the cup and then downed its contents in one gulp. After a moment, he frowned and examined the cup more closely. "Odd. This tastes not like other *arrack* I have sampled."

"Ah. Well, doubtless each village hath its own recipe, which the herbalists guard jealously. Or so Timóteo has told me."

"And we know the good little brother never lies, eh?" Lockheart nodded toward the Padre. "Have you thought to take the map from him?"

"Your pardon?"

"The *arrack* has addled your wits, lad. The Padre is insensate and no one is here to see. Search his clothing for the sorcerer's map and then, whether he lives or dies, we are the better prepared to continue on."

"I had not thought of that."

Lockheart shook his head. "You are a brave lad, but you lack a scoundrel's cunning. Your master has ill-prepared you for a tradesman's life."

"You may have the right of it," said Thomas, wondering if he had miscalculated the dose of *datura* and ruined his chance.

"Go on, then," said Lockheart, pointing at the Padre. "Have a look 'round him. I will give warning if we should be spied upon."

"Very well." With a last glance at Lockheart's face, Thomas shifted onto his knees and bent over the Padre. Carefully, as if he might wake the Inquisitor, Thomas pulled aside the collar of the robe. The Padre wore nothing about his neck. Thomas began to pat the hems of the sleeves with a growing disgust, as if he were robbing the dead. Then he noticed a small pouch attached to the cord around the Padre's waist. He touched the pouch and felt, amongst a few coins, a small, cylindrical object. He loosened the pouch strings and pulled out the rolled up map. "I believe I have found it, Andrew."

Thomas turned around, to see the Scotsman slumped against the wall, staring slack-jawed at his lap. "Andrew?"

There came no reply and Thomas waved his hands before Lockheart's eyes. They did not even blink. Slipping the map into the drawstring casing of his trousers, Thomas quickly tugged open the neck of Lockheart's Hindu tunic. He found a chain on which hung a silver pendant. But he also found a leather lanyard on which hung a little leather pouch. He tugged it open and found it was filled with a brown powder. *Aha. You are yet the scoundrel I have thought you.*

Thomas closed the pouch and removed the lanyard from Lockheart's neck. He held the pouch dangling before him a moment, mindful of the power he held in his hand. *O divine sap, what a troublesome temptation thou art.*

He turned and quickly checked the Padre's breathing and pulse. They were very light, but still present. *He yet lives so I must not use thee now. But what to do with thee until thou art needed?* Thomas thought to wear it on his person, but if Lockheart were to wake before he used it, the Scotsman might snatch it back from him.

Thomas saw movement out of the corner of his eye and turned his head to see Timóteo peeping in. "I thought I had told you to rest."

Sheepish, Timóteo slunk in. "I could not sleep. I worry too much about the Padre."

"Very well. You can do me a service. Come here."

Timóteo came beside him but his eyes widened as he saw the leather pouch Thomas held. "Is . . . is that the *pulvis mirificus?*"

"Yes. But we do not need it yet. I want you to keep it with you, as you are near the Padre most often."

"M-me?"

"This must be kept in a safe place, Timóteo. You are trusted and no one will suspect you."

Eyes wide with awe, Timoteo crossed himself and bent his head to receive the lanyard.

As Thomas placed it over the boy's head, he thought, *The boy accepts it as if a sacred object. Gonsção said Timóteo had read the Santa Casa's records and knows something about the powder.* "You seem afraid, Timóteo. What is it?"

"No, I am not afraid, Tomás. But the Padre thinks the powder is evil. I do not know that he will like our using it on him."

"If it will disturb him, then we will not tell him what we have done. The one man I have quickened with this substance believed only that he had awakened from slumber, and that is what we will tell the Padre." Thomas dropped the loop of leather over Timóteo's head and tucked the pouch beneath his robe. "There. Timóteo, the Padre told me once that you had read—"

"Is he dead yet?" said Joaquim, strolling into the alcove.

Thomas shut his eyes and sighed. "You are like a raven circling over a battlefield, Joaquim. You come hoping to find some unfortunate who has fallen to make a meal of him."

"What a terrible thing to say, Tomás, when I am showing concern over our poor Padre. Hmmm, he does not look too appetizing. We must be sure to keep him from the crows, lest we poison the poor birds, eh?"

"Senhor!" said Timóteo.

"Oh do not looked so shocked, little brother," said Joaquim. "His journey to heaven will buy us our journey home. You would be eager too, if you had any sense."

Timóteo lifted his chin. "I am not returning to Goa with you. I will not abandon our quest."

"Fine! Stay and see how far you get on your quest. Stay and be eaten by tigers or killed by brigands. I doubt the

Santa Casa will miss one acolyte. What is the matter with Frater Andrew here? He does not look well either."

"He is drunk," said Thomas. "It is nothing unusual."

"Ah, no doubt he is celebrating the thought of returning to civilization as well. By the way, Tomás, the Domina Agnihotra is asking for you. She wishes to speak to you right away. You might as well take the chance to see her now, for it may be your last."

"Yes," said Thomas darkly, "I should speak with her." Turning back to Timóteo, he laid a hand on the boy's shoulder. "As you cannot sleep, you may as well keep vigil here. Come and tell me if there is any change in him."

"I will, Tomás."

With a final glare at Joaquim, Thomas stood and walked out of the alcove.

Aditi had lodged with her train in a large house that was set back from the street. Thomas was fairly certain one of the Goan soldiers watched where he went, but he no longer cared. If he could counsel patience to Aditi, some lives might be saved. If not, then at least he might secure her protection.

The serving girl admitted him immediately and showed Thomas to a room whose entrance was covered by a cloth curtain. The girl pulled aside the curtain and bowed, gesturing for him to enter. As the cloth fell back into place behind him, Thomas found himself in a room draped with broad lengths of calico and silk, to resemble a caravaneer's tent. Light came from oil lamps hung from the ceiling. The outer world seemed far away—an effect Thomas found pleasing.

Aditi sat in a mound of pillows, wearing only a long, sheer silk jacket. Her braided black hair hung over her left shoulder. "Tamas! I am glad you have come to see me." Her smile was bright but fleeting. "I have been hearing rumors. Perhaps you can tell me if they are true."

Thomas crossed to a cushion beside her. "What is it you have heard, Aditi? Perhaps I can allay your fears."

"Or perhaps give me hope, Tamas. I have heard that the priest of the Orlem Gor lies near death."

"It is true he is still very ill, but I expect that he will recover."

Aditi frowned. "My servants say he is very pale and hardly breathes."

Dear God, does she want the Padre dead as well? But it is natural that she should be an enemy of anyone from the Santa Casa. I should not tell her I have gotten some of the resurrection powder, nor what I plan to do with it. "Yes, but I have treated such fevers before and I know the signs of returning health."

"You are helping him get well, this man who keeps you prisoner?"

Thomas sighed. "My master taught me healing arts, not killing ones. I have no wish to hasten any man's death. But listen. It will not go better for me if he dies, for his soldiers would then return to Goa, and they intend to take me with them."

"Ah." Aditi stared pensively at him.

Puzzled by her minimal response, Thomas added, "They will hand me back to the inquisitors of the Orlem Gor if I return with them."

"Tamas, have I not said that I came with this caravan because of you? You will not see the Orlem Gor again. I promise you this." She reached out and stroked the back of his arm.

"I am most glad to hear it. But if I were to try to escape with your caravan, the soldiers might come after and do harm to you and your merchants."

"I see. They would fight to take you back."

"They may. And I wish no one to die on my account. So you see, it is better that the Padre will become well again soon."

"Ah. Do you want the Orlem Gor to find the *rasa mahadevi*, Tamas?" A tint of steel appeared in her blue-grey eyes.

"What? No, Aditi, of course not."

"Then why do you befriend that boy monk who serves them?"

"Whyever not? He has a great interest in herbs and medicines as I do. What harm can there be in showing kindness to him?"

Aditi paused and then slowly smiled, "Ah, Tamas, we do not think alike, you and I. I find your philosophy strange. I have lived as long as I have by knowing very clearly who my enemy is."

"The boy is not my enemy, Aditi. He is as trapped in this expedition as I. And the Padre is not all you think him either. But it is no matter. Once in Bijapur, I can be cut loose from them and need serve them no longer. That is surely better than dissolving the expedition out here, where there is greater danger to everyone."

"True," murmured Aditi, regarding him coyly. "In Bijapur, many things become possible."

"Precisely. If you will still speak to the Sultan for me, and he takes me into his service, I may eventually earn enough to make the pilgrimage to the city of your Mahadevi."

Aditi shook her head. "There is so little you understand. You do not need wealth to be a pilgrim. Here in India, holy seekers wear and eat next to nothing. You will need practice." In one graceful move she slid up beside him and began tugging his shirt out of his slops.

"Aditi, this is not a good time for love play."

"Shhh. We must take our chances where we can, Tamas. Who knows when we may have private hours together again. Now that there is light, I may see whether your curls below are as golden as those above, nai?" She plucked at the drawstring of his slops and the rolled-up map he had hidden there fell out.

Thomas tried to grab for it, but Aditi was quicker and snatched the rolled parchment up.

"What is this, Tamas?" She unrolled the map and gazed at it for long moments.

Thomas fell back against the pillows and sighed. "It is De Cartago's map."

"I thought you said the priest of the Orlem Gor had this."

"He did. I stole it from him while he lay unconscious."

"Clever Tamas. But you have no need of this, since I can lead you where you wish. And we do not want anyone else to have it, nai?" She stood and went to the nearest oil lamp, and put the tiny scroll into the flame.

Thomas almost leapt up to stop her, but he checked himself. *Wherefore should she not burn it? I am not going to search for the resurrection powder and I care not if others do. She is right— 'tis best the Padre cannot have it.*

The sound of running feet approached the cloth curtain. "Tomás!" Timóteo cried. "Tomás! Where are you? Come quickly! Tomás?"

"I am in here, Timóteo." Thomas retied his slops and stood.

"It is the Padre, Tomás. It is time. Please hurry."

Aditi caught his sleeve as Thomas headed for the curtain. "Why did you tell him you are here?"

"He would not have come if it were not urgent."

"But why do you go? If the priest is about to die, should you not stay so we can hide you from the soldiers?"

"Because there is more I may yet do to save him. Fear not. If all fails, I will return." Thomas pulled her hand off his sleeve and kissed it, then turned and departed through the curtain.

Aditi heard their running footfalls echoing away through the house. *One more thing he may do? What more can he do for a dead man, unless. . . . He has more of the* rasa mahadevi! *Oh, I am a fool! A weak fool!* Aditi put her left hand to her forehead and felt a burning in her right. She looked and saw the smouldering stub of parchment still in her fingers and she dropped it on the rug. Swearing softly, she stepped on the glowing remains with her sandalled foot and stuck her scorched fingertips into her mouth.

A bad omen. I must not be so inattentive. It is now clear he is lying to me. He had the map, and he did not like it when I burned it. He has the blood. What other lies has he told me? How many more will now learn of Her secret? Ai, why did I not kill him while I had the chance?

In the dim torchlight of the street, Thomas and Timóteo ran to the alcove where the Padre lay. Joaquim was there ahead of them, waiting at the entrance. Other *soldados* passed to and fro behind him, carrying away the Padre's possessions.

"You are too late, herbalist," said Joaquim. "The Padre is dead, may God rest his soul. You had best pack up quickly. The *sargento* wishes to leave before the sun rises."

"If you please, Joaquim, let Timóteo and I pray over the Padre before he is moved."

"You may pray all you like while you pack."

"No! That would be . . . improper. Let us see him now. I ought to examine him one last time. There are stupors that have the semblance of death, and Padre Gonsção may—"

"What love do you have for the Padre," sneered Joaquim, "that you take such care of him? He, who tormented you in the Santa Casa, and forced you onto this journey to nowhere?"

"He has never harmed me, nor spoken a word of anger to me. He risked his life to help me when I fell down the mountainside. It was because of him that I had a hope of release from the Santa Casa. It was because of him that I confessed and became a true Catholic. Surely one of the Mother Church such as yourself can see what I owe to this man."

Joaquim raised his eyes to Heaven. "Ay, the *convertados* are always the worst. Go on, go on, but be swift."

Before the *soldado* had finished speaking, Thomas and
Timóteo ran into the alcove. They knelt at the Padre's side
and Thomas felt for a pulse at his neck. There was none.
Thomas waited until there were no soldiers in the alcove,
then whispered, "Give me the pouch."

Timóteo pressed it into Thomas's hand, clearly happy to
be rid of it.

"My thanks. Now pray, loudly, if you please."

Timóteo began, and Thomas looked over his shoulder.
Joaquim was arguing with another *soldado* at the entrance.
Thomas tugged the pouch open and, pinching the Padre's
jaws to open the mouth, poured the brown powder between
his lips. Some of the powder spilled onto Gonsção's chin and
cassock but Thomas could not spare the time to be tidy.

When the pouch was empty, Thomas tucked it under the
pallet and joined Timóteo in prayer.

He hadn't known what to expect. The apprentice-boy on
the *Whelp* had seemed to merely wake from sleep, while the
sorcerer De Cartago had spasmed and shook as though his
limbs were possessed by demons. Long seconds passed as
Thomas and Timóteo prayed, and Thomas began to fear that
Heaven had chosen not to return Gonsção's soul to his body.

The Padre gasped, as though he were a drowned man
washed ashore, and his eyes opened. ·

"Thanks be to God," breathed Thomas.

Timóteo stared, ashen-faced, his prayers dwindling off to
silence.

Padre Gonsção turned his head and looked with aston-
ishment at Thomas. "Magister Chinnery?" he rasped.

"We had feared the worst for you, Padre," Thomas said,
"but God has been merciful, and your fever has passed."

Grasping the edges of the pallet, Gonsção managed to sit
up. "Timóteo," he said, upon seeing the boy.

Timóteo crossed himself, saying, "Mater Maria. A
miracle."

"How do you feel now, Padre," said Thomas.

Gonsção frowned and blinked. "I . . . I appear to be well."

"It brings me joy to hear it. You have been in a very deep slumber. The *soldados* had given you up for dead. Can you stand? Let me help you." Ignoring the pain in his shoulders, Thomas grasped the Padre's arm and tried to help him off the pallet.

Gonsção was shaky at first, like a man twice his age. But as he stood and stepped forward, he seemed to gain more strength.

Thomas guided him outside where Joaquim was still arguing with another soldier. Thomas cleared his throat.

Joaquim looked at him. And at the Padre. *"Madre do Deus,"* he breathed.

The other soldier, presumably the sergeant, turned pale as he saw them. He uttered a longer string of epithets that were not reverent.

"Deus lhe dê boa manha tambem," said the Padre with a wry smile.

"Sim, Padre. Obrigado," the sergeant said, scowling. He spit onto the ground and strode away.

Joaquim began to laugh. But there was despair in his laughter and it was not a pleasant sound. "Ay, Padre, truly the angels are protecting you and your quest. We had given you up for dead and were preparing to bear your sorry body back to Goa."

"It would seem," said the Padre, with a glance at Thomas "that this world is not yet done with me."

"Indeed, you have powerful friends watching over you, Padre." Joaquim removed his helmet in a deep, Goan bow to Thomas, then turned and walked slowly down the street.

"So, Padre," said Thomas, "what is your will? It is yet night and you might get more rest before we need set out again."

Padre Gonsção rubbed his chin, looked down at his hand

a moment, then absently dusted his fingers on his robe. He stared up at the stars in the sky, as though he regretted not being among them. "A small meal, I think. And then we should get onto the road again, before our escort loses heart and abandons us. It will be less unpleasant to travel in the night, while the air is cooler."

"Do you feel well enough to travel?" said Thomas. "While your recovery seems miraculous, the body does need time to—"

The Padre held up one hand. "Let us speak no more about it, Magister Chinnery. I will give you such thanks as you deserve at another time. Go and ready your mule."

"Very well, Padre." Thomas turned and walked down the street, his heart lighter. *Thanks be to God, or to the goddess Mahadevi, or whatever powers have brought this miracle about. I need not see Goa or the Santa Casa ever again, and there shall be no battle over me.*

At the far end of the street, Lockheart emerged from another alcove, rubbing his head. The Scotsman's gaze fell on Thomas and for a moment, Lockheart only stood and glared. Then an enormous grin spread across his face. He strode over to Thomas and gave him a great bear hug. "Well now, well now, 'twould seem I misjudged ye, Tom. You're a better rogue than ever I thought." Putting his face close, Lockheart growled softly, "Did you use all of it?"

So he knows. Ah, well. "I fear so."

"Tch. Well, what's done is done."

"Forgive me. I did only what was right," Thomas said. "No men need die for my rescue and one man but lives beyond his time."

"And I've but the headache for your pains. 'Twould seem you have an unerring hand upon the tiller of our expedition, lad. You'll steer us true and straight, though gods and man defy you. A veritable Ulysses."

"I trust our journey will prove less hazardous than that of Homer's tale."

"Do you? Have you not already met our Circe?" Lockheart glanced toward the house where Aditi lodged, and placed his finger alongside his nose. "Beware, Tom. Methinks she may be transforming you into a swine e'en now."

XI

MYRRH: This is a costly, aromatic gum brought forth by small trees, which grow in the East. It hath been used since ancient times for anointing priests and consecrating temples. The taste of this spice is very bitter. An infusion of myrrh is good for wounds and sores of the mouth. A tincture of myrrh soothes coughs and ailments of the lungs. The ancient Greeks believed drops of the resin were tears shed by a woman turned into a tree after being punished for disobeying a goddess....

The Mirza Ali Akbarshah swayed in the *howdah* atop his elephant, now almost used to its rolling gait. The landscape around him was becoming more green and lush as they neared the city of Bijapur, which lay only one day ahead. He could see why Akbar and his sons itched to push the empire south. There was much wealth to be found here.

Behind him, the Mirza could hear some of his men singing as they marched or rode. Jaimal had apparently spread word of the silver reliquary of the nameless *shahid*, and now the men's thoughts were filled with visions of treasure. The Mirza was pleased to have their enthusiasm once more, but he worried about the consequences.

The derwish Masum rode with him, occasionally regaling the Mirza with Sufi tales, or reciting unfathomable poetry. Since viewing the stone hand at the *ziarat*, the Mirza had felt unease, and wished to keep the mystic nearby. *The legends say leaders are well-guided by Sufi advisors. Perhaps Masum will help me to understand the mysteries I may encounter.*

If the hand was only a cunning sculpture, and the Mirza chased only stories reinforced by false clues, his fortunes were at an end. His ambitions would be cut short by a disappointed Emperor, and his life perhaps cut short by disappointed soldiers.

But if the hand had once truly been flesh . . . The Mirza was ever of the Faithful, upholder of the Law, respectful of the Five Pillars. But he felt an inner tremor at the thought that he might experience a tangible manifestation of the Divine. Only the Prophets were said to be capable of *mujizat*, miracles, and the Prophets were of another age. But saints might have *karamat*, charismatic gifts, and perhaps that was how the stone hand had come to be.

"You have been silent a while, my Lord," said Masum. "Would you like to hear another story?"

"No, Masum." The Mirza pinched the bridge of his nose and sighed. *Whoever said the company of a Sufi brought good fortune did not also say how much patience such company required.* "However I do have a question to ask of you. What do you know of this Ibrahim 'Adilshah, Sultan of Bijapur?"

"He is a wise and learned monarch, Lord Mirza. He has welcomed refugees from near and far to settle in his land. My own *pir* came from Persia, and many artisans came from the south when Vijayanagar fell. Although it was his uncle who fought the great battles that brought peace to Bijapur, it is this Ibrahim who has made a glory of that peace. His city is the most beautiful in the Deccan."

"Have you met the Sultan?"

"Oh, no, Lord Mirza. I have only seen him pass by in procession. He is quite magnificent in appearance."

"I understand. It is true that Ibrahim drifts from the True Faith, as is rumored of the Shahinshah Akbar?"

"That is a subject much debated among the *ulama* and the *sheykhs*. It is said the Sultan does not always make the proper observances, but he has built beautiful new mosques. He has not proclaimed a faith of his own devising, as your Emperor has, but Ibrahim's personal worship is rumored to be . . . unusual. The Sultan gives more than a little honor to the Hindu goddess Sarasvati, because of his devotion to music and poetry. It is said he keeps an idol of her hidden within his palace."

"Music. Poetry," muttered the Mirza. A *pattamar* had arrived at their camp that morning with a message from the Sultan, welcoming the Mirza and his men into the kingdom of Bijapur, and directing them to the best encampment site near the city, as well as which caravanserai would have lodging for the Mirza and his officers. The message had been in the form of a poem. The Mirza could have dealt with the warlike Ibrahim I who had brought peace to Bijapur. But a monarch who wrote poems?

"Poetry is the language through which the soul speaks," said Masum. "My *pir* values the art as well."

"I see. What does your *pir* say about dreams?"

"A dream is a journey, my Lord, to an inner land that is but a mirror of our own. In that land, one may be guided by the angel of philosophers. Dreams may show the way onto the path to Paradise and to God."

"Ah. Well. I have had a dream . . . much the same dream every night since we visited the tomb. Perhaps you can interpret it."

"I am but a *murid*, Great Mirza, and I do not yet have the wisdom of a *pir*. And my *pir* would say that you must meditate upon your dream yourself until your soul comprehends it. But," he tilted his head with a gentle grin, "I confess to being curious. I would like to hear this dream."

"Very well. I dreamed of an enormous cup that was filled by five streams. The cup had five sides and was held in the hands of a beautiful woman. She said that if I drank from one side, I would be poisoned. From another side, I would taste sweet wine that intoxicated. From the third side, I would receive clear water that refreshed and purified. Drinking from the fourth side, I would taste blood. And from the fifth and last, I would receive only ashes and dust."

"Ah," sighed Masum, his eyes shining.

"Well?"

"Have you thought upon its meaning, Great Lord?"

"I have. Some of it seems to be a warning. Yet the cup is a Sufic symbol, is it not? The many sides could reflect the teaching that the Divine is to be experienced in all his forms."

Masum seemed delighted with this, as if the Mirza were a child uttering his first clear words. "This is a worthy interpretation, my Lord. And, to us, the woman is a symbol of divine manifestation. That fact that you are asked to drink from the cup . . . well, it is through the mouth that the Divinity enters and consumes from within."

"Ah." The Mirza did not feel enlightened, but his apprehension grew.

"Again, I must remind you that I have not yet walked the full Path of the Suf, nor should this *howdah* be thought my *khanagh*. But there is one more interpretation of the dream to be considered."

"And what is that, Masum?"

"I believe you, perhaps all of us, will be offered a choice. How you choose will have serious consequences."

"That is a very safe interpretation. Leading this army makes such choices a daily occurrence."

"You misunderstand, Great Mirza. I do not mean the minor actions in a mortal life. All men are like the dust in the cup, we can be blown afar by the breath of God. One path may bring nourishment to the soul, another sweet oblivion." He held out his cupped hands and opened his mouth as if to say more. Then Masum sighed with a rueful smile and looked away.

"What is it?"

Masum shook his head. "Forgive me. I am a poor teacher. I speak beyond my place."

It was clear he would not be coaxed into further explanation. The Mirza looked out again at the fields and groves. A flock of doves sprang from one of the trees, circled his elephant and flew off toward the southeast, sunlight shimmering off their wings.

Are there concepts greater than my mind can hold, greater than words can express? Is that what silences Masum? Yet he feels I should come to know them. Why? Is not the following of the Law enough? Are not the responsibilities I bear to my family, my men, and my Emperor enough? Do I owe yet more to Allah? Or does the Divine offer me that which I cannot yet see?

Troubled in ways he did not understand, the Mirza let silence fall like a curtain between himself and the Sufi mystic.

Hot, dry wind blew Brother Timóteo's hair askew and red dust filled the sky, obscuring his vision. On occasion, he would catch frustrating glimpses of high, stone walls and glimmering domes in the distance. He tried to put up the hood of his brown robe only to have a gust snatch it off him, pelting sand in his eyes. "Where did this wind come from, Frater Andrew?" Timóteo shouted. "This was a nice, calm green valley when we entered it this morning."

"It is the dry season," said Brother Andrew. "The camel drivers told me that, in this month, the djinn of the Deccan deserts become jealous of Bijapur's fertility and try to reconquer the land."

"The Padre says such tales are pagan nonsense," said Timóteo. The ends of the leather reins he held flapped in the wind and suddenly slapped him in the face. "Ai! Mater Maria!" he cried, and then crossed himself. *I should not have spoken so soon. Perhaps demons are at play here after all.*

After seeing the resurrection of Padre Gonsção, Timóteo could no longer discount any wondrous tales. If a man could be brought back to life with the powdered blood of a legendary creature, who knew what other tales might be true?

Timóteo turned in his saddle and looked back at the Padre, who rode behind him. The Padre was huddled over his horse, the hood of his black cape pulled low over his face, the ends of the cape fluttering behind him like great black wings.

As though a demon of Death follows me. Timóteo shuddered and turned round again in his saddle. *It is just my imagination.* The Padre had been different in his behavior since his revival. He had become more silent and distant, though he seemed in good health. *Madre Maria, I hope he is not possessed.*

Timóteo's burro stopped abruptly and one of Sri Agnihotra's serving girls appeared beside him, her *shal* wrapped tightly around her head and shoulders.

"You! Little monk of the Orlem Gor. Sri Agnihotra wants to talk to you."

"Me?"

"She needs you to translate something. She's over here by the side of the road. Come."

Timóteo looked around, but Brother Andrew and the Padre were too far away to shout at. He could not see Tomás at all.

"Come on!" The girl tugged on his sleeve.

"Very well! I'm going." Timóteo slipped off his burro and led it by the reins, following the girl through the swirling dust as best he could.

The palanquin was not far away and Timóteo knelt beside it. The purple curtains had been replaced by thick wool felt, and Timóteo was envious of the Lady's protection from the wind and dust. He wished he could crawl into the palanquin just to be someplace sheltered and safe for a while. But the Lady had not seemed a generous sort and the Padre would be furious, so Timóteo banished the thought from his mind.

"Sri Agnihotra!" said the girl he had followed. "I have brought the little monk."

"Good. Go wait with the others and send the messenger here." The voice still did not sound like that of an old woman, but Timóteo knew he had not seen enough women, of any age, to be an accurate judge. "Little monk, are you there?"

"Yes, Sri Agnihotra."

"Good. I called for you because I wish to speak Marathi and to be clearly understood."

"Yes, Sri Agnihotra." From around the other corner of the palanquin, a thin, dark-skinned man wearing only a dhoti appeared.

He bowed to Timóteo, and said, "I am here at your summons, Lady."

"Good. Little monk, this is where our caravans part company. I must go on into the city, where I will speak to the Sultan and arrange a meeting for your priest. My merchants must go about their business. This messenger will guide your people to a caravanserai nearby, where you may take shelter, and prepare yourselves for a summons from the Sultan."

"Yes, Great Lady. The Padre, if he were here, would thank you for all your assistance."

"Thanks are not necessary. I have done as my dharma required. Go now, and get yourselves out of this wind."

"Thank you, Sri Agnihotra." Timóteo stood.

"Oh, little monk? One more thing."

"Yes, Lady?"

"Tell Tamaschinri . . . tell him I hope to see him again soon."

Timóteo could not help smiling, even though he knew he should not approve. "I will tell him, Sri Agnihotra."

"Good. Go."

Thomas stood on the crenellated parapet of the caravanserai gazing at the huge black basalt walls of Bijapur. With the fall of evening, the wind had died down and the dust had settled, although the remaining haze made for a glorious sunset.

The serai was located about a mile west of the city. What little of Bijapur itself showed above its walls, the glimmer of golden domes and tips of graceful spires, tantalized Thomas like the shimmer of mirage on a desert, or the first sight of land to a man who had been too long at sea.

Somewhere in its midst was Aditi, with whom all his hopes lay. *Mayhap, e'en now she sits at the foot of the Sultan and speaks for me, preparing the way for my journey home, though she knows it not.*

Thomas was ready for the expedition to end. Since his resurrection two days before, Padre Gonsção had become aloof, allowing only Brother Timóteo to attend to him. Joaquim and the other *soldados* had become sullen and short-tempered, drinking and gambling in the evenings, quick to start fights among themselves. They paid little attention to Thomas anymore, except to now and then glare at him hatefully. *Mayhap Joaquim and his fellows hoped I'd try to escape and give them cause to kill me. Then they might convince the Padre to abandon the quest. But no matter. We are here and we shall all be free of this fools' journey anon.*

"Beautiful, is she not?" said Lockheart, coming up behind him. "A jewel of a city set within the copper of the desert. Be proud, lad. Few of our land have seen this sight."

Thomas nodded. "A tale worth the telling to those at home." *Where I hope to be headed 'ere long.* "But where have you been these past days, Andrew? I have hardly seen you. This is hardly proper behavior for a hired nursemaid."

"After your clever scheme with the Padre, lad, I think you have little need of one. But I have been keeping company with Sri Agnihotra's merchants. It is they who know this land and its people. Much may be learned by listening to them. For example, you've noticed, no doubt, that this serai was vacant awaiting only our arrival?"

"A stroke of good fortune."

Lockheart shook his dark curls. "The camel drivers think not. This is high caravan season, and by rights there should have been no room at all. They suspect the Sultan may have ordered this serai to be vacant for us."

"Even better. His Majesty already favors us."

"Think again. To the caravaneers, it is never a good sign to have a potentate too interested in your business."

"Mayhap they are unused to having a foreign delegation in their midst."

"Or they have their noses to the wind. You'll notice, we occupy only one quarter of this serai, yet no other caravans have been allowed in."

"What of it? We are given privacy."

"Or we are cut off from outside aid. Or the extra room is being held for someone else."

Thomas laughed. "Does our journey so want for excitements that you must seek intrigue everywhere? Can you not occupy yourself with duller pastimes?"

Lockheart clicked his tongue. "You are failing your lessons in roguery, boy. And I had thought you such a promising pupil. We are foreigners here, and not well-loved by the populace. A cunning mind and quick eye are necessities for survival."

"So I am learning, Andrew."

"Are you? When you take so little interest in your lodging?"

"Because I do not expect to be here long. Perhaps as we speak, there is one within the Sultan's palace who serves my interests and may secure a position for me, thus freeing me from this expedition and the Padre's gentle care."

Lockheart raised his brows. "Indeed? How can you already know one within those walls unless . . . the Domina Agnihotra?" His puzzlement became a smile. "You have used your charm to beg a boon of her. I eat my words, Tom. You are a rogue indeed to use an old woman so."

Thomas looked around to ensure no one else was near. "Not so far a rogue, Andrew. She is no crone. In truth, if you can keep a secret, she is none other than the fair Aditi, whom you have met before."

"The very same we plucked from De Cartago's ship? What a marvel! Methought I recognized her voice as she scolded the thief, but thought it happenstance. How can this be?"

"I know not how she learned of our expedition, but she joined it in order to give aid to my escape."

"Wherefore did you not tell me this?"

"She is yet sought by the Santa Casa. I dared tell no one for fear of what the Padre might do, should he learn of it."

"But we are many miles from Goa."

"For aught I know, she may be of such value to them, that the Padre might have turned back at once to deliver her to the inquisitors. Or had the soldiers take her prisoner and force her secrets from her on the road."

"Methinks he would not be such a fool. And yet," Lockheart mused, stroking his beard, "if anyone were to know the source of our resurrection powder, 'twould be she. Ah, but by now you surely have cozened it out of her. Forgive me, lad, for ever thinking you wanted wit. You have been bent upon the greater prize all along. No wonder you had not thought to steal the map from the Padre. You had no need of it!"

"No need," agreed Thomas, truthfully.

"In that case," Lockheart said, holding out his hand, "will you give it me?"

Thomas stared at him. *You want the powder for yourself.*

"Forgive me, Andrew, but I no longer have it. The Lady Aditi has taken it from me. For safekeeping."

Lockheart's hand closed into a fist. He turned and gazed again at the city walls. "You've placed your trust in a leaky basket, lad. Remember this same Aditi was the adamant-hearted creature who slew Master Thatch, and betrayed De Cartago despite his fondness for her. Wherefore should you believe she will show to you greater constancy?"

"Such thoughts do not trouble me," said Thomas. "Had she wished me ill, she had all manner of chance to do me harm and did not." *And I've no other choice. So long as she speaks me fair to the Sultan, my plans are set and I am halfway home.*

Aditi bowed until her forehead touched the rug on which she knelt. Ordinarily she would give such obeisance only to the Mahadevi, but there was much she wanted from Ibrahim 'Adilshah. She wished to make the best impression.

Though her thoughts whirled and jangled like a dancer's bracelets, she kept her movements still and her gaze straight-forward. She had no fear of the 'Adilshah, for he was only a mortal potentate. But she felt more and more she was stray-ing from her duty to the Mahadevi. Once her divine adop-tive mother learned of Aditi's failures, who could say what retribution She would deliver?

"So, Sri Aditi," said the Sultan, reclining upon pillows, an asoka blossom in his hand. "It has been a long time since you have graced our *durbar* with your presence."

His words were ironic, for few of his court would ever know she was there. They were meeting in a tiny, dark room of the royal residence, the *Gagan Mahal*, lit only by one nar-row window set high in the wall. The blind musician, Gand-harva, was playing his *vina* softly in a far corner of the room. Aditi pretended not to know him, and he had not acknowl-edged her.

"I go where my dharma requires me, Majesty."

"As do we all. But your beauty and talents have been missed. I trust all is well with She whom you serve?"

"Her strength and health never waver, Majesty."

"Of course, of course. I understand you have brought to me a most unusual gift. Strangers from Goa and further west."

"You are well informed, Majesty."

"It is a poor *raja* who does not have the ears of elephants. But given the dangers of the road, it is fortunate these strangers had you as a guide to help them arrive safely."

Is he chiding me? What has Gandharva told him? "For the Mahadevi, all things are possible. I am only Her servant."

Ibrahim stared at her a moment. "Yes, yes, but what do you . . . what does She expect me to do with these westerners? They seek audience with me, you say. What do they want?"

"They will ask you the whereabouts of the Mahadevi. As you do not know this, you will send them away no wiser."

The sultan examined the *asoka* blossom in his hand. "I thought it was the wish of the Mahadevi to only be known to those who are ready for such knowledge. Even I am not permitted to travel to Her sacred city, wherever it is, and sit at Her feet and receive Her wisdom. How did these Goans come to know of the Mahadevi at all?"

Aditi paused. "You have heard, have you not, of the dreaded Orlem Gor of the Portuguese? Some followers of the Mahadevi were captured and tortured in that horrible place. That is how they know."

"The Mahadevi did not have the power to still Her followers' tongues?"

Aditi clenched her fists, but hid them beneath her skirts. "Their tongues were stilled, Majesty."

"But not soon enough, it seems. And here you are, helping these priests of the Orlem Gor. Perhaps your goddess wishes to become better known. Perhaps that is why a Mirza of the Emperor Akbar comes here from Lahore with a small army, also seeking the Mahadevi."

Aditi held herself very still. *A Mughul army comes as well? Ibrahim must not know I am surprised by this. But, ai, Mother of All, what are you doing to me?*

"Ah," said the sultan, smiling, "is it possible I know something you do not?"

Aditi smiled her coldest, most knowing smile. "Do not deceive yourself, Majesty. Do not let pride blind your eyes. All is as the Mahadevi wishes."

"Why?" shouted Ibrahim. He jumped up from his divan and paced along the dais. "Why is She allowing these people to come here? Why now? Is this to test my loyalty? Is it to prove I am still worthy of Her support? Have you any idea what the Muslim clerics will make of this? How much trouble this will bring me?"

Ah, good. His fear makes him talkative, and he does my work for me. Aditi inclined her head. "It is good to see your wisdom has not faded with the years, Majesty. You yet have the eyes of an eagle and see things clearly."

"Do I?" Ibrahim sat down again heavily, arms crossed. "Was the building of a temple to Her, in the very heart of the city, not enough?"

"Any king can build temples, Majesty."

"I do *puja* before Her avatar's likeness every day!"

"Worship is important. But it is easy to lay offerings before an image and chant prayers."

"Not with *ulama* spying on me and condemning me and threatening uprisings! You should tell your Mahadevi *that.*"

"I am sure She knows."

Ibrahim nervously tore the *asoka* blossom to pieces and tossed it to the floor. "Must I keep paying," he muttered, "for one favor given long ago?"

"It is true that years ago, the Mahadevi returned something very precious to you," said Aditi. "But think what else

She may have done on your behalf? Was not Vijayanagar destroyed to bring further greatness to Bijapur?"

"That was during my uncle's reign."

"To the Mahadevi, past and future are one. She knew what was to come. Had Vijayanagar not fallen, would you not now be wearing armor on horseback, instead of enjoying music and poetry?"

Ibrahim sighed. "You have made your point. So. I have a plan for dealing with these two expeditions. But I am only a mortal and it may fail. If it results in Emperor Akbar sending his main force south, or should it bring Portuguese armies from the west, I shall expect the Mahadevi to provide protection."

Aditi tilted her head and smiled. "Do you wish to bargain with the Mahadevi? Fear not, you will receive all the assistance you deserve."

Ibrahim tapped his fingers on his knee. "That, my dear, is precisely what I fear."

"Do not doubt yourself, Majesty. I have every expectation that you will do well."

"I thank you for your confidence in me."

"There is a thing more."

Ibrahim rolled his eyes and sighed explosively. "What?"

"There is one among the Goans whom you are to take particular note of. His name is Tamaschinri, from a country he calls Ingland. You will know him by his yellow hair and fair skin. His eyes are a color like mine. He will wish to enter your service, and you should consider this."

"Should I? And what does this Tamaschinri do?"

"He is an herbalist and a healer."

"Feh. We have no need of herbalists in Bijapur. Most of what they call medicine is poison, or fakery. Unless . . . does this man have the Mahadevi's gift of healing?"

"He has used Her gift. But you must not expect him to do so again."

"Strange. Well, is he a soldier? Can he fight?"

"No. His arms were damaged by the Orlem Gor. It will take some time for him to heal."

"Hah. A poor healer he must be, if he cannot heal himself. Is he a musician?"

"No."

"A poet or philosopher?"

"No."

"An artisan of great skill?"

"No."

"A strategist, then. Or a war engineer? Or a weapons maker?"

"He is a man of peace, and knows none of these things."

"Then what use am I to make of this man?"

"That is not important. There is purpose in what I ask. But consider this—he has knowledge of a country you have never heard of. More of his people may someday come to India, first for trade, later perhaps for conquest. I have learned these English can be a fierce and cunning people, when there is something they dearly desire. It may serve you, and your descendants, to learn all you can from him." Aditi did not know, in fact, if another like Tamas would ever set foot in India, but Ibrahim would not know either, and he might find the argument convincing.

The Sultan regarded Aditi some moments, chin in hand. "So. I will take note of this yellow-hair, for whatever mysterious reasons you or your Mahadevi may have."

Aditi bowed. "Again, you show great wisdom, Majesty."

"Hah. Will you be staying in Bijapur a while, Sri Aditi, or does your dharma call you elsewhere?"

"Your hospitality is praised throughout Sind," said Aditi. "I would not insult such a gracious host by departing so swiftly."

Ibrahim pursed his lips. "You do me too great an honor. Well. I will not be so ungracious a host as to hasten your departure. Please consider yourself a guest in my house. But understand, my court is filled with suspicious clerics and noblemen always seeking ways to discredit me. I must ask you to remain within the areas proper for women, and not to behave in an unseemly manner. I will supply you with servants who will see to all your needs, so that you need not wander. I will let it be known that you are . . ." he gestured vaguely with one hand, "a distant cousin or something."

Aditi, in one graceful motion, stood and bowed. *So. While I am here, I am to be part guest, part prisoner, and part relative. I am gaining new challenges by the minute.* "Your Majesty need have no fear that I will be an indiscreet guest. Did the Mahadevi not send me to be of service to you? I look forward to the pleasures of your hospitality, and to the chance of having further conversation with so accomplished a lord. And I should like to tell your *vina* player that his skill is excellent, most pleasing to the ear. I wonder if he knows the Song of the White Dove. It has been too long since I have heard such divine music. I long to hear it again."

Ibrahim raised a brow and turned to the blind musician. "Know you such a song, Gandharva?"

Gandharva tilted his head, pausing to consider before replying. "I believe I used to know such a tune. I will attempt to relearn it, and then play it for you, Lady, once I am certain of the notes."

"That is most gracious of you," said Aditi.

"If there is nothing else?" said the Sultan. He clapped his hands twice and a girl servant appeared silently from behind a gilded lattice screen. "Show my guest to suitable quarters within the *zenana* and make her presence known to the Begum Shah."

The girl bowed deeply and gestured for Aditi to follow her. Aditi gracefully strolled from the chamber, head high, as if she had no care in the world. *Great Mother, are You testing me as well as Ibrahim? How am I to stop an army of the northern Empire, when I could not turn away a gaggle of western*

*barbarians? Is their meeting by your design? Ai, I hope Gandharva
can send his message. Send me word, Great Mother. Let me know
your will.*

After she had gone, Ibrahim turned back to Gandharva. "She has changed since we last saw her, don't you think?"

"As to that I could not say, Majesty."

"Oh. Your pardon. Your eyes. But I am certain she is more cautious, less fiery, than I remember her. She seems to have great faith in her Mahadevi. Did you say you knew her well, Gandharva? She did not seem to know you, or pretended not to."

"The Mahadevi, it is said, has a thousand eyes and one does not necessarily see much of another. I have spoken to her once or twice, but it would not surprise me if she did not remember me."

"How many blind *vina* players are there in the world? And what did she mean about 'The Song of The White Dove'?"

Gandharva smiled. "The music of Bhagavati is like that of no other place, Majesty. The Lady is homesick, no doubt, from living among foreigners in Goa. She wishes to hear familiar sounds from home."

"I see. When you remember this song, I would like to hear it as well."

"It would honor me to play it for you, Majesty."

Ibrahim reclined on the divan again, but was unable to find a comfortable position. "Have you any advice to offer on her words? Her secretiveness disquiets me. Do you think she is telling the truth?"

"I think it would be wise to heed her words, Majesty."

"Do you? What if your Mahadevi has decided to expand Her domain? Bijapur has prospered these many years. Perhaps She regards it as a cultivated field now ripe for harvesting."

"The only territory the Mahadevi would conquer is that of the heart and mind. She has no need of land, or warriors to win and hold it."

"Does She not? Then why does She permit the Portuguese and the might of Akbar so close to Her domain? Does She want to play us all against one another, weakening us? Or is this a game of Aditi's, kept secret from the Mahadevi? The Maratha *sardars* are numerous here—Aditi might have powerful support among them. By bargaining with the foreigners, does she plot to set herself up as queen? I wish Chand Bibi had stayed—I could have used her wisdom, as well as some of her army. I am not a man of war, Gandharva. It pains me to think I may be hearing the rumble of Shiva's chariot."

"If you will forgive me, Majesty," said Gandharva, "I fear you may be like a child in a dark house; frightened by every shadow, you invent monsters lurking there. I respectfully suggest you need to light more lamps before you peer into dark corners. From what little I know of Sri Aditi, she is devoted to the Mahadevi and would never betray Her."

Ibrahim sighed. "You may be right. But what of this yellow-hair she asks me to take into my service? It seems a bizarre request, is it not? Why should I have a foreign herbalist in my court?"

"Perhaps it is not for your sake that she asks, but for his."

"Ah." Ibrahim stared up at the window a moment. "An interesting point, Gandharva. She wishes to separate this one from the rest of the expedition. So that they do not benefit from his knowledge? You don't suppose . . . she fancies him?"

"Again, I submit Your Majesty is attempting to drink from mirages. Until you see this man yourself, you cannot know what he is."

"You are right, my friend. I can make no good plans without more knowledge. I will counsel myself to patience. When you next pray to your goddess, kindly petition her to give me guidance."

"I will surely do so, Majesty. Know that the Mahadevi watches and gives aid to those who serve her."

"It is reassuring to be so looked after," said Ibrahim, ironically contemplating Gandharva's sightless eyes. *And I must, in like wise, keep close watch upon Her servants.*

XII

JASMINE: This plant grows in the East and is very like a vine. It is oft found in gardens there, for it brings forth white flowers that exude a sweet perfume. A tincture of the flowers soothes frights and cares, though oil of this plant is said to excite the senses. A tincture of the leaves eases ailments of the eyes. Because it is thought a flower of beauty and womanly sweetness, it is under the care of the Virgin Mary. It is said that to dream of jasmine is to dream of good fortune....

Thomas stood on the balcony outside his second-story room, overlooking the center of the serai, squinting in the morning sunlight. He had not slept well. The *soldados* in the room beside his had been drunk and loud until late in the night. And some new party had entered the serai, causing much shouting and bellowing of camels, as well as blasts on what had sounded like an ill-blown trumpet.

He now beheld the source of that sound: a great, grey behemoth with enormous ears and a fantastical nose. Atop it was a small, gilded, brightly painted pavillion, furnished with rugs and pillows.

So that is an elephant. The drawings I have seen of such beasts do it no justice. No wonder Hannibal could terrify Rome with an army of them. I wonder whose creature that is, and what important personage arrived in the night. Doubtless Andrew shall tell me.

Thomas heard pounding footsteps on the balcony and turned to see Timóteo running toward him. "*Boa manha*, little brother. I have not seen you in some while. Has word come from the sultan yet?"

"No, Tomás," Timóteo said as he clumped to a halt. "No word. The Padre wishes to speak to you—" The boy gasped and his eyes grew wide as he looked into the courtyard. "*Elefante!*"

"A marvelous beast, isn't it? Haven't you seen one before?"

"Only from a distance. Whose is it? Do you think I might ride on it?"

"I am hoping Brother Andrew might tell us. Have you seen him?"

"No, Tomás. But I have not been away from the Padre much."

"Ah. Is the Padre well? I have not seen him leave his room at all."

Timóteo looked up with a guilty expression. "I do not know. His body seems well, but his spirit . . . I do not think he likes what we did, Tomás."

Thomas frowned. "I wonder what he experienced after he passed over from the fever. If we have snatched him from Heaven, I can understand that he would not be pleased." *Although, if an Inquisitor may pass the gates of Paradise, I am concerned for the nature of God.*

"I asked him what he saw after death, but he would not tell me. He said God does not intend for the living to know."

"That is what I would expect him to say. The first time I used the powder, it was to revive a ship's carpenter's ap-

prentice . . . a boy not much older than you. He said he saw
a white temple full of serpents, or something of that nature.
The vision did not seem to frighten him."

Timóteo blinked. "Where were the serpents?" he demanded.

Thomas was a little taken aback. "In the temple, as I
have said."

"But where in the temple?"

"I . . . I do not know. He did not say."

Timóteo sighed and went back to staring at the elephant. "Senhor De Cartago was going to tell me. But I
wouldn't listen."

"You talked to Senhor De Cartago after his resurrection?"

Timóteo nodded. "I was his *avocato*. But I failed, and he
died again unrepentant."

"You cannot blame yourself for that. But he said nothing
of the World Beyond?"

"Only that everything I had been taught was lies. But he
was trying to frighten me. I think there was a demon's spirit
in him."

"Do you think the Padre has been in same wise possessed?"

"I do not think so, Tomás, but he is changed. Please go
talk to him."

"Yes, I see I must. If he is merely melancholy, perhaps I
may in some way lighten his spirits."

"Enter," called the Padre as Thomas knocked on his
door, and Thomas stepped into the dim room. It was a large
guest-chamber, one of the best the caravanserai had to offer:
airy, and with a good view of the city. But Gonsção had set
out only a plain pallet and a low table, on which were only
one candle and a bible. The rest of his quarters were bare.

The Padre sat in a corner, murmuring over the rosary in
his hands. His hair had not been combed in some time and

he was allowing a beard to grow. His face seemed older, his skin more sallow.

Thomas crossed the room and sat before him. "You sent for me, Padre?"

Gonsção left off his prayers and looked up. There was a distance in his gaze that Thomas found disconcerting.

"I did, Magister Chinnery. It has been too long since we have spoken, and since I have been returned to this world, I sense that I must keep some connection with it."

Not knowing what else to say, Thomas murmured, "I am pleased to see you are well."

Gonsção tilted his head. "There are many things I no longer understand about you, Senhor. It would seem you have had some *pulvis mirificus* with you all this time, or you knew of some other source. You are familiar with its use, yet you restored my life, knowing I have sworn to destroy it. I no longer know what you intend for our expedition. You have become a puzzle to me."

Thomas opened his mouth but found no answer forthcoming.

"Did you think I would believe your lies that I had been naturally healed of the fever? Did you think I would not know the truth? You must be an ill-experienced sorcerer indeed."

"I am no sorcerer," Thomas said. " 'Tis true, I found a little of the resurrection powder—"

"Where?"

Why should I not tell him? Let Andrew answer for himself. "Brother Andrew had it."

Gonsção chuckled darkly. "Of course. And Sadrinho believed we had taken it all from him in the Santa Casa. What fools we were. Go on."

"I only used it to spare the expedition. If you had died, the soldiers would have given up the quest and returned to Goa, taking me with them."

"So Timóteo told me. I understand, Magister, your wish

to not return to the Santa Casa. Sadrinho would not have taken your failure well, and he is not a just man. But I am of two minds about you. You were willing to spare the expedition, no matter the cost of my soul."

"There would have been bloodshed, Padre. The merchants and your soldiers would have fought and perhaps killed one another. That is what I sought to prevent!"

Gonsção shook his head. "It is clear there are some matters of faith that still elude you. Flesh is but a brief vessel for the soul, which is eternal. Yet you seem to find flesh more worthy of protection."

Thomas sighed and looked away, unable to face him. "I am a simple apothecary, not a theologian, Padre. I have devoted my life to the study of substances that are of benefit to man's physical form. You have a better understanding of spiritual matters than I. I did what I felt right. If your continuing existence is abhorrent to you, you may leave it at your will."

"And thereby commit the further sin of suicide. Truly, you must despise me, seeing how eager you are to have me precede you to the fiery Inferno."

"No! That was not my intent at all!" Thomas slapped the floor for emphasis.

"Forgive me, Magister, but how can I know your intent when I can no longer trust the slightest thing you say? Did you think I was not aware of your taking the map from me? The fever made me immobile, but not entirely unaware of my surroundings."

Thomas tried very hard not to seem surprised. "I do not have the map, Padre. Perhaps what you sensed was part of a fever dream."

"Perhaps. But in any case I no longer have the map. And you were the only one near me other than Timóteo. What am I to think?"

"Please believe me, Padre. I have meant no harm to anyone. I wished only to bring us all to Bijapur in safety."

"So. We are here. What is your intent now?"

"My intent is to consult with the Sultan for the next direction our path will take."

"And will we be taking the same path?"

"Whyever not?"

"As I have said, I no longer know what your motives and plans are, though it is apparent my death is not among them. Are you thinking of abandoning the rest of us here?"

"I have no plans to seek the powder on my own, if that is what you mean."

"That is not what I asked. But I see you are unwilling to make your thoughts known to me. Therefore I must let events play out as they will. But know this. As I have been granted an unnatural extension of my life, I will devote it to the continuance of the search, whether you help me or not. And my intent when I find the source of the *pulvis mirificus* remains the same, Magister, whether you wish it or not. Your use of it to revive me has not changed that. If anything, it has made my resolve all the firmer."

"I understand, Padre."

An uncomfortable silence fell, into which the Padre finally spoke. "Since you have nothing more to tell me, please leave me. I wish to continue my meditations."

Thomas stood. "Very well, Padre. Shall I send Timóteo to keep you company?"

"No. I prefer solitude."

Thomas bowed to him, in the Hindu fashion which was becoming habitual to him. When he went outside, the bright sunlight momentarily blinded him.

Something pounced on his sleeve. "Tomás, come and see!"

"Timóteo? What is it?"

"I have found out who has brought the elephant. It is a Mughul prince from the north, where the Emperor Akbar reigns."

"A prince? So we are sharing our lodgings with royalty."

"Come, I will show you where they are roomed."

Thomas let the boy lead him along the inner balcony to the other side of the serai.

"There, Tomás, at the last door."

Two turbaned men, armed with great curved swords stood before the door at the far end of the row.

"Ah. There is not much to see, Timóteo."

"He was standing outside, not long ago. He is tall and thin, and very splendid."

"Well I do not think they would appreciate our waiting here staring at their door in hopes that he will emerge again."

"There is another newcomer, Tomás. Down there. Only I do not think he is a Mughul."

"How can you tell?" Thomas looked down and saw, in a corner of the courtyard away from the animals and stables, a man in a white wool tunic with hair sticking out from under his turban and a rather unkempt beard.

"From the turban, and the style of *jama* he wears. Oh, I see now. He is a Sufi."

"What is a Sufi?"

"They are a type of *muçulmano*, but strange. They come into Goa now and then. Sometimes they sing and play the tambora, sometimes they dance around and around."

"Does the Padre know you are so familiar with a heretic faith?" Thomas teased.

"I am not! Oh, look, he is setting out things."

The Sufi sat cross-legged, beside a small brass brazier. He was pulling from a pouch at his side various leaves, twigs, and small bricks of a golden substance. He crumbled one of the leaves into the brazier and grey smoke rose from it. Folding his hands into his lap, the Sufi swayed from side to side, humming.

"He is an herbalist too, Tomás! Let's go talk to him and see what he knows."

"Er, I do not think we should disturb his—Timóteo?"

But the boy had already dashed over to the descending wood stairs and was clattering down them.

Best to stop the boy before he bothers the man too much. Reluctantly, Thomas ran down the stairs after him. As he reached Timóteo's side, the Sufi opened his eyes and looked up. He smiled and, placing his palms together, bowed from where he sat.

"He is speaking Dahkni," said Timóteo. "He says he was praying for a vision, and here you are."

"I imagine I am something of a sight," murmured Thomas, running his hand through his hair.

"He asks our names." Timóteo bowed to the Sufi and introduced himself. He pointed to Thomas and said, "Sri Tamaschinri."

"Tamas," repeated the Sufi, who touched his own hair and then laughed.

Thomas chuckled as well. "I was told once that my name meant darkness. I suppose it is ironic with my pale hair."

The strange man burbled more, and Timóteo translated, "He is saying something about his philosophy. He says the soul is the darkness into which the light of the Heart must shine. He says that to see the world dark is to be a stranger to the unity of the world. But to be in darkness is to be moving toward the light. I do not understand what he means, Tomás."

"He plays a philosophic fugue upon my name. The man is clever, clearly."

"What is a fugue?"

"A complex form of music. But what is he called?"

"He says his name is Masum al-Wadud, and he is from Shahpur Hill, not far away."

"Did he arrive with the prince who now occupies this serai?"

"Yes, he says he serves as advisor to the Mirza Ali Akbarshah, emissary from the Padshah Emperor Akbar."

"Tell him we are honored to be sharing quarters with so eminent a personage. And so long as we are here, ask him about his herblore."

"Ah, yes." Timóteo babbled with the Sufi, who became very animated. He spoke of the items in front of him with excited gestures of the hands.

After this had gone on for some time, Thomas cleared his throat and said, "Translate, if you please, Timóteo."

"Oh. Your pardon. He has been saying that he knows the Greek medicines taught by Ali Ibn Sina."

"Ibn Sina," Thomas repeated, finding the sound familiar. "Ah! He must mean Avicenna, the ancient Persian physician."

The Sufi bobbed his head up and down. "Avicenna. Acha!"

"He says he is sorting the substances he has gathered recently into their taste groups. That is how he categorizes them, in the ayurvedic manner. That piece there is rauwolfia root. It is bitter. That dark bark is licorice root, which is both sweet and bitter. That yellow stuff is myrrh, like the gift that was given to our Lord, yes? It is both bitter and pungent."

Thomas laughed. "Slow down, Timóteo. This is too much to learn at once. Did you tell him how we in the west arrange our herbs by those which are cool and those which are warming?"

"I did. He has heard of the method, but he does not understand it."

The Sufi was rummaging in a large leather satchel that hung from his cloth belt. He came up with a triangular piece of white material. The mystic handed it to Thomas with soft words and a bow.

"He is making a gift to you," said Timóteo. "He says it

is cuttlefish bone, which is hard to find this far from the sea. He says it is good for stomach sickness."

Thomas slowly accepted the white piece of bone, also with a bow. "Alas, I have nothing to give to him in turn."

"Maybe I have something." Timóteo pulled his cloth sack from his belt and pulled out a shriveled leaf. "Here's a grape leaf from Goa's arbors. I am sure it is rare around here." There was a bit of vine still attached to the leaf, stuck on something in the pouch. Timóteo tugged hard and a tiny leather pouch popped out . . . the one that had contained the *rasa mahadevi*. It plopped on the ground in front of the Sufi.

Thomas stared, horrified, for a moment, then whirled on Timóteo. "What are you doing with that?"

Timóteo jumped back. "I didn't want the *soldados* to find it. So when they moved the Padre's pallet and I saw it, I picked it up."

The Sufi, meanwhile, had taken up the pouch and was examining it closely. He put a finger to the brown powder that coated the rim of the pouch, and sniffed at it. Then he brought the powder-coated fingertip toward his outstretched tongue.

"No!" cried Thomas, catching the Sufi's wrist just in time. "Timóteo, warn him! Tell him it is deadly poison, quickly!" Wide-eyed, Timóteo spoke urgently to the Sufi. The mystic said, "Ah," and lowered his hand with a sigh. Thomas released his wrist. Very carefully, the Sufi wiped his finger on a piece of burlap pulled from his satchel. Then he placed the pouch in the burlap and folded the cloth with agile fingers.

"He thanks you for your gift, and your warning, and asks what is its medicinal use. Tomás, what shall we tell him?"

Thomas sighed. *Ah, the vagaries of fate. But it would be surpassing rudeness to take it back, and there is only a tiny portion left.* "Tell him it is to be used only when all hope is lost."

"He understands, and asks what it is called."

"Oh, what's the use of deceiving. It is called *rasa mahadevi.*"

"Are you certain we should—"

"Just tell him!"

"*Rasa mahadevi,*" repeated the Sufi, with no more reaction than a curious quirk to his brows.

At least it has no mystical significance for him. Mayhap he will forget about it 'ere long.

A Mughul came toward them and shouted at the Sufi. Masum stood and hastily gathered his things, bowing and speaking to Thomas and Timóteo all the while.

"He begs our pardon, but he is called away to see a visitor at the gate. He says he will speak of us to his Mirza and perhaps arrange a meeting so that we may share a meal and share our knowledge further."

Thomas bowed back to him in the Hindu fashion. "Tell him we would be honored to meet his prince. It has been . . . enlightening speaking with him and I look forward to having more of his acquaintance." *Dear God, I hope we have not already done too much.*

Aditi strolled aimlessly through the water gardens of the zenana, in the Palace of Delight, feeling she had had enough of the 'Adilshah's hospitality. Truly, how many hours could one spend listening to stories, admiring the fragrance of flowers, playing games of shatranj, watching dances, eating sweets, teasing the eunuchs, sucking on a smoky hookah, playing with monkeys, dandling babies on one's knee, before a woman would go mad?

It had not been all tedium. The 'Adilshah Begum, Taz Sultan, was an interesting woman, not unaware of politics, and skilled in poetry. And her daughter, Malika Jahan, was lively and bright, making sketches of palaces and mosques because her father promised to build her one when she decided on a design she liked. But for the rest . . .

Aditi sat on a stone step beside a latticework wall and gazed out over the gardens. There were hundreds of women in the *zenana*, most of whom would be fortunate to meet with Ibrahim once in a year. *Still,* thought Aditi, *their life here is much better than what they might face back in their villages. There are worse fates than boredom. Who is to say that a caged bird does not have a better life than a bird who is free to fly through the jungles and face the fangs of tigers?*

For herself, Aditi preferred tigers to cages.

The twang of *vina* strings close beside her jarred her out of her thoughts. It had come from the other side of the latticework wall.

"Who is there who dares to incur the Sultan's wrath?" said Aditi, imitating the harem guardian's call.

"It is only I, Gandharva, Sri Aditi. The eunuchs let me by, assuming my blindness makes me harmless."

"A good thing they do not know you well."

"Please do not disabuse them of their foolish notions. I came to bring news. The Goans have arrived at Bijapur and are now lodged in a serai just outside the city walls. I have heard the sultan intends to invite them in tomorrow and bring them to the Gagan Mahal."

"Ah. I must see if I can move my lodgings there as well. Perhaps the Begum Shah can help me. Has there been any sign of the northern general yet?"

"Akbar's Mirza arrived in the night, though his army is camped to the north of the city. His party is also lodged in the serai."

"Along with the Goans? Why?"

"Who can say? The 'Adilshah is anxious and is beginning to suspect plots everywhere. I suppose he wants to have his eyes on everyone at once."

"I do not know if that aids our cause or not. Have you answer for my earlier request? Did you send a messenger dove?"

"I made the attempt. But then heard that I had been watched and a skillful bowman brought it down not far from the palace."

Aditi cursed under her breath, then said, "So Ibrahim now has the message in his hands. Do you think he will understand it?"

"Only if he reads Hellenica," said Gandharva. "And considering our good sultan has only a poor grasp of Persian, and no western tongues at all, I think it unlikely."

"That would be fortunate. Were he to know, it would only add to his suspicions. Ai, how I needed the Mahadevi's guidance, and now I must spend who-knows-how-much-longer, on my own."

"Aditi, have I not told you how clever you are? You could not have survived as long as you have without such talents. Have faith in yourself, as the Mahadevi surely has in you."

"I can only hope, Gandharva, that Her faith has not been misplaced."

XIII

HEMP: This plant grows in the East, where it is known as
ganja. It has long, toothed leaves, and brings forth tiny
blossoms in late summer. The resin of this herb is good for
easing spasms and pain of all sorts. It soothes coughs and the
headache, and stimulates the appetite. It will aid movement of
the bowels, and a paste made with the oil will smooth the skin.
Care must be taken in its use, howsomever, for hemp will
produce visions, and the illusion that one's surroundings are
either far more pleasant, or more terrifying, than they truly
are....

The Mirza Ali Akbarshah turned as the door to his serai
quarters opened. Masum walked in, followed by an austere man in a long kaftan and simple turban.

"Lord Mirza," said Masum, "I have brought a learned
alim to speak with us. He is Abu'l Hassan, a Qadiri Sufi, and
he has something of importance to tell us."

The Mirza bowed to the *alim.* "You are most welcome to
my lodgings, Sheykh Hassan. Please be comfortable and
share some tea with us."

The *alim* crossed the room quickly and, with a brief
bow, seated himself at the low table, opposite the Mirza. "I
regret that I may not stay long, and that I must speak my

business in impolite haste," said the *alim* in elegant Persian, denoting his many years of study, "but I do not wish the Sultan to know I am here, or to suspect for what purpose I have come."

The Mirza nodded to Jaimal and his eight men, all the escort he had brought to the serai, other than Masum. The men checked outside the windows and stationed themselves at the two doors to the room. "You need not fear eavesdroppers, Sheykh Hassan. Please speak freely and I shall listen."

"I thank you, wise Mirza. It is known in the palace that you come seeking stories of a pagan goddess who has the powers of life and death."

"That is correct."

"You are, yourself, among the Faithful?"

"I am a follower of the true Law. And this one," he indicated Masum, "is setting my feet upon the Path."

The *alim* nodded, and leaned forward, one elbow resting upon his knee. "What I have to tell you, Lord Mirza, is not spoken from anger or jealousy. Nor am I a traitor to the kingdom of Bijapur. I bring you this information only to set matters right, and perhaps to stop the spiritual degradation of my king and countless others."

"I understand," said the Mirza. "Never would I think so ill of one so learned. Please continue."

"I have been privileged to serve the Sultan Ibrahim 'Adilshah for many years, counseling him to be aloof to pagan influences. Alas, he has chosen to pay little attention to my counsel in recent years, and this is why. Some years ago, the Sultan's daughter, Malik Jahan, was dying of fever. Ibrahim became very distraught, for he is quite fond of her, even though she is a girl-child. He brought healers and physicians from all over Bijapur and beyond to try to save her. None of them could do her good. All of us prayed for her recovery, night and day. Alas, Allah, the Merciful, was determined to take her and she died."

"A great pity," the Mirza said, but the *alim* held up his hand.

"The tale is not finished. On the day of her death, a blind brahmin came to the palace, offering to help. He was told he was too late, but he would not be discouraged. He claimed to be a *shushena*, one with the skill to revive the dead, and he told the Sultan that the child might yet live again. He advised Ibrahim to bring an idol of the pagan goddess Sarasvati into his palace, and place the body of the girl before it. I and my brethren protested such a heathen act, but the Sultan loved his child and was determined to try anything.

"So that very night, the Sultan lay the child before a likeness of Sarasvati and the blind brahmin prayed over her body. The following morning, the brahmin presented the girl to the Sultan, alive and happy, as if she had only been asleep for a day."

"Ah, a miracle," said Masum.

"Sorcery," said the *alim*, scowling. "It is because of this that heathen influence flourishes in Bijapur, as you will see. It is because of this foul magic that Ibrahim has built temples to pagan goddesses, and devotes his idle hours to music instead of study of the Qu'ran. Although he claims to be of the Faith, Ibrahim has strayed dangerously from the Path."

"Most regrettable," said the Mirza.

"Indeed. For this reason, I have come to speak with you. I am told you seek the evil *rani* who sent the brahmin to corrupt our sultan. We suspect, even now, one of her djinn haunts the palace, to whisper in the Sultan's ear."

"By any chance," asked the Mirza, "is this brahmin who healed the child still in Bijapur?"

"No. He fled shortly after her resurrection, rather than face our questioning."

"I see. Unfortunate, for we might have convinced this sorcerer to tell us more about the one who sent him."

"She can be nothing else than a demon spawned by a son of Shaitan to wrest Ibrahim from his faith. Find this witch-queen, Lord Mirza. Find and destroy her. But do not let her continue to poison the soul of our Sultan. In the name of Allah, the Supreme, who hears and judges all, I set you this holy task. If you succeed, there can be no doubt you and your men shall earn their place in Paradise." The *alim* stood and bowed again, as if to leave.

"Please, Sheykh Hassan," said the Mirza, standing also, "I would be honored if you could stay and join us for midday prayers."

"Ordinarily, I would be pleased to, Highness, but today I cannot. As I have said, I must return to the *Gagan Mahal* before it is known where I have been. May the All-Seeing guide you." The *alim* turned and swiftly departed.

"So," said Jaimal, standing behind the Mirza, "it is a *jihad* after all."

"Perhaps," said the Mirza, "if his story can be credited."

"I am not sure that the *sheykh* has a clear vision of the matter," said Masum. "He has seen a thing which has disturbed him and therefore he is quick to find evil and blame it for all he does not approve of."

The Mirza gazed down at the mystic. "No story we have yet heard is a clear vision, Masum. All are shadows of the same object, but cast by different lights. We will not know the truth until we cast light upon the thing itself. But I will tell you this. Whatever doubts I may have had about our journey, I have them no longer."

Timóteo pounded on the door to the *soldados'* quarters.

"What is it?" someone yelled in slurred Portuguese.

"Senhores, word has come! The sultan has summoned us to his palace."

"What is that you say?"

Impatient, Timóteo pushed the door open and rushed in. Most of the twelve soldiers were lying on the floor in one attitude or another. *Sargento* Cateloso was bending over one of them as he turned and regarded Timóteo with an angry glare.

"What do you mean barging in like this?"

"Senhores, the *sardars* are here. They have come to guide us into Bijapur. We must pack up our things quickly and go with them."

The *sargento* stood, scowling. "Quickly? We must jump at the Sultan's orders, must we? Little brother, I have four men here, sick with the same fever the good Padre had. How am I to move them quickly, eh? Unless you and your *Inglês* can work another miracle, these men can go nowhere."

"I . . . I will gladly pray for them," said Timóteo. "But the Padre is prepared to go and he is having our mules and horses saddled. You cannot let him go into Bijapur unprotected. What of the quest?"

"What of it?" said the *sargento*. "The Santa Casa has some crazy idea for an expedition and hires convicts to guard their emissary." He knelt down close to Timóteo's ear, his breath heavy with the stench of palm wine. "I tell you, little brother, your Padre may be more safe away from us than with us. We do not like this Deccan, with its thieves and tigers and ugly people. We do not wish—"

"I will go," announced Joaquim Alvalanca, standing a bit unsteadily.

The other *soldados* looked at him as if he had lost his wits.

"Why not?" he went on. "There is nothing to do in this serai except drink and piss with the camels. At least in the city, there may be women. And more variety of drink. Who is with me?"

The *sargento* said, "You—Estevão, Gonsalo, Carlos, Salvador. Go with him. The rest of you stay."

"Only five?" protested Timóteo.

"Be happy, little brother, that it is not *none*. Now begone! They will meet you at the front gate when they are ready."

Angered by the *sargento*'s attitude, Timóteo only said, "May God forgive you, Senhor," and ran back out the door.

Two hours later, Timóteo sat on his burro, impatiently waiting for the *soldados*. Tomás and Frater Andrew were already on their mules, waiting at the gate, but they had little to pack. Padre Gonsção was there also, seated on a splendid dapple-grey stallion, sent by the Sultan as a gift. The *sardar* escort, four richly dressed Hindus on beautiful black horses, waited just outside the gate with puzzled expressions.

Why do they shame us so? though Timóteo of the *soldados*. *Where is their "gentleman's pride" they talk endlessly about? Madre Maria, forgive me, but I wish they had never come with us.*

Timóteo sighed and looked around for sign of the missing soldiers. His gaze strayed upward and he saw the Mughul prince again, leaning on the railing outside his quarters, watching them. Beside the Mirza stood the Sufi Masum. The Sufi smiled and waved at Timóteo. Timóteo smiled and gave a little wave back. The tall Mirza inclined his head to him. Timóteo bowed back. *It is a shame we could not stay longer. I wish I could have asked him for a ride on his elephant. I think he would let me.*

There came a clatter of hooves on the courtyard flagstones, and the five late *soldados*, led by Joaquim, came riding up. Timóteo was glad they were not swaying in their saddles.

They formed up the line quickly, then. The four servants of the Sultan would be in front. Behind them rode the Padre, Timóteo beside him. Thomas, Joaquim, Brother Andrew, and another *soldado* rode behind the Padre. The rest of the Goan soldiers were behind them. With a cry in Marathi, the four *sardars* wheeled their horses and led the party out of the gate of the serai and onto the main road into Bijapur.

The road was swarming with travellers on foot, palanquins, oxcarts, camels. And, coming right toward them, two elephants, bearing gilded *howdahs* like the one in the serai.

"Is it not proof that God has a sense of humor?" Joaquim said from behind him. "Look at the ears he gave those beasts! And that nose!"

As the behemoths passed by, Timóteo was amazed by the silence and grace of their walk. The *mahout* of the second elephant waved his hooked guide-stick in greeting to Timóteo. Timóteo grinned. Unable to take his eyes off the beasts, he turned nearly all the way around in his saddle to watch them.

He then caught Padre Gonsção scowling at him and he immediately turned forward and sat up straight.

The *sardars* ahead of him were laughing, not unkindly, at him. "If you wish to see a wonder, boy," said one of them in Dakhni, "just look ahead of us."

The echoing *tok* of his burro's hooves on wood brought Timoteo back to his immediate surroundings. They were riding over a broad bridge that spanned a wide moat, and led to a gate in the wall. One of the *sardars* turned and said, "This is the Macca Gate. It is only one of five into the city."

The gate was enormous, to match the walls; more than twice the height of a man, made of beams six inches square, fastened with iron clamps and studded with iron spikes a foot long. To each side of the gate rose a tower with arrow-slits and small cannon bristling their tops. Men with spiked helmets, wearing armor of colorful padded cloth, with curved swords at their sides, stood to either side of the gate, watching those who passed through with narrowed eyes.

"Ah," whispered Timóteo. "It *is* a wonder."

"What is he staring at? Ai!" said Joaquim as he caught sight of the gate. "With such walls, a king would not need an army."

"Please be quiet," said the Padre to the *soldado*. "Timóteo may act the child, but it is not fitting that you should."

"But I am sure our guides do not know Portuguese, Padre."

"Some foolishness transcends language, Senhor Alvalanca."

Passage through the gate was slow, as the entry was choked with people and animals going in and coming out.

The lead *sardar* called out to the gatekeepers in the name of Sultan Ibrahim 'Adilshah, and the guardsmen began to roughly shove men and oxen, women and camels, aside until a pathway was cleared for the Goan party to pass through unhindered.

As they emerged onto the main thoroughfare of the city, Thomas was amazed at how broad and clean the street was, finer than any avenue in London. There was no slop in the gutters, for one thing, and many merchants were busy with brooms sweeping their doorsteps and sprinkling them with water. Each shopfront had a shade tree in front of it, clearly planted by design. Dividing the street was a broad strip of gardened earth on which grew tall palms. Beneath the palms, poorer merchants sat at ease behind their wares, which were laid out on blankets in tidy array.

And the buildings! Many were constructed from black or ruddy red stone, their windows filled with delicate latticework. Domes of a blinding white or shimmering gold rose above the palaces and the mosques. Lintels and pillars were carved with images of vines, or trees, or lotus blossoms. Glancing into archways, one could sometimes glimpse a recessed garden with a fountain in the center, tended by women in bright-colored *shals*. Walls were adorned with colorful tile, whose patterns formed intricate arabesques.

"It is an amazing skill of these Mohammedans," said Lockheart in his ear. "That which looks like a butterfly, or sailing ship, or leaping gazelle, is in fact a line from their holy

scripture, done in such cunning calligraphy that it may take
whatever shape the artisan wills."

"Seems a fanciful treatment of the sacred, methinks,"
said Thomas.

"They do not think the delightment of senses to be a sin,
lad. A philosophy I consider most enlightened."

"It has somewhat to recommend it."

The denizens of Bijapur themselves seemed decorous
and pleasing to the eye. Merchants fanned themselves idly
while they gossiped. Rich men in bejeweled jackets and tur-
bans rode by on well-fed steeds. Poor men in clean, plain tu-
nics strolled at ease on the avenue. Women, some veiled,
some not, wearing diaphanous skirts and short upper garments that left their midriff bare, walked gracefully with pots
on their heads or hips, or children by their side. Hindus wearing only a loincloth and a thread over their shoulders sat on
the street corners in silent meditation.

Thomas stared at it all in amazement, filled with the
growing, unsettling notion that he had come to a land more
civilized than the one he called home.

They turned south, off the main thoroughfare, and rode
over another moat, through another ring of thick stone walls.
From the splendor of the buildings and gardens within the
fortifications, this was clearly the domain of the nobility of
Bijapur. Another turn, and before them stood a hall with a
huge archway, giving view to an enormous atrium with long
rectangular pools and flower beds, surrounding a raised platform within.

Lockheart spoke briefly to the noblemen who led them,
then turned and said, "This is the *Gagan Mahal*. It is where
we will be lodged and also be meeting with the Sultan. They
say it is quite an honor that we will be staying here."

They dismounted outside the *Gagan Mahal* and were escorted under the enormous arch. The courtyard and garden
paths within were as clean and well-trimmed as the avenues

outside. "How wondrously well cared for all this is," Thomas murmured to Joaquim beside him.

Joaquim hawked and spat on the ground. "They are fastidious, these Muslims and Hindus, no? It is like a country filled with fussy housewives. Who could live like this?"

Thomas did not reply, but it occurred to him that living in such beautiful surroundings might do things to a man. *Perhaps, if Aditi has been successful speaking on my behalf, I might have the chance to learn what it would do.* He wondered what it might be like to serve one of these silk-turbaned lords. To ride a fine horse, live in a marble confection of a palace, perhaps to have a foreign woman as wife or mistress. Whether it would be blissful enough to make a man forget home altogether.

Like the voyage of Ulysses indeed. Might Bijapur be my Land of the Lotus Eaters, promising sweet forgetfulness? Will I have the strength to withstand its beauty? Or do I hope that I will not?

XIV

MANDRAKE: This puissant plant is also called
Mandragora, or Satan's Apple. It has large leaves that lie on the
ground, purple flowers of a bell's shape, and brings forth yellow
berries. The most powerful part is its brown root, which, at times,
takes the shape of a man. The Mohammedans call it the Devil's
Candle, for it is said to glow in the night. Some say it shrieks
when pulled from the earth, or that it grows where men have
been hanged. Some say it prophesies, or reveals secrets. The
rootstock is used to ease ailments of the lungs, to induce sleep,
to cure melancholy, and as a purgative, but great care must be
taken for it is also a deadly poison. It is said mandrake is used in
a witch's most powerful spells. A tincture of the root in wine
will incite the lust or venerie....

The Mirza Ali Akbarshah admired the nearing walls of Bijapur from atop his swaying elephant. *Ibrahim the First was
a fine martial engineer. Many men and many large guns would be
needed to breach those walls. If I return with nothing else, this information may well be of use to the Emperor.*

The invitation to the Sultan's palace had come in the afternoon, not long after the westerners had departed the serai.
The Mirza could not help but wonder if it was entirely coincidence. "Masum," he said to the Sufi seated beside him,
"did the Goan boy tell you for what purpose his party has
come to Bijapur?"

"We did not have much time to speak, Lord Mirza, so alas

he did not. His companion, Tamas, is learned in herblore and healing, as I am, so they may be here for trade."

The Mirza shook his head. "That cannot be the whole of it. The boy was dressed as some of the Christian monks do, and I heard that there was a Christian priest among their party, though I did not see him."

"Then perhaps the Sultan has invited them to share their philosophy with him. I have heard your Emperor Akbar often does the same."

The Mirza allowed himself a brief chuckle. "Indeed, groups of Jesuits have come to Agra and Lahore. But when Akbar would offer questions about their faith, it would lead to great arguments among the Christians, as if they could not decide even among themselves what was truth. They did not acquit themselves well, I have heard."

"Perhaps Ibrahim has summoned them for his amusement, then, although I hope he is not so unkind."

"So long as they are not intended as our amusement as well, I will not let it concern me."

"Ah. Our guides are leading us to the Shahpur Gate, Lord Mirza."

"Is there some purpose, do you think, in taking us to a farther gate? Did they want us to see the might of their walls for some time?"

"I cannot say, Lord Mirza. It is possible this entrance is closer to the Sultan's palaces. Perhaps the more direct route has been blocked. Perhaps this one is the proper size for elephants."

The Mirza could see that the elephant and the *howdah* would pass easily beneath the Shahpur Gate. And the way seemed to be remarkably clear of other travellers, such that their *sardar* escort needed only to nod to the guardsmen beside the gate towers as the escort, his elephant, Jaimal, and eight well-chosen Mughul horsemen passed through.

The sultan's invitation had specified that he bring only

ten men with him, pleading difficulties of lodging and feeding many at the palace. The Mirza suspected the true reason was fear, but thought it no matter. Intimidation was not the method he intended to use to coerce the Sultan into assisting their search. *And Ibrahim would not dare attempt treachery against an emissary of the Padshah Emperor, particularly when I have an army stationed nearby that is large enough to do great damage to surrounding farms, and disrupt trade for miles.*

The Mirza felt the muscles in his back ease as they entered the city, for it was not unlike Lahore. The avenues were narrower and the people perhaps less prosperous, but in other ways there was a comforting similarity.

Not far from the gate, the Mirza could see a high watchtower.

"That is the Upli Buruj," said Masum. "I have heard there are cannon in it that are twice as long as a man is tall, and many powder chambers to serve them."

No doubt Akbar's Deccani generals already know of this, but it would be wise to remember it.

As they headed toward a citadel in the center of the city, there was an unsettling feeling growing in the Mirza, although he could not pinpoint what it was. And then he understood. Amid the latticework and calligraphic tiles and polished stonework on the buildings around him, there were pillars that seemed to have stone vines clinging to them, whose column caps were stone lotuses in bloom. Even the mosques, when seen close up, had plant motifs worked cunningly into the structure, as if the building were an organic thing, grown out of the earth. It seemed to him vaguely obscene. *It is as though the same karamat that produced the stone hand of the nameless* shahid *had been at work here.*

"I see the Lord Mirza admires the skill of our artisans," said Masum, proudly. "Did I not tell you the best have come here from everywhere to lend beauty to Bijapur?"

"Ah, the style, I confess, is different from what I am used

to, Masum. I expect Jaimal will not like it." The Mirza glanced down from the *howdah* at Jaimal who rode beside the elephant. As he thought, the lieutenant was frowning at the buildings.

The wealth of this place cannot be denied, thought the Mirza, *despite its strangeness. Akbar shall not leave this plum unpicked for long, if fortune gives him any chance. But that is not my concern, nor should I excite Ibrahim's fears with even a hint of it. I must not let the djinni of distraction, as Masum would say, lead me astray from my goal.*

Aditi wandered the upper gallery of the *Gagan Mahal,* peering down through the gold-inlaid stone latticework at the great courtyard below. It was galling to have to remain in the upper stories, the only area of the palace where women were permitted. But the Begum Shah had protested that it was the best she could do, given that many guests would be arriving. *More likely, Ibrahim wishes to keep watch upon my actions.*

Aditi was only able to catch a glimpse, now and then, of Tamas and the rest of the Goan party when they entered the palace. She wished she had kept one or two of the Marathi girls who had accompanied her palanquin on the road from Goa. She could have used them to deliver messages, or gather information for her. But she did not wish to endanger the Marathi girls by exposing them to palace politics. Aditi had released them to the care of local *sardar* families, who would treat them well.

Now Aditi was served by one of the Begum Shah's hand-women—an unsmiling, narrow-eyed creature named Krodha. Aditi was certain the woman was a spy, by the way she was closely watched. *So, Ibrahim does not trust me. Well, he is not un-wise in this. But it is annoying. I must do something to escape her meddlesome company.*

Aditi sighed and sat on the floor beside the latticework window. *In Bhagavati, I could walk anywhere, speak to anyone, do just as I please so long as I did not disturb the Mahadevi. How long it has been since I enjoyed such freedom. And home is so close. Mere days away. Great Mother, may my work here be done quickly so that I may come home soon.*

She noticed Tamas walking with Lakart toward the baths. She wished she could hear their conversation. *What is it about him? By all good sense, I should have killed him. What god or demon stayed my hand? Does Kṛṣṇa toy with me, making me long for a man who should be my enemy?* In so many stories she had heard since a child, love is a man's glory but a woman's doom. She was beginning to feel the truth of it.

Her thoughts were shattered by shouts and the blaring of trumpets that came from the grand arch of the *Gagan Mahal.*

"What is that?" Aditi said to Krodha.

"Ah, that would be the arrival of the emissary from Emperor Akbar, my lady. This is good news. There will be music tonight, and dancing and fireworks. We will be able to watch the entertainments from the balconies here."

Entertainments were far from Aditi's mind. *How many men has this Mirza brought? How much about the Mahadevi does he know, and how did he learn it? How much more will Ibrahim tell him? Will I have any power to stop him at all?* The thoughts overwhelmed her until she wanted to shake her fretwork cage and roar like a lion.

"My lady, what is the matter? Doesn't any of this interest you?"

Be calm, be calm. Blind emotion will not further our cause. Where is that cleverness Gandharva has praised us for? Ah. But if there is music planned, Gandharva will be among the musicians. He may discover much that I cannot. How ironic that I think of asking him, a blind man, to serve as my eyes.

Aditi turned to Krodha and tried to put on a more humble demeanor. "Forgive me. You must think I have been terrible to you. It is only that I have been . . . distracted. You see, and please tell no one I have confided this to you, I came to Bijapur hoping to catch the Sultan's eye."

Krodha raised her brows. "Hah! You are far too old."

"I know, but truth is never a barrier to hope, is it?"

"How can it be that you are unmarried at your age? How can your family have neglected their duty to you, or you your duty to them?"

"It is a long story. But my true parents died when I was only a child. And my stepmother . . . has been preoccupied with other things."

Krodha nodded as if she understood all. "Stepmothers will slight children who are not their own kin. She would not offer a proper dowry for you?"

Aditi gazed with an appropriately sad expression at her feet. "No."

"Fortune has not been kind to you, Sri Aditi. Now, me, I was married at twelve! To a wealthy silk merchant's son."

"How wonderful for you," murmured Aditi, trying to hide any hint of sarcasm. *And how you love feeling superior to me.* "Does your husband live here in the *Gagan Mahal?*"

"Oh, dear me, no. He lives above our shop, and often travels with our son to find goods to sell."

"Ah, a son," said Aditi, in an appropriately wistful tone. "You must miss them."

"No, no, my husband is a brute and the boy is growing up just like him. You see, I am three-times blessed, Sri Aditi. To be married and have a son and to rarely suffer their company."

"Indeed, Lakshmi has smiled upon you." *And now I know why you are so sour.* Aditi gazed out again through the latticework and sighed. "Do you think, Krodha, that we could have a musician come to entertain us this afternoon? Music does much to ease sorrows and my spirits do need comforting. There is a blind *vina* player whom Ibrahim has recommended to me, a fellow named Gandharva. I love the sound of the *vina*. Could we have him play for us?"

"Well, musicians will be in much demand today, because of all the visitors. But I will see what I can do."

"And some wine, to refresh us?"

Krodha tilted her head semi-disapproving. "Well, given this is a festive evening, I suppose no one will begrudge us a little wine."

"You are very kind."

From a balcony of the Palace of Delight, not far from the *Gagan Mahal,* the Sultan Ibrahim also heard the shouts and trumpets. "What do you know of this Mirza Ali Akbarshah?" he asked Haidar Khan, one of his most trusted generals.

"I have heard little of him, Majesty. What little I have heard indicates he is competent enough. But I cannot think that the Emperor Akbar would have sent a superior general with such a small force to conquer a legend. This suggests the Mirza is possibly a troublemaker. Someone the Emperor wanted out of the way for a while."

Ibrahim nodded, sipping cardamom tea from a porcelain cup. "That is a reasonable assessment. Although we have heard that at times the mighty Akbar does not follow reason. Looked at another way, if this Mirza Akbarshah is a superior general, he needs only a small force. And if his true purpose is to spy, then it is better for him to claim a purpose that makes him appear to be a buffoon, no?"

"Is his purpose so foolish?" asked the general, running a hand over his greying beard. "I have known you a long time, Ibrahim. Do you truly fear he is a spy? Or do you fear that he may succeed at precisely that which he claims he has come to do?"

Ibrahim smiled tightly. "Never let me think you are too clever, Haidar. You know how feeling the fool upsets me. But sending a mediocre general with a small force to capture a mythical goddess? Really, it is too ridiculous to be believed. Therefore, he must be up to something else. I want you to pay a courtesy visit to his encamped troops and see what you can learn there. You know how to read an army. Do it tonight, while we entertain the Mirza."

Haidar Khan bowed. "As you wish, Majesty. When do you expect to meet him in formal audience?"

"Tomorrow. Morning. Early."

The general raised his bushy grey brows. "So soon?"

"It will put him off balance. And if he is a spy, we do not wish him to dawdle too long among us. I mean to send him on his way as soon as possible."

"Your strategy has some merit, Majesty. If he is a spy."

"If he is not, Haidar, then his fate must be in the hands of a greater power than I." *The longer the Mirza remains among us, the more his story may spread, the more certain factions in Bijapur may suspect my strange alliance with the Mahadevi. The* ulama *think I am simply misguided. Oh, the uprisings it would cause, were they to learn otherwise.*

Aditi looked up as the carved wood doors were unlatched and Krodha ushered Gandharva, his *vina* slung over his back, onto the balcony.

"My lady has requested my presence?" he said in a neutral tone.

Aditi jumped up and took his hands in hers. "Ah, at last! I have heard so much about you that meeting you is like finding a long-sought treasure. I am honored that you have agreed to play for me. Come, make yourself comfortable." She took his elbow and guided him to a rug piled high with cushions.

"My lady is too kind," Gandharva said with just a hint of irony. "I fear I cannot stay long—all of the musicians in the palace have work tonight. But I hope to please you in what little time I have."

"Just having you here adds to my happiness," said Aditi. She sat down close beside him.

There came a gentle rapping at the doors again. "Ah," said Gandharva. "That will be the refreshment sent by the Sultan."

"He is kind to think of me at this busy time."

"He wishes you to be comfortable and content with your accommodations."

"And not cause trouble?" Aditi muttered under her breath as Krodha was occupied taking the large brass tray from the servant at the doors.

"As you say."

Krodha returned with the refreshments, which included a ewer of *sendi* palm wine, a pot of clove tea, a plate of stuffed dates, a bowl of sliced mangoes and bananas, and silver-wrapped sweetmeats formed from carrot, pistachios, and rose-petals.

"Ai, what an elegant treat!" said Aditi. "Perhaps Ibrahim thinks kindly on me after all. You must have some, of course, Krodha. Now, good musician, I have languished here feeling lonesome. Please play for me a song of love."

"As my lady wishes," said Gandharva. "Shall I sing of Kṛṣna and the dairy maids?"

Aditi giggled, trying to seem a fool. "Rather, I would prefer to hear of your namesakes, the Gandharvas, those godlings well-versed in wine and love potions, who are so handsome that they are irresistible to women. Do you know any songs about them?"

The blind musician smiled. "I would be a poor Gandharva if I did not, my lady."

"Do you think that is appropriate, Sri Aditi?" said Krodha, frowning.

"There is only us here, by ourselves. Everyone else is involved in their own business. Who should care if we take what pleasures we wish?"

Krodha tilted one shoulder in half-acceptance and poured the *sendi* into two cups.

Gandharva launched into a lively song that described the godlings meeting the lascivious water-nymphs, the Apsaras, on the shore of the great sea. Their subsequent embracing and lovemaking (joyfully described over several verses) so churned the ocean's waters that the sea-foam became a potent aphrodisiac, one drop of which would be sufficient to drive a man or woman mad with lust.

When he finished, Krodha, arms wrapped tightly over her knees, said, "That song was outrageous! Disgusting!"

"Oh, no no," said Aditi. "It was wonderful! Ah, to have some of that sea-foam now. What use I could make of it." She slid over to Gandharva and placed her arms around his neck. "Your song makes me wish to be close to you. I need something from you."

Gandharva set the *vina* aside, an amused expression on his face. "I am at my lady's disposal."

"Sri Aditi?" said Krodha, growing shock on her face.

Ignoring her, Aditi placed one of her long legs around Gandharva's waist and whispered in his ear, "Speaking of potions, do you have any *rasa mahadevi* with you?"

"As always, my lady," he whispered back. "Why?"

"I have need of it." She ran her hands down his back. "Where is it?"

"In a vial, in a pouch in my *shalwar.*" He smiled. "But you will have to get it yourself."

"Sri Aditi, what are you doing?" cried Krodha.

"I believe she desires something that is in my trousers," said Gandharva.

Aditi fought down the urge to box his ear and began to undo the ties of his tunic. "Do not raise your hopes too high, my friend," she whispered. She slid her hand within his tunic, down his chest, feeling the warmth of his skin. She felt along the edge of his *shalwar* trousers until she found the pouch. Aditi then shifted her hips until her body blocked her hands from Krodha's sight, and retrieved the vial, deftly tucking it into her own skirt band as she removed her belt-sash.

"It is not my hope that is rising, as you have by now discovered," said Gandharva. He placed his hands on her hips, and rotated his thigh between her legs. "Are you sure you wish nothing more of me? It has been a long time since we were so close. The Mahadevi gave me my name for a reason, as you know. The palace girls here have taken pity on me, and taught me many a pleasant thing."

Aditi felt a twinge of desire that made Gandharva's offer tempting. . . .

"Sri Aditi!"

After placing a passionate kiss on Gandharva's neck, she whispered, "Not for me. Not right now. But can you do something for that harridan, to calm her?"

"Ai, the things I must do for the women in my life. I can please her, but only if she comes to me willing to be pleased."

Aditi leaned back from him and turned toward Krodha. "No need to be jealous, Krodha! Gandharva tells me he can easily pleasure two women at once."

"I am a married woman, Sri Aditi!"

Aditi left Gandharva's embrace and sat beside the serving-woman. "Yes, and your husband is far away and treats you terribly." Aditi ran her hands over Krodha's hair, down her shoulders. "It is so unfair. You still are quite lovely, yet no man appreciates you." Aditi quickly passed her hands over Krodha's breasts, noting with some amusement that her nipples were erect.

Krodha chewed on a thumbnail, staring at Gandharva who was stretching a welcoming, beckoning arm toward her. "But . . . but it is unseemly!"

"Are the gods who know the joys of love unseemly,

Krodha? Only they will watch and judge, for no one else will ever know. I, surely, would never betray you. Gandharva can pleasure a woman in ways that bring no child. You will not be shamed. Go on. You may have him first. You have worked so hard. Accept this gift he offers you. You have earned it."

Taking Krodha's arm, Aditi guided her over to Gandharva's lap. Then Aditi returned to the brass refreshment tray. As Gandharva began his gentle work, Aditi warmed the clove tea over a small brazier. She tried not to laugh, as he exclaimed softly, poetically over Krodha's soft skin and supple form. As Krodha cried out in rising joy and surprise, Aditi stirred the tea leaves and cloves in the bottom of the pot. As Krodha thrashed in the final throes of ecstasy, Aditi placed a thimbleful of the *rasa mahadevi* into a cup and poured the clove tea over it.

As Krodha lay panting and sighing in Gandharva's arms, Aditi took the cup and went to her. "There, now, isn't that better? Here, this tea will cool the fires in your blood and let you rest."

"Indeed," gasped Krodha, her hair in disarray and clothing askew, "I am thirsty." She took the cup eagerly in both her hands and drank it all in one draught.

Aditi took the empty cup again as Krodha closed her eyes. The serving woman leaned against Gandharva and gradually her breathing slowed, until there was no breath at all.

"You have killed her?" said Gandharva, disbelief in his voice.

"I did not use all the powder. I will revive her with the rest later, fear not. But I had to speak to you without her knowledge or interference. I am trapped here, Gandharva. I need your help to learn all I can about Tamas, about the Mirza, about what Ibrahim intends to do with them. I am not as free to wander as you."

Gandharva chuckled. "You are trapped, seeking, 'darkness,' " he said, playing upon the meaning of *tamas*, "while

I am trapped within darkness. What a poor pair of spies we make."

He carefully slid from beneath the dead Krodha and set her head down gently on the carpet. "I will do all I can for you, Aditi. In exchange."

"In exchange for what?"

He reached over and put his arms around her waist. "Krodha may have found release, but I have not. Have pity on your poor, blind friend, and help me, won't you?"

"Release? There is not enough powder for both of you," Aditi teased.

"You know that is not the oblivion I meant," Gandharva said, cupping her breast in his hand.

"Well, you have done me a service."

"I would do you another."

Aditi admitted to herself that her desires were somewhat stirred, and she did like Gandharva, and he was very skilled. Who knew when she would next have the opportunity for pleasure again? "Very well, my friend, but you must tell me things." She lay down beside the dead woman and guided him on top of her.

"Anything my lady wishes," Gandharva said between kisses. "Do you wish poetry? Compliments? Lies?"

Aditi laughed and gasped as his hands slid up her legs and his fingers plunged deep within her. "Information! Where are the Mirza's men staying? Will they be entertained by dancers? When? Where will the dancers be going? Will the monks of the Orlem Gor be seeing them too?"

Gandharva pressed his warm, stiff member into her and between sighs, thrusts, and moans told her all he knew of the evening's preparations for entertaining the Mirza and the Goans.

Aditi took her own pleasure as it came, admiring Gandharva's skill. Yet, to her dismay, she found herself continually wishing he were someone else.

XV

ROCKET: This vegetable brings forth yellow-white
flowers in summer and has long leaves that have a peppery
taste. In the autumn, it bears pods of tiny yellow seeds. This
plant has been known since ancient times, and eating the fresh
leaves will be an aid to digestion and a cure for the scrofula or
King's Evil. The flower has a sweet scent by night, but has none
in the day, and therefore Rocket is thought a plant of deceit....

Thomas leaned back, floating in a huge, steaming, bathing
pool, the aches in his shoulders and legs seeping away
into the hot, rose-scented water. The swirling patterns on the
blue-and-gold tiles on the ceiling led the mind away from
problems of the world, into a pleasant stupor. The laughter
of the Goan soldiers, who were teasing and petting the dark-
eyed serving girls who sponged their backs, was distant,
unimportant. Wisps of steam danced around him on the
water's surface, as if spirits lost in thoughtless celebration.

Before the bath, Thomas and the others had been fed a
feast of roast chicken, fish and rice, fruits, and flat bread. He
had eaten until his belly could hold no more. Now Thomas

felt as though he wanted nothing other than to drift in this warm, carefree daze forever. His only wish was that Aditi might be with him, to share such bliss. *Some part of heaven must be sweet as this. The easing of all pain, the lack of want. If death be this gentle, 'tis no wonder the Padre resents me so for snatching him from it.*

A hand touched his shoulder. "Ho there, lad."

Thomas flailed in the water in startlement. His legs sank, kicking uselessly, his breath sputtering in the hot water. Reaching back, his hand found the edge of the pool, and he drew himself up, coughing.

"Your pardon, Tom. I'd not meant to drown you. Methought this a good time for talk, now that we are re-freshed from the journey."

"If you wish," Thomas grumbled.

"I was wondering where your thoughts lay this eve'n."

"If you must know, I was thinking on death."

"A grim subject for one so young and hale."

"Not grim at all. I was finding the prospect almost pleasant."

"Were you? Dear me, lad, has our journey so dispirited you, that you long to be rid of life?"

"No, fear not, Andrew. I wished only to be rid of care. Which I was, until short moments ago."

"Alas that I should bring the weight of the world back down onto your shoulders, Tom, but there are matters of im-port to be discussed. As our Goan friends are distracted, and neither the Padre or the little brother are nigh, this may be our best opportunity."

"Oh, very well." In truth, Thomas had been dreading what he knew Lockheart was about to ask. *Is it time that I should tell the truth, and admit my plans to depart for home? Or must I continue to dissemble until I have the security of the Sultan's protection?*

"Here we are in Bijapur, the first portion of our quest completed. My wonderment is, what shall be the next?"

Thomas sighed and leaned back against the edge of the pool. "What would you, Andrew? What do you advise?"

Lockheart rubbed his soggy beard. " 'Tis a temptation, of course, to think on desertion and hope that, from here, a route may be plotted home."

Thomas tilted his head and raised a brow. *Might his plans be similar to mine own?*

"But I have thought on this, and found many a disquieting point. To be the only returning survivor of our expedition with nought to show for it . . . There would be questions, aye there would, as to the fate of the Queen's envoys, and if the answer mislikes the Crown, a cozy prison cell awaits."

Thomas smiled to himself. "True, Andrew. You might have much to answer for."

"Ah, but the prospects would not be so fair for thee, either. Think you Master Coulter will take kindly to your failure, after all he had invested in the voyage?"

"I would hope he would be understanding. Calamity at sea is not unknown. And I could bring back valuable lore about the land and peoples I have seen."

"The Dutchman Linschouten has covered the same territory, lad. Would your knowledge offer anything new?"

"As to that, I could not say."

"Naturally not. And what might your good Protestant Master Coulter make of the tale of your rough confession and conversion to the Church Catholic?"

Thomas winced. "That is unfair."

"Mayhap. But now let your mind wander another path. What say we journey on, in search of the resurrection powder. Think on your reception at home, with the greatest gift an apothecary could want. The power to cure all, and the wealth and fame it would provide. Not to mention immortality for yourself and your family."

"I had such thoughts when I resurrected Nathan and beheld what the powder could do. But after seeing the risen De Cartago and the miserable Padre, I find I have them no longer."

"If common greed will not persuade you, what of duty? Think on what disaster will fall if the Santa Casa finds the source. Spain has made great show of wishing to conquer our fair isle. With immortal armies supported by the powder, think you England would prevail?"

"The Padre wishes to destroy the source, not to claim it."

"So he says."

"And I believe him."

"I am amazed, Tom, that you, who has suffered the madness of the Inquisition, are so trusting."

"Think what you will, but I would wager my life on it. However, I would not stop you from seeking this powder on your own, if that is your wish."

"No, no. Our fates are cojoined, Tom. Whither you go, I perforce must follow."

Thomas sighed again, more heavily, becoming irritated by Lockheart's presence. He turned and flung his leg out onto the rim of the bath and pulled himself, dripping, out of the water. "I will think on this, Andrew. But give me leave to have some peace awhile. We will talk again anon." He stalked off in search of a towel.

Padre Gonsção found a corner of the enormous chamber the Goan party had been given for their quarters, behind a column with a niche where he could place a rough crucifix made from two tamarind twigs. In this corner, he would be less distracted by the heathen splendor of the palace around them.

"Padre," said Timóteo behind him, "I would like to go to the baths too."

"No," said Gonsção. "The public baths are a lure to sensuality. You may use a damp cloth here, if you need to clean yourself."

"Oh. Padre, one of the servants who served us supper said there would be music and dancing ladies later this evening. May I—"

"No!" Gonsção sighed and stood, ignoring the creaking of his knees. "I am sorry, my son. I am sure I must seem a horrible old ogre to you, but I have my reasons. You are not aware what danger we are in, body and soul, in this place. I have seen how the wonders of this land catch your eye, but you must beware, Timóteo. These people may seem kind and hospitable, but they care little for the state of our souls. That must be our concern."

He placed his hands on the boy's shoulders. "I need you to be my steadfast ally, Timóteo. There may be no one else we can count on to continue with us in our quest. Half our Goan soldiers have already abandoned us and may, even now, be on their way back to Goa. I do not know the depth of loyalty of those who remain. Brother Andrew would seem to have forsaken his vows, assuming he ever took any, and has assumed the habits of the natives. He will assist us only so long as it serves his purposes, whatever they may be."

"Tomás will not abandon us, Padre. You may count on him as well."

Gonsção shook his head. "I would like to think your faith in him is justified, but I have grave doubts."

"He could have gone back to Goa when you were sick, Padre. He could have let you die!"

"You are young, so I will forgive that outburst. But Senhor Chinnery had no wish to face the Inquisitor Major's wrath, for which I cannot blame him. Brother Andrew has some influence with him, and may turn him against us. We must not expect that he will travel with us any further."

"But he must!" said Timóteo. "How will we find the source if he does not?"

"You may not remember, Timóteo, but there was a map that was taken from Senhor Chinnery while he was in the Santa Casa. A map drawn by the sorcerer De Cartago. Senhor Chinnery took this map from me while I was ill, for reasons that are unclear to me. But it is no matter, for I had read the map before and committed it to memory. There were three dots upon it. If the first dot was indeed Goa, and the second Bijapur, then the third must be our goal. And its distance, if the map is accurate, is but half the length of the line between Goa and here, meaning only a six-day journey. If my orientation of the map is correct, it is to the south and east. Therefore, we may have no need of Senhor Chinnery's guidance."

"But what of the traps he says await us?"

"I suspect, my son, that Senhor Chinnery invented them as a way to ensure his place on the expedition. But if not, we will face them as they appear, and pray for God's help."

"If we must, Padre, but I am sure Tomás will be with us. You will see."

Gonsção sighed. "I hope so, my son. Now go and wash yourself. There is cool water in the basin over there."

Nodding, disconsolate, the boy shuffled off.

Gonsção turned again to the niche and knelt before it. He reflected how, before his illness, his faith had been a practical matter, a part of life like the air he breathed, and central to his work. But now he had seen what lay beyond the portals of death, and faith had become a matter of more urgency. Gonsção recalled seeing a white light leading him on through a dark corridor. On the other side, he found himself on a hill overlooking a beautiful blue sea. He was aware of a white building behind him. But when he turned to look at it, he saw. . . . *No. I must not think on it. Must never speak of it. No one must ever know what I saw.*

Thomas sat with his back against a slender column of brown basalt and watched the sun set. He now wore a clean silk tunic and the loose trousers they called *shalwar*. He was trying very hard to get drunk on a drink called *charas*, juice of the herb called *ganja*, and *boja* beer. He hoped to bring back the state of bliss he had felt before in the baths. He was not being entirely successful.

The problem was, Lockheart had stated some important points. To return to England with nothing but a forced conversion would not win him favors from Queen or Master. *Master Coulter might even deny me the hand of his daughter Anna.* Not that it was tragedy in itself, for Thomas found he had little fondness left for her, but the thought stung his pride. *I could dissemble about the conversion, but they would wonder how I 'scaped the Inquisition without it. Worse, if my denial is discovered, would I be exiled? Or executed? I could reconvert*—the thought of what this might do to the status of his immortal soul was dizzying and Thomas tried to put it from his mind.

He looked around him at the garden of the wing of the palace given for their use, and regarded his fellow travellers. Joaquim and two other Goan soldiers had accomplished what he had not and were drunkenly attempting to sing, talk, or gamble and not doing any of them well. Two *soldados* were missing, off to tryst, no doubt, with willing Hindu maids.

Some musicians had arrived while Thomas wasn't paying attention, and Lockheart was engaged in eager conversation with a blind fellow who held a bulbous instrument that seemed to be a stringed fretboard suspended between two large gourds. Other musicians were settling in, cleaning their flutes, tightening their drums, and otherwise preparing to play.

Poor Timóteo. He would love to see this. And the Padre—you would think with a lutemaker as a father, he would have some interest. But candlelight flickered in one window of their quarters from which Thomas could sometimes hear a murmur of the Padre's prayers.

Thomas felt a small pang of guilt. *But wherefore should I be troubled? For enjoying a pleasant rest after an arduous journey? For returning the Padre to a life that he cannot himself enjoy?* Thomas took another swig of the *charas* and laughed at himself. *Thou consummate fool. I have 'scaped the dreaded Inquisition and reached the haven I sought. Here my arms may heal and I may live amidst beauty until I decide what to do. Surely the Padre cannot continue without me. Wherefore should I be melancholy on such a glorious evening?*

From somewhere above and to the right, there came the tinkling of bracelets and tiny bells, and the swish of garments of silk. *Ah! The dancers.* Thomas sat up and the Goan soldiers nudged each other making anticipatory noises. The blind musician set his strange instrument across his lap and began to play a droning chord. The drummers on the balconies overhead joined in, the flutists with them. The very air seemed stirred with the music, and Thomas felt his blood quicken with the sound.

Down a nearby marble staircase, the dancing girls descended. Each wore a jacket of the sheerest silk over a short-sleeved blouse that left the midriff bare. They wore colorful narrow trousers that clung to their legs, hiding none of their shape. All were barefoot, save for golden chains with bells around their ankles. Each girl wore a necklace of black stones and pearls, and copper bracelets on her upper arms and wrists. They each were bedecked with elaborate earrings and jewel-trimmed mantles of the same fine silk as their jackets. As they danced down the stairs, twirling and undulating, sinuous as snakes, Thomas thought each one prettier than the last.

"Beguiling as sirens, are they not, Tom?" said Lockheart in his ear. "Know you that their movements, their every pose and gesture tells a story to one who can read them."

"The story they tell me, Andrew, is that I have lacked female company for too long."

Lockheart laughed and clapped Thomas on the back. "Hah. Behold! Their charm is great enow to draw the dragon from his lair."

Thomas looked where he nodded and saw Padre Gonsção standing at the door of their quarters, frowning and restraining a wide-eyed Timóteo. Unable to stop himself, Thomas joined in Lockheart's laughter, letting it spill out until it was spent.

And then he glanced up at the last woman in the line of dancers. She seemed different from the others, not dancing quite the same as they were, and her gaze had stayed on Thomas a long while. He caught a glimpse, through her mantle, of the dancer's eyes and, with a flush of joy, Thomas recognized her.

"Aditi!" he called out. "Aditi, you've come to dance for me!"

Her brows rose with alarm and she swiftly padded over to him. "Shhh. Do not speak my name, Tamas. Others should not know I am here."

"Oh. Forgive me. But I am happy to see you."

"Perhaps I should let you lovers be," said Lockheart, with a wink, and he moved off to a discreet distance.

"I am happy to see you, Tamas," whispered Aditi over the drumming. "I came to learn if you are well. I spoke to the Sultan for you, as you wished. He has said he will see what he can do with you."

"Sweetest Aditi," said Thomas, somehow unable to control the loudness of his voice, "You are truly an angel!"

"You are drunk."

"Am I? Huzzah, I have succeeded then! Pray, grant me

more sweet oblivion in your arms, for there is much I would forget."

Thomas put his arms around her waist, ignoring a protesting ache in his shoulders.

"You should take more care, my love," said Aditi, gently taking his arms off her. "There is still danger near." She tilted her head to indicate the Padre.

Thomas followed her gaze. The Padre was staring at them, pale with amazement and fury. "Oh, mark him not. He is jealous of the worldly pleasures that he denies to himself. We are far from Goa. What harm could he do you now? Stay with me, Aditi. Have we not reached a haven of rest, where we no longer need hide our affections?"

The line of dancing girls was slowly departing through a scalloped archway across the pavillion. Aditi leaned close and kissed Thomas's cheek. "I must go. If fortune is with us, we will speak again soon." She easily slipped out of his encircling arms and ran off to join the other dancers.

Thomas leaned back against the pillar with a sigh of disappointment.

"So," said the voice of Padre Gonsção behind him, "that is the mysterious Aditi."

"What are you babbling about, you self-appointed eunuch?"

"I will assume it is the demon of drink speaking with your tongue and therefore take no insult. But if you will indulge me, I have something to tell you." The Padre sat down beside him. Thomas could smell the Inquisitor's bodily reek in a way he'd never noticed before.

"You need bathing."

"You need to listen. I would normally tell this to no one outside of the Santa Casa. But when we were seeking the members of the sorcerer De Cartago's cabal, there is one we heard of whom we never found. She was known only as Aditi, and was said to be the instigator of the cult . . . someone who brought low into pagan sinfulness a governor and a vice-regent of Goa. It would appear she has claimed yet another victim."

"Perhaps Aditi is a common Hindu name. What of it?" Thomas tilted his head back and closed his eyes, wishing the annoying Padre would go away.

"I had thought it very odd that the woman in the palanquin leading our caravan was so interested in you. But now I understand. I admit you had me fooled. You are a clever man, Magister Chinnery."

"Heh."

"But I am left wondering, has Aditi led you and me here to take us away from our goal or toward it? I am sure she has no wish for the Santa Casa to find her beloved goddess. Perhaps she is misleading both of us."

Thomas chuckled. "You are trying to get me to mistrust her."

The Padre shrugged. "Who am I to say if you should trust her? I do not know what she has promised you, or you to her."

"That which she promised me," Thomas said thickly, "she has already done. And you have me wrong, Padre. To gain her help in leaving Goa, I told her I sought to learn of the Mahadevi. But I have no intention of turning pagan, you may rest assured of that."

"Ah. So it is you who are deceiving her. Clever fellow."

"It is but a gentle deceit. I had no evil intent."

"No, no, I quite understand," said the Padre.

"As our cause is great and holy, is it sinful, do you think, to deceive her so?"

A bitter laugh erupted from the Padre. "I would not let it concern you, my son. I have despaired of your salvation for some time now. So. You never wanted to find the source of the *pulvis mirificus* at all, did you?"

Thomas paused. "I would prefer to speak no more of

this. You will know my mind in full tomorrow, after we have met with the Sultan. Believe, however, that I have meant no harm to you or Brother Timóteo, and I wish no harm to you now."

Gonsção put on a rictus grin and stood. "How reassuring you are, Magister Chinnery. I have learned a valuable lesson from you. Meanwhile, you have surely earned this respite from care. Enjoy your worldly pleasures while you may." The Padre patted Thomas on the shoulder, hard.

"Ow!" Thomas winced and rubbed his shoulder in bewilderment as the Padre strode back into the guest chambers.

The Mirza Ali Akbarshah reclined in a nest of pillows in a pavilion on the north side of the Gagan Mahal, watching the stars. He and his men had endured the hospitality of the 'Adilshah, bathing and eating and blandly admiring the gardens. After the many days on the road, the change was pleasant, but it only made him wish he were back in Lahore rather than this backwater sultanate.

He sipped his clove tea and regarded his companions a moment. He had chosen the men who accompanied him for their good sense and sobriety, and he was not disappointed. His men did not touch any manner of alcohol offered. They spoke to each other only of inconsequentials, nothing an eavesdropping ear would find interesting. The Mirza already suspected Ibrahim might call them to join him at early prayers, or give them audience in the morning, hoping to catch them unready. It was a common trick—the Mirza had used it himself once or twice.

A group of musicians had arrived from some other part of the palace and were arranging themselves. Masum was guiding, and eagerly talking to, a blind fellow carrying a *vina*. The Mirza was somewhat relieved that the garrulous Sufi had found another ear to pour his stories into.

Jaimal came over and sat beside the Mirza. "Why do we not send them away?"

"Come, now, Jaimal, there is no need for such an obvious insult to the Sultan. We have no cause. Yet."

"But there are dancing girls on their way. Does this Ibrahim think to ensnare us with his kingdom's beauties? It is unseemly. We should send those away at least."

"Ah, but Jaimal, would it not be worthwhile to determine that our girls of Sind dance better than these Deccani women? Besides, the Sultan might wonder what sort of men we are if we fear a troupe of dancing girls."

He won a grudging smile from Jaimal. "You are right, my Lord. Very well, let them come."

Before long, there came the jingling of jewelry and the musicians began to play—it was a form of drum-heavy music the Mirza was not familiar with. The girls entered, wearing *cholis* and *peshwaz* of reasonably good quality. Their dancing was graceful, but the Mirza did not know the meaning of the local gestures so he could not tell whether they were describing a story of sisters defeating a gang of bandits or washerwomen beating clothes in a river.

Their movements blended well, clearly they had danced together often, except for the last woman in the line. She seemed slightly older and her movements were not always in accord with the others. She seemed to be watching the Mirza and his men intently with unusual blue eyes.

Aha. Of course. That is the Sultan's spy. Well, let her watch all she likes, she will see or hear nothing of interest from us. The Mirza smiled and nodded at her.

The woman responded with a dazzling smile, nearly missing a step. The dancers circled the pavillion five times, and the last woman edged closer to the Mirza each time she passed, trying to show off some portion of her anatomy to good favor, not bothering anymore to match whatever story the other dancers were telling.

"You would seem to have that one's eye," said Jaimal.

"At the very least," said the Mirza. "I think I will play along with her game and see what she intends."

The dance ended with a shrill trilling of flutes, and the girls dispersed toward the men. The dancer/spy ran and slid to sit at the Mirza's feet, narrowly beating out two other hopeful girls. The Mirza was vastly amused.

"Have you enjoyed what you have seen, Great Lord?" said the woman, speaking perfect Court Persian in a honeyed voice.

"I could not take my gaze from you," said the Mirza, "so distinct was your grace. You stood out from the rest."

The woman gazed down with studied modesty. "My Lord does me too much honor."

"Impossible!" said the Mirza. "But surely, so well-spoken a lady as yourself is no simple dancing girl. You must be . . . ah, I have it. You have been a high-caste courtesan, have you not?"

"Ah, you have me there, my Lord. I have indeed served as such a one in the past. In the north, in Rajasthan."

"What could have brought you to such a pass, to now serve as a simple dancing girl?"

The woman turned her large blue-grey eyes up at him. "I am forced to admit the truth; I came here solely to entertain you, my Lord."

"Now it is you who do me too much honor."

"Impossible," sighed the woman, voice heavy with desire. "I have heard the Great Lord comes to Bijapur seeking stories. I have many tales to tell."

"Amazing," the Mirza said to Jaimal, "to find such a diamond among plain rubies. Come, my dove-eyed beauty, sit beside me and tell me what you have heard."

The woman nearly entwined herself onto his lap. "You seek a powerful *rani* who gives the gift of immortality to any man who can spend a night with her and survive."

"That is an . . . interesting variation on what we have heard, my lovely. Does your tale describe where this *rani* might be found?"

"Far, far to the south, my Lord, in the Nigiri Mountains, where the mist never leaves the forest treetops, her city is hidden in the deepest caverns of an ancient volcano. It is guarded by ten thousand demons. Only the bravest of men can enter, but once you do, you never wish to leave."

"You spin a wondrous tale, pretty one."

"I suppose you will tell us," said Jaimal, "that the cave is paved with gold and emeralds, that honey runs in rivers down the mountainsides, that the birds sing *ragas* in praise of the queen, and that the trees bear fruit all year long."

"Ah! You have heard this story, I see."

"Something similar, yes," said the Mirza. Out of the corner of his eye, he saw Masum sit beside Jaimal. *So, the Sufi wishes to hear her tales too. I wonder what he will make of her.*

The dancer leaned close to him. "And where, may I ask, did you learn of this story, you who come from so far away?"

"I fear my answer is dull, comely one, for I only learned of it when my Emperor ordered me to embark on this journey. As to where he learned of it, well, you would have to travel all the way to Lahore and ask him to have the answer."

"Your Emperor did not make it clear to you?"

"No, nor would I ask him to. Kings do not like querulous servants, as a rule. However, there are some who said a goddess with hair like fire appeared to him in a vision, driving a sky-borne chariot, drawn by four tigers, demanding that Akbar go in search of her and send her tribute."

"But you—" suddenly, the woman's attention was caught by something Masum was doing.

The Mirza followed her gaze and saw that the Sufi seemed to be taking little balls of wax and applying them to a leather pouch that was coated in brown dust.

"What is that?" the woman whispered. "What are you doing?"

Masum smiled. "I have been told it is called *rasa mahadevi*, my lady. The one who gave it to me said it is a deadly poison, to be used only when all hope is gone. There is not much of it, however, so I am trying to gather all I can in a way that it is not lost."

Her stare was intense. "It is indeed a most deadly poison. Who gave it to you?"

"A westerner with yellow hair. Where he got it, I do not know."

"Was his name Tamas?"

"Why, so it was, my lady. Have you met him?"

The woman slapped the floor and growled something that the Mirza did not understand, though he was certain it was most unwomanly. Without any further word, she stood and left the Mirza, pausing only to say something to the blind *vina* player before departing the pavillion.

"That was very strange," said Jaimal.

"Yes," said the Mirza, looking where she departed. "Ibrahim seems to have made a poor choice of spies. Do you know what might have upset her, Masum?"

The Sufi shook his head. "I cannot imagine, Lord Mirza."

"Ah, well." The Mirza stood and clapped his hands. "The entertainments are at an end."

Aditi ran softly, silently toward the palace wing where the Goans were lodged, pulling from the waistband of her skirt a small, thin dagger. The atrium outside the Goan's chambers was silent, except for the calls of nightbirds.

Thomas lay sprawled on the flagstones, light from the moon and distant torches glimmering in his golden hair. For a moment, Aditi wondered if someone had done her work for her. And then she heard him snore. *This time, Tamas, Kṛṣṇa will not stay my hand. You have betrayed too much, giving the* rasa mahadevi *to the Mughuls. How much did they pay you? What did they promise you? No matter.*

She approached his sleeping form, dagger raised—

"Ay, *inglês!*" The door to their chambers banged open and one of the Goan soldiers staggered out. "The Padre says you must come in right now, you naughty boy," he said in slurred Latin.

Aditi ducked behind an *asoka* tree as the soldier grabbed Tamas under the arms and lifted him up. Thomas groaned and leaned on the soldier, muttering incomprehensibly. Together, the two managed to stagger inside.

Aditi stamped her foot, cursing, and ran back to her latticework eyrie. Gandharva was already there, removing a broken string from his *vina*. "Well?" he said, as she entered.

"Fate has hindered me again. He was alone, but a soldier took him inside before I could kill him."

"Ah."

"Ai," sighed Aditi, sinking onto a cushion beside him. "What a night."

"So it was. I think my fingertips shall become like stone, if they do not fall off first. How did you fare with the Mirza?"

"I learned no more from him than Ibrahim told us. I tried to tell him lies about the location of the Mahadevi's city."

"Did he believe you?"

"No more than I believed him, I suspect."

"You could not . . . convince him with your charms?"

Aditi glared at Gandharva even though he could not see it. "To what purpose? The Mirza is no fool, to be led by the snake in his trousers. No doubt he would have made use of me, but it would be no more to him than blowing his nose."

"Ah, these northern lords known nothing of the social graces. It must be that stifling Faith of theirs. What of the one who had the *rasa mahadevi?*"

"He is an unkempt Sufi with the expression of a friendly puppy. I do not think he knows what he has. He has been told it is poison, and therefore may do nothing with it."

"Ah, you must mean Masum. He is from the Chisti compound on Shahpur Hillock. I spoke with him before I played for the Mughuls. I think you have more to fear from him than you know."

"Why?"

"Because he feels divinely inspired in his search, and therefore will not let matters of material want or lack of knowledge hinder him."

"I see."

"He says he learned of the Mirza's quest through dreams."

Aditi sighed and slapped a pillow. "What are we to do, Gandharva, when the Mahadevi herself confounds us?"

"Do not blame the Mahadevi for what may be the work of demons, or mere coincidence. You and I are like travellers on a raft in a river. We have come to a place where other streams enter and cause clashing currents, and there are rocks hidden beneath the water. The imprudent traveller would try to force his course, and risk being tossed from his raft to drown. The wise traveller will work to keep her craft from overturning, and seek the calmest water, but otherwise let the river have its will. Thus the wise will still be afloat when the flow of the river becomes clear and straight."

"Your stories are charming, Gandharva, but they do not serve to guide me."

"Ah. Just as well, then, that I shall never become a Suf'."

Aditi stared out beyond the balcony, to the starlit roofs of Bijapur. "The Mahadevi cannot guide me either. I have become unsure of my purpose, Gandharva. I find myself wishing only to return to Bhagavati."

"You are tired, Aditi."

"Yes, but it is more than that. I have become weary of this

life. What I do. Do you think the Mahadevi would permit me to no longer be her ears and mouth?"

"I cannot foretell what the Mahadevi will or will not allow. But you have yet a piece of unfinished business."

"What is that?"

"Your servant whom you promised to revive." With one foot, he gently nudged the body of Krodha.

"Oh. Yes. I had nearly forgotten." Aditi retrieved from under the tea-tray the vial of *rasa mahadevi* she had taken from Gandharva. She unstoppered it and poured the last remaining grains into Krodha's mouth.

After a few moments, Krodha shook, as if in the throes of night terrors. Then she gasped and sat up, eyes wide.

"Ah, there you are, sleepy one," said Aditi, leaning casually against Gandharva. "We were wondering if you had decided to stay in Shayapura forever."

Krodha put her hands to her face and her arms as if in wonder that she still possessed a body. "I . . . I must have slept deeply indeed. Such dreams I had." She looked at Gandharva. "You are still here?"

"He is back," said Aditi, "from his other entertainments. It is quite late. Past the middle of the night."

Krodha stood. "I should go."

"But why?" said Aditi. "Who will serve me my morning meal?"

"I will send another." Krodha wrapped her *shal* tightly around her shoulders and headed for the door.

"Have we frightened you so, good Krodha," said Aditi, following after her, "that you must run from us?"

Krodha turned back and stared at Aditi. "I have a warning for you."

"A warning?"

"In my dream, I was in a place unknown to me. A temple of white stone, with tall pillars. There was someone, a queen of the Nagas, I think, who spoke to me. Her words were foreign, but I understood her. She said I was not to be admitted into Paradise, for it was not yet my time. And that I was to tell you that you have committed a sin against the gods. What was her word . . . *hubis*, I think."

"Hubris?"

"That is it. She said you would suffer for it. I do not know what the dream means, Sri Aditi, but I no longer wish to serve you. I think it would bring bad fortune. I will send another." Krodha departed through the lattice door, shutting it firmly behind her.

Aditi felt frozen in place, the latticework patterns swimming before her eyes. "Did you hear her, Gandharva?"

"I did. You wished for a sign. It would seem you have been given one."

"Surely the Mahadevi understands what I have done and why."

"Mmmm. The Mahadevi may not care what your needs are. Gods are fickle that way. Or it may not have been the Mahadevi who spoke to Krodha in her death dream. Or it may just have been a hallucination and nothing more."

Aditi passed a hand over her eyes and her dizziness faded. She walked back to Gandharva and reclined on the pillows beside him. "How do you escape madness when you hold so many conflicting thoughts?"

"By not dwelling on any one of them too much. Each moment is what matters to me. To think on the future or the past is to dwell on lies and illusion."

Aditi turned her head and regarded the bright, burning stars. "Whoever spoke to Krodha was correct. I am punished already. For I do not think I will be getting any sleep tonight."

XVI

🌿 ROSE: This is the queen of flowers to peoples of all lands. Every part of the plant hath curative use. Attar of rose eases sleep and preserves youth. Infusion of the dried petals cures the headache, and mixed with honey it purifies the blood. Its fruit eases pains of the chest and throat. The red of the rose is said to be its blush from when Eve kissed it in the Garden, though its thorns grew to remind us of Man's Fall. To Mohammedans, the flower is a sign of virility, and it sprang from the sweat of the Prophet as he journeyed to Paradise. Among Hindoos, the rose won a contest between the gods as to which flower was the most beautiful. And to the Greeks of ancient times, the rose was stained by the blood of Venus, whose feet bled upon the thorns as she searched for her love Adonis. A rose hung over a council hall signifies that guests therein may speak freely, without fear. Fallen rose petals, or blossoms out of season, are evil omens....

Although the sun had not yet shown itself over the walls of Bijapur, and although the songs of the muezzin and the sonorous prayers still echoed with comforting resonance through their spirits, the Mirza and his men stood waiting by the door.

The Mirza smiled at the slap of approaching footsteps. "Did I not tell you?" he said softly to Jaimal.

"I am glad my Lord did not ask me to place a wager," the lieutenant said with a grudging smile.

The door opened and the well-dressed servant it revealed took one step within and then stopped suddenly in surprise.

"Good morning to you," said the Mirza. "We are ready for our audience with Sultan Ibrahim."

"Ah . . . ah . . ." stammered the servant.

"That is why you have come, is it not?" said Jaimal. "To summon us to his august presence?"

"Indeed, my lords, it is. Did someone come before me to tell you?"

"We knew," said the Mirza. "How is no matter."

"Of . . . of course, my lords. But you may take your time. His Majesty has no wish to hurry you."

"But we are ready now. You may lead us to him directly."

"Uh . . ."

"That is," said Jaimal, "if His Majesty is ready for us."

"But of course he is," said the Mirza. "It would be a poor host to invite his guests before he, himself, were ready."

The servant's cheeks were beginning to turn a shade of crimson. "If my lords will be so good as to follow me." He bowed and led them into the corridor.

The Mirza noticed that Masum was the last to leave the room, just as he had been the last to arise from his prayer rug. *His feet must be finding the spiritual Path*, the Mirza thought with an inward smile, *for he is having difficulty staying aware of the earthly one.*

The servant led them in a circuitous route around the perimeter of the *Gagan Mahal* before finally guiding them to the enormous stone platform at the center of the palace. To the west was the great arch, through which any passersby could see the meetings that were taking place. There were no walls or pillars near the platform, the Mirza noted. No places for soldiers to hide in ambush. It provided an atmosphere of openness, safety, honesty, and trust.

Either we have nothing to fear from Ibrahim, thought the Mirza, *or he is more clever than I expected.*

A temporary reflecting pond had been constructed on the platform, and filled with white lotus. Pots of jasmine, roses, and chrysanthemums lined the perimeter of the platform. At the eastern end stood an octagonal dais covered by a canopy of red-and-green silk. On the dais was a plush, wide chair with short legs and a high back. At present, the chair was empty.

Before the dais were several large, richly woven carpets, and it was here, to the right side of the dais, that the Mirza and his men were invited to sit. The Mirza wondered at the arrangement but did not openly protest.

Behind the curtained back of the dais, a servant called out, "Make way, all who hear, for The Most Radiant Sovereign, Highest Royal Majesty, Ibrahim 'Adilshah, Supreme Lord of Bijapur, Favored of the Almighty, Jagat-Guru, Noble Teacher, Defender of the Women, and Keeper of the Faith."

The Mirza turned toward the dais and bowed from the waist, motioning for his men to do likewise. He did not go to his knees, for he wished it to be clear that this was a meeting between equals.

The back panel of the curtain parted and, behind two servants, the Sultan Ibrahim stepped in. If he had dressed hastily, there was no sign of it. The portly sultan wore an elegant yellow silk *jama* with a golden *kammerband* and jeweled belt studded with sapphires, over yellow *shalwar* trousers. His bejeweled *pagri* turban of gold cloth was entirely correct.

"If it will please His Most Royal Majesty," the servant went on, "may I present the emissary from our neighboring kingdom to the north, His Highness, Mirza Ali Akbarshah."

From his bow, the Mirza said, "I bring you greeting, Majesty, from The Imperial Shahinshah Allahu Akbar, Khalifah, Ruler of all Sind. May He who is the Provider of all things shower you, your family, and your kingdom with peace, harmony, and those blessings you surely deserve."

The Sultan briefly embraced the Mirza. "I am honored to receive the emissary of my illustrious neighbor; may the

Most Generous and Merciful look kindly upon the Shahin-shah's family, his lands, and his people. Please be comfort-able, all of you." Ibrahim seated himself, cross-legged, on the broad seat of his chair.

The Mirza and his men sat on the rugs to the Sultan's right hand, as they had been instructed.

Other men joined the Sultan on the dais. "This is Qasim Firishta, my court historian. I have invited him for I think this may be an occasion of some importance. And this is Nur Al-Din Muhammad Zuhuri, my court poet, here so that this happy meeting may be recounted in pleasing language. And this is Gandharva, a most skilled musician, for I can never be without music."

The Mirza recognized the blind *vina* player as the one who had entertained his men the night before, the one whom the strange dancer-spy had spoken to before she hastily de-parted, but he chose to make no comment upon it.

"I trust you will forgive me," said Ibrahim, "for calling upon you so early. I fear my business will make this day quite full. But I wanted to be sure to greet Your Highness at the first opportunity."

"I fully understand," said the Mirza. "Besides, dawn is an auspicious time for discussing great undertakings."

"You are gracious indeed," said Ibrahim. "But since I have been so unkind as to call you so early, allow me to make amends by offering some modest refreshment." He clapped his hands and servants came onto the platform bearing plat-ters of silver. These were piled high with slices of passion fruit and pomegranate, honey loaves sprinkled with poppy seeds, quail eggs spiced with turmeric and saffron, bowls of spiced pickles and steamed lotus hearts. Tea spiced with co-riander and cinnamon was poured into little silver cups and set before the Mirza and his men.

There was an awkward moment as the others waited for the Mirza to begin eating. *If Ibrahim had wished villainy, he could have had us slain as we slept. We should not fear poisoning now.* He plucked up a slippery slice of passion fruit and popped it in his mouth. Then he gestured to his men that they may do the same, which they did with great eagerness.

After eating, some time was passed in discussing the health of the Emperor, the weather in Bijapur and how its crops fared, Ibrahim's family, and other inconsequential chatter, neither the Mirza nor the Sultan wishing to reveal too much nor say too little.

"But can the rumors we have heard be true," asked the Sultan at last, "that a general of your wisdom and ability comes to the Deccan not in search of martial glory, but chasing folk tales?"

The Mirza smiled. "The Shahinshah has great respect for the wisdom of his people. And if what he has learned bears fruit, there will be as much glory in it as in conquest. Imagine, if you will, O wise Majesty, that there exists somewhere an immortal queen, who may be willing to share the knowledge she has gathered over centuries of life, perhaps even the knowledge of eternal life itself. What king would not wish to find such a queen?"

"But my good Mirza, such stories have been told for as long as men have had mouths. Have they ever proven true?"

"Who is to say that some of them have not? Perhaps this queen has merely kept her secret well for a very long time. Perhaps she has had assistance in keeping her secret by those who have received her aid, those for whom she has destroyed enemies, or returned life to a dying child."

Ibrahim narrowed his eyes just a little. "An interesting supposition. But I think the good Mirza plucks fruit from the trees in the garden of his own imagination."

"Why think you so?"

Ibrahim sighed and leaned back in his chair, clasping his hands across his belly. "Were I to find such a queen, I would do all I could to marry her and thereby join our kingdoms and our knowledge and our blood. I expect any royal prince would do so."

"Perhaps she will not accept any mortal man as husband."

"If this queen is so powerful on her own," responded Ibrahim, "why has she not conquered all of Sind to reign in place of your Emperor?"

As the Mirza paused to consider his answer, Masum sat forward and said, "Perhaps, Majesty, her long life has taught her not to value war or conquest, but to value peace and learning. She hides herself decorously, at the top of a distant mountain, as the wisest *pirs* are said to do, and invites those who thirst for knowledge to seek her out."

Ibrahim raised his brows.

"This, Majesty, is Masum Al-Wadud, a Suf—"

"A *murid*," Masum corrected.

"From your own Shahpur Hillock," the Mirza finished.

"Ah, a Chisti?" said the Sultan. "I am a great admirer of the poetry produced by your sect. You must tell me some while we await the others who will join us shortly."

Masum beamed. "Most gladly, Sire."

"Others?" said the Mirza.

The wails of the Mohammedan criers still echoed through his mind as Padre Gonsção crossed himself. He tried to cover the heretic's cries with Christian prayer, as he knelt before the cross he had placed in the niche. *Does God suggest the torments that await heretics in Hell by the voices that call them to their misbegotten prayer? How can men of good sense answer such a call?*

Knees creaking, Gonsção stood and looked around at the others. He fought down a burst of gloating at seeing Magister Chinnery, eyes bloodshot and face pale, still lying on his pillows and moaning with the headache. *Such are the wages of sin, Magister.*

The former Brother Andrew sat scowling and rubbing his head, but seemed in better form. *Someone who is all too used to sin and its effects.*

The *soldados* were in various states of sleep, bleary wakefulness, or sobering pain. Occasionally one would groan, "Must you pray so loud, Padre? Ai, my head!"

Timóteo knelt beside Gonsção, eyes shut in prayer. At least he was still untainted by this place. *If Goa might be compared to a good woman fallen, Bijapur is an exotic, strutting harlot. May you, at least, not succumb to her temptations, my son.*

Footsteps approached the door and it was flung open without a knock. The *soldados* groped for their swords. Gonsção stared at the dark, turbaned servant who bowed in the doorway. "Timóteo, ask him what he wants."

The boy obediently stood and spoke to the servant, then turned back to the Padre, surprise on his face. "He says the Sultan has summoned us. We are to have audience with him this very hour."

"How fortunate, then, that my loud prayers have awoken everyone," said Gonsção dryly. "We will be ready all the sooner."

At further words from the servant, Timóteo added, "He suggests that we hurry. The Sultan does not like to be kept waiting." Softly, the boy confided, "I wish I might have stayed in prayer longer, Padre. There was much I had to ask."

Gonsção placed his hand on the boy's shoulder. "God will surely have audience with you again, Timóteo. But this may be our only chance with the Sultan."

He waited the long minutes it took for the others to find and pull on their clothing, throw water on their faces, and force themselves into a reasonable state of wakefulness.

The servant guided them along a straight corridor that lead from their wing to the central atrium and the enormous platform at its center.

The Sultan was already present, sitting cross-legged on

an overstuffed, oversized chair. *No one seems to have taught these people how to use furniture properly*, thought Gonsção. Ibrahim 'Adilshah, in the Padre's estimation, was a large but not unhandsome man, built square but tending toward fat in the middle. He had a firm, square jaw fringed with a well-trimmed black beard. His nose was a sharp angle with slender nostrils, and his eyes and lips were large. He looked resplendent in yellow-and-gold cloth, and wore more jewels than any European princess.

There were three men seated behind the Sultan, one of whom was the blind musician Gonsção had noticed at the entertainments of the night before. *This Sultan cannot even conduct business without sweetmeats and melodies. Truly, he follows a sensual faith. Yet I must deal with this man. How I wish Sadrinho had sent someone else.*

A group of Mughuls sat on some rugs to the Sultan's right, watching the Padre's group approach with barely concealed curiosity and wariness. The remains of a meal was scattered on silver platters in front of them, and a scent of spiced tea hung in the air. The man sitting nearest the Sultan's dais was tall and austere, with a well-trimmed beard and elaborate turban. The shorter, darker man beside him scowled at the Goans as they approached. The man to his right, who wore a tunic of white wool and whose beard was more unkempt, smiled broadly and bobbed his head. "Tamas, Timóteo," he greeted them.

Gonsção turned to Brother Timóteo. "You know this man?"

"We met him in the serai, Padre. He is an herbalist like Tomás."

Gonsção glared at the young *inglês*. "I see someone should have looked after you better, Timóteo."

Magister Chinnery said, "It was a chance meeting, nothing more."

"We will discuss it later." Gonsção motioned for Brother Andrew to walk beside him, and together they went before the Sultan. Gonsção went down on one knee and bowed low, motioning for the others to do the same.

The servant who had led them to the platform proclaimed their arrival in his lilting language.

Brother Andrew frowned. "Strange, he is not speaking Persian."

"No," said Timóteo in a loud whisper, on Gonsção's other side, "he is speaking Marathi. He said, 'His Radiant Majesty, Shah of Bijapur, beloved of Heaven and his people, greets you and welcomes you to his humble dwelling.'"

"Alas," said Brother Andrew, "that is not a language I know."

Timóteo went on. "He further says that these other men are emissaries from the great Mughul Emperor Akbar. Their leader is the Mirza Ali Akbarshah."

"Why are they here?" said Gonsção.

"We must first introduce ourselves," said Brother Andrew. "Speak what you will, Padre, and I will try him in Persian."

"Very well. Tell him I, Father Antonio Gonsção, of the Dominican Order, Emissary of Cardinal Albrecht of Spain and Inquisitor Sadrinho of Goa, thank him and greet him in return."

Brother Andrew turned and translated to the Sultan in what Gonsção presumed was Persian. But this caused Ibrahim to scowl slightly, and the Sultan turned to his servant. The servant provided retranslation in another tongue.

"Most astonishing," whispered Brother Andrew. "It would seem the Sultan does not know Persian at all."

"Perhaps he refuses to learn it," said Timóteo, "because Persian is the tongue of the Mughuls."

Gonsção looked at the boy. "I do not understand. If these other men are of the Mughuls, why does he not speak in a tongue that favors them?"

"The boy has a point," said Brother Andrew. "The camel drivers told me that the Deccanese kingdoms hate the

Mughul empire, for they know Akbar seeks to someday conquer them."

"This situation becomes more complex every moment," murmured Gonsção.

The Sultan smiled and gestured to indicate they should sit on the rugs to his left. The Mughuls who sat to his right watched silently, except for the odd fellow with unkempt beard who stared at Gonsção as though he were seeing a two-headed horse.

The *soldados,* also silent and wary, seated themselves on the rugs and cushions, keeping Magister Chinnery close among them. Gonsção reluctantly selected a flat, square cushion and eased himself onto it. *Is it some unshakable habit of barbarism that leads these people to conduct their business out of doors, sitting on the ground? I have spent too many hours kneeling to bear this well. God grant me patience.*

Brother Andrew placed himself between Gonsção and the Sultan to serve as interpreter, but Gonsção kept Timóteo beside him in case more direct interpretation became needed.

Gonsção gestured to Joaquim to present the gift they had brought for the Sultan. The *soldado* took up the cedar box and went forward, on his knees, toward the dais. The servant stopped Joaquim a sword's-length from the foot of the dais and took the box from him, placing it at the Sultan's feet. At the potentate's nod, the servant opened the box.

The Sultan leaned forward as the servant reached in and slowly lifted a cloth covering what lay inside. The Sultan reached in as if to take up the silver-bound book within. Suddenly, he snatched his hand back as if it had been bitten by a snake. His eyes rolled in dismay and his right hand strayed toward the curved dagger in his sash. Then he closed his eyes, and with a sigh, sat back, waving his hand dismissively. The servant closed the box and took it away.

Gonsção was perplexed. *What could distress the Sultan so*

about a copy of the Bible? I had heard this king was receptive to those not of his faith.

Food was brought for them on silver platters: unrecognizable fruits and vegetables as well as rice and eggs. The *soldados* snatched up the food as soon as it was set before them and gobbled it down. Gonsção noticed the Mughuls across from them staring in disapproval. *What a sordid sight we must make.* Despite the growling of his stomach, Gonsção chose to forebear from tasting any of the repast. He wished to focus his attention on the meeting.

The leader of the party who sat across from them turned to the Sultan and spoke tersely.

"Do you understand him, Timóteo?"

"He says he is curious about our presence and wishes to know what we are doing here. I do not think he is pleased to see us, Padre."

The Sultan smiled genially and spoke with warm enthusiasm. "It would seem His Majesty plays games with us both," said Brother Andrew.

Timóteo continued. "He says that the wise and generous God has presented him with an honor like no other he has ever known. Our two parties have come from different lands, with different faiths, yet seeking the very same thing."

"The same thing!" Gonsção and the Mughul prince exchanged appalled glances. *It is as Sadrinho feared. Already the Mughuls know of the resurrection powder. Alas for Portugal. If Akbar finds the powder, Goa is lost. Alas for Christendom, for if all Islam finds it, we are lost.*

"The Sultan says the Mirza was sent here following tales of an immortal queen who lives in a hidden fortress."

"Tell him we had heard it was a pagan goddess."

The Mughul leader spoke, and Timóteo said, "The Mirza said they have heard similar tales also. He asks if we know where she is. What shall I tell him?"

Gonsção paused. *This is not information I wish to share. Why would the Sultan wish to help the Mughuls if they are enemies? How did they learn of the powder, I wonder? Did the mysterious Aditi seduce their Emperor also?* "Tell them we learned of it from a sorcerer in Goa, who learned it from a woman named Aditi."

The barest twitch of the Sultan's bejeweled hand betrayed his recognition of the name. Gonsção could see no such reaction among the Mughuls.

"The Sultan asks if these persons gave you knowledge of the location of the hidden city."

"Tell him we have some idea of where to look."

Again the Sultan spoke at length with expansive gestures, nodding and smiling at both parties.

Timóteo translated, "He says this is very good news, for the Mughuls have need of this knowledge. And they, in turn, can offer us protection. The Deccan is a dangerous place to strangers, and the Mirza has brought an army of five hundred men. If we join our expedition with his army, our small group need fear no harm."

An army! Dear God, preserve us. How am I to stop a multitude from taking the source of the powder? "Please thank His Majesty for his concern for our safety, but we go with the protection of the Lord Christ and his Heavenly Father, and we need none other."

As Timóteo translated, Gonsção noticed the wild-haired Mughul pointing at him and speaking to the Mirza.

Brother Andrew chuckled.

"What is amusing?" growled Gonsção.

"That fellow, Padre, is a Sufi, a Mohammedan mystic. He says you must be a Sufi also, because you are wearing a robe of white wool, as he does. You see, 'Suf' is Arabic for 'wool.' "

Gonsção narrowed his eyes at the mystic. "Please inform him of his error. A robe of wool was also worn by our sacred Lord, Jesus Christ."

Brother Andrew smirked and spoke directly to the mystic. The Sufi smiled and replied to Gonsção in his unintelligible tongue.

"He says that is natural, for the Nazarene was a wise teacher, as was their Prophet, Mohammed, who also wore the white wool. He is glad you and he have these things in common."

Gonsção sighed and turned away.

The Sultan spoke again, and Timóteo translated, "His Majesty is pleased that already we are finding bridges between our two peoples. He says he has always believed that peoples of different lands and faiths can learn from one another."

"That is ridiculous!" snapped Gonsção. "How would any man ever be able to distinguish Truth if all beliefs and customs are given equal validity?"

Timóteo raised his brows, but spoke to the Sultan. "His Majesty suggests that the best bread is made by winnowing all grains together and baking them in the same oven."

"Tell him Truth is like gold dust scattered amongst those grains. If it is sifted among many other grains, a great treasure is lost. It must be kept separate and pure to retain its value."

The mystic across from him babbled again, and Brother Andrew said, "Our Sufi friend suggests that bread is more valuable than gold, and that bread of but one grain is less healthful than a loaf made of many ingredients."

"Is he a madman? Even his fellow Mughuls frown at him."

"Mystics are often mistaken for madmen, Padre."

The Sultan laughed and clapped his hands. Timóteo said, "His Majesty is pleased at our philosophical discussion and says it bodes well for our expedition. He asks what he may do to further our plans and help us on our way."

This is idiocy. "Did he not understand you at first, Timóteo? We are declining his offer. Please make that clear to him."

"Wait," said Brother Andrew before Timóteo could begin. "Padre, if you will hear some counsel, I suggest it would not be wise to insult the Sultan by refusing to travel with the Mughuls. We do not know what agreements he has made with them or—"

"That should be none of our concern."

"Please listen, Padre. So long as our Mohammedan hosts feel we are useful, they will be courteous and hospitable. And I will point out that, if our small band leaves alone, the Mirza's army might come after us in any case. If they harm us after the Sultan has placed us in their 'care,' they risk incurring his wrath, as well as violating their own custom of hospitality, which they take very seriously. Also, by going with them, we may find some opportunity to prevent their getting the powder, which we might not if we travel alone."

Gonsção sighed. *Blessed Almighty, who looked after Daniel in the den of lions, look after us now.* "You have made an excellent argument, Brother Andrew. I cannot fault it, much as I would like to. Timóteo, please tell His Majesty that we will accept his help in providing our expedition with supplies and knowledge of the Deccan, and we will welcome the Mughuls as allies in our search."

The Sultan beamed and threw his arms wide with joyous exclamations. He then extended his hand toward the Mughul Mirza, and spoke at length to him.

An argument broke out among the Mughuls, which Gonsção presumed was similar to theirs. Both the mystic and another man who sat beside the Mirza spoke rapidly and emphatically to him. The Mirza himself sat calmly, rubbing his beard, until his men ran out of words. Finally he turned to the Sultan and bowed, making his reply.

The Sultan stood and shouted praises to Allah, which Gonsção presumed meant that the Mughuls had also agreed to comingle their forces. Ibrahim came down from the dais and stood between the parties, one hand extended to each.

Understanding the gesture, Gonsção stood and took the hand extended to him. The Mirza did the same, while the other Mughuls glared at him as though he were mad. The Sultan placed the Inquisitor's and the Mirza's hands together—almost as though it were a marriage—and made more lofty declarations.

Timóteo translated, "His Majesty says that this must truly be the work of the Divine. That two groups of men, foreign in thought and deed to one another, should join together in the search for that which is sacred and beautiful. He pledges all his help to this blessed quest, and asks only that we keep him informed of our progress that he, too, may learn of the wonders we discover together."

So that is part of his scheme, thought Gonsção. He nodded and looked the Mughul general in the eye, trying to determine what sort of man he must now deal with. But from the Mirza's dark, weathered face he gained no clue.

"His Majesty thanks you all and now releases you to return to your quarters to prepare for your departure. He does not wish to delay you an hour longer than needed to see that you leave well-provided."

The Sultan turned and with a wave of the hand dismissed the Mughul party, allowing them to leave first. The Mughuls departed the platform with dark glances at the Goans as they passed.

Gonsção bowed, expecting to also be dismissed, as the Sultan spoke to him. "His Majesty says we may also go, may God go with and advise us. He asks only that the yellow-hair named Tamaschinri remain for a private audience."

Gonsção whirled to face the *inglês*. The young man blinked, but his surprise seemed false. *And when was this bit of treachery arranged?* "It would appear that the Sultan has some interest in you, Magister Chinnery. You have great skill in charming the natives of this land."

"No need for suspicion, Padre," Brother Andrew said quickly. "Thomas merely has some specific questions for the Sultan based on the clues that De Cartago had given him."

"Indeed?" *Are you part of this plot as well?*

"Of course!" said Timóteo. "He is going to ask the Sultan about those traps we should watch out for, and maybe trick him into revealing what he knows about the *pulvis mirificus.*"

Magister Chinnery smiled wanly and nodded. "Yes, of course."

"Well, then," said Gonsção, "you must have Timóteo stay to be your interpreter, as Brother Andrew does not speak the Sultan's language."

The young *inglês* looked stunned—it was clearly not a turn of events he had expected. Gonsção decided to drive home the advantage. "And a good thing, for I need to talk to Brother Andrew myself. It appears there is much more I need to know about local politics and custom if we are to travel with the Mughuls. Oh fear not, Magister, I will not leave you unguarded. Joaquim may stay to make sure the Sultan does not try to harm you."

"But Padre," said Brother Andrew, "Timóteo, skillful interpreter as he has proved to be, knows little of the local customs. He may give insult without intent."

"Then I trust the Sultan would forgive him because of his age. And I expect Timóteo, who has lived on this continent all his life, may know a little more than a Scotsman recently arrived, no? Come, let us not tax the Sultan further with our company. Magister Chinnery, I await your report of the interview with much anticipation."

Gonscao noted the sorrow in the young *inglês'* eyes as he looked at Timóteo. *So. The boy's regard still matters to you. Good. May you see the pain of your betrayal in the boy's face as he speaks your words to the Sultan, and may the pain have echo in your heart.*

Motioning for the *soldados* to follow him, Gonsção descended from the platform, thoughts gathering in his mind like storm clouds.

XVII

BLOODSTONE: This is green chalcedony that is flecked with red spots. Some say the spots came from the blood of Christ as it dripped from the cross onto green jasper. When worn in an amulet about the neck, it cures the hemorrhage. In a poultice mixed with honey, it will lower swellings and tumors. Some say that to carry bloodstone will make one see through lies and illusions, yet will make every word of the wearer believed. It brings peace amid chaos and can soothe the wrath of kings. No power or obstacle may keep the wearer from his fated goal. It can bring visions of what is to come. Yet bloodstone will also summon tempests, earthquakes, and destruction....

Thomas watched the Padre and Lockheart leave the Sultan's audience platform. A haze of cold bewilderment fogged his mind, as if the world of this day were completely different from the one he had inhabited the night before. *Where yesterday all was hope and beauty, this chill morn brings only melancholy and shattered illusion.*

Thomas's head ached from over use of drink and his arms ached as they always had since leaving Goa. He had had no appetite for the strange repasts brought by the Sultan's servants. The fairy-tale palace now seemed alien and bizarre . . . frightening in its unfamiliarity. Thomas found he longed most for a bowl of warm pottage by a kitchen fire, and to walk

London's muddy, sloppy streets in a cold November rain, hearing all around him speaking a tongue he knew.

"Senhor," said Timóteo, tugging at his sleeve. "Tomás, the Sultan says he is ready to speak to you."

"Ay, be gentle with him little monk," said Joaquim with a sly smile. "Our Tomás has sampled too many of the good things and now he is paying."

"Your pardon," Thomas said, trying to stay aware of the here and now. "I am ready, if I must be." He walked to the rug in front of the Sultan's chair and knelt, then bowed in Hindu fashion. Joaquim and Timóteo knelt to either side of him. Thomas felt confined between them as if again in a cell of stone and iron bars.

The Sultan Ibrahim dismissed his historian and his poet, allowing only the blind musician to remain on the dais with him. Then he leaned forward on his chair and spoke toward Thomas.

Timóteo turned his head sharply, his eyes wide with shock. "Tomás, his Majesty says that someone has told him that you wish to leave our expedition to enter his service. This cannot be true, is it?"

Thomas sighed and stared down at the twisting arabesque patterns in the rug beneath him. *Shall I shatter this boy's trust for a spirit-fogged illusion that I belonged here? Whatever had possessed me yesternight? My arms are no use. I cannot be a soldier and know nothing of warcraft. My only skill is in administering herbs that grow thousands of miles away. Aditi wants me to seek her "goddess," Andrew wants me to find the powder for my trade's sake, Joaquim for his freedom's sake, Timóteo and the Padre for God's sake. Who am I to deny them all? What have I to offer the Sultan for aid in getting me home? And were I to strike out on my own, I might well become a highwayman's prize and then a rotting corpse along some forgotten jungle road.*

Betraying Timóteo's trust seemed the most hurtful thing of all. Thomas had never been openly admired, looked up to, by anyone in his life. *One day Timóteo must learn that the world can be a cold and evil place. But let it not be from me.*

"Tomás," said Joaquim softly in his ear, "are you asleep? Pray do the little monk the kindness of answering him. And be sure that you make it the right answer."

"Your pardon, Timóteo. Please tell the Sultan that he has been misinformed. I do wish to speak with him, but for reason of learning more about this land, particularly the Deccan to the south and east, and the goddess who produces the powder that brings the dead to life."

Timóteo smiled, visibly relieved, and translated Thomas's words to the Sultan.

Ibrahim sat back, surprised at what the Goan boy was saying. He stroked his beard and stared at the yellow-hair. Could the foreigner be playing him for a fool? *The young man seems sober, almost ill. There was some consternation among them before their priest left, and the soldier beside the yellow-hair has a threatening smile. Might Aditi have been lying to me?* He turned and asked Gandharva, softly, "What do you make of this?"

"Perhaps the young man has changed his mind, Majesty."

"No." Sudden revelation struck Ibrahim as if Sarasvati Herself had breathed upon his face. *Aditi does not want him as part of the expedition. But why? He says he has questions about the Deccan. Has he some special knowledge without which the Goan expedition would fail? But the priest said his knowledge of the Mahadevi comes from her. Does she secretly favor the yellow-hair and plan to destroy the other westerners? Or does she plan to destroy him to aid the others? I must learn what business she has with these Goans.*

"Is he quite certain?" said Ibrahim to the boy. "My court is open to scholars and travellers from all lands. And I can offer protection, if he feels others might prevent his choosing to stay."

There was the slightest hesitation in the yellow-hair, and

a swift glance toward the soldier at his left, before he replied that he was certain. *So. Perhaps the young man is being coerced or is a captive. Perhaps Aditi wished him rescued. Clearly I must speak with her again. But why did the Goan priest reveal that he knew of her? By the Merciful, what a tangle this is!*

Turning to Gandharva, Ibrahim murmured, "I am finding more and more that I must speak again with Sri Aditi. Could you possibly find your way to where she is lodged and tell her to come to me as soon as possible? Do so in a way that others do not hear you, and do not give her cause for alarm."

"Of course, Majesty," said Gandharva, standing and bowing. "Although, you understand, I am limited in my abilities. I may be slow."

"Do what you can," said Ibrahim.

"Majesty." Gandharva bowed a final time and departed through the curtained canopy.

"Very well," Ibrahim said, turning back to the Goan boy-monk. "There is little I can tell you about the lands to the south and east. It is a desolate land, peopled only by poor villages, or so I am told. I cannot think why anyone would believe a goddess reigns there. Particularly you, who are Christians and therefore profess to worship The One God, as those of my faith do."

The yellow-hair spoke to the boy a long while before the boy translated. "Majesty, you are correct. We do not believe that we seek a goddess. But Sri Chinri has heard of such things as the fabled Philosopher's Stone, which grants wisdom and immortality. It may be that someone has found this marvel and is using it to advantage, ascribing its power to a goddess, so that it will be accepted by pagans."

Ibrahim rubbed his bearded chin. "That is . . . an interesting supposition." *What if this Mahadevi business is all a sham? Aditi and Gandharva might be liars, or even have been duped themselves into believing it. Perhaps that is why I have never been permitted to visit the hidden city. Perhaps there is no hidden city at all.*

And yet, my daughter was revived from death. Might it have been the power of some mineral, and not a deity, that revived her? How embarrassing to think that the disapproving clerics may have been right all this time.

Attempting to keep his growing distress from his face, Ibrahim went on. "To be truthful, my young friend, I believe you and the Mirza Ali Akbarshah to be on a foolish chase. However, as I am bound to be a gracious host, I will not impede your search in any way."

The boy translated the yellow-hair's reply as, "We are grateful for all the assistance Your Majesty chooses to give."

"I ask but one thing more," said Ibrahim. *Now that Gandharva has left, let us see what can be learned from this.* "I am unfamiliar with your western tongues, and I have a missive here that I cannot read and would like translated. Would you do me the kindness of looking at it and telling me what it says?"

The yellow-hair nodded his agreement, and Ibrahim pulled from a fold in his *jama* a slip of palm leaf. It was the one his servants claimed had come from a messenger dove released by Gandharva. None of his other advisors could read the script, but his historian suggested it might be an ancient western language. Ibrahim handed the leaf to his servant, who handed it to the boy-monk. The boy's eyes widened and he gave it to the yellow-hair, talking excitedly.

The yellow-hair looked at the palm leaf a long time. Ibrahim was unable to read his expression. At last, the yellow-hair handed the leaf back to the boy and spoke softly but emphatically to him.

The boy returned the leaf to the servant and said, "Sri Chinri says that the words on it are Greek, but that the message is nothing more than a prayer."

"Which deity is it a prayer to?"

The boy consulted a moment with the yellow-hair. "The message does not specify one, Majesty."

"What does the petitioner request from his deity?"

"Only good health and good fortune, Majesty."

Ibrahim regarded the yellow-hair for some moments. The foreigner looked down, not meeting his gaze. *He lies. He knows more but will not say. I can presume that Gandharva was sending a message to the Mahadevi. Or someone posing as the Mahadevi. But for what purpose? To request aid or report on my actions? Do he and Aditi work together or oppose each other? Was he trying to tell the Mahadevi of Aditi's treachery or request divine aid for their plot? What will the Mahadevi do? It is time I confronted Gandharva with this, as soon as he returns. Though it will be painful. He is such a good musician. And I have thought him a friend.*

"Then that shall have to content me." Ibrahim sighed and stood. "Come, let me show you some of the *Gagan Mahal*, on your way back to your quarters. It is considered a wonder of architecture for this region, and I never tire of sharing it with visitors."

"You are certain?" Aditi said to her new serving-girl, Pramlocha.

"Most assuredly. This message came from the westerners' quarters, Sri Aditi, for you."

Aditi unfolded the scrap of parchment and noted the message therein was, curiously, written in Latin, not Greek.

> Dearest Aditi, come to our rooms at once.
> I will be alone. I have spoken with the Sultan.
> I must talk to you.
>   Your Admiring One

She did not know if it was his handwriting, but the parchment was surely an indication it was from Tamas. "Will you lead me there?" she asked Pramlocha.

The girl hesitated and looked away. "I am not supposed to let you wander."

"It would not do to insult the Sultan's guests by refusing, and I will not be wandering but going to one place only."

Pramlocha clicked her tongue, but did not move. "I do not like these foreigners. They stink."

"So they do. But this one says he has something important to tell me. Perhaps it is something the Sultan will need to hear. But I cannot know unless I speak to this man. The Sultan will be most displeased if important information is lost because a serving-girl does not like his guest's smell."

With a heavy sigh, the girl said, "Very well. I suppose I must. This way."

Aditi followed her new servant along a back passageway, pretending she did not know where they were headed. She saw Gandharva at a distance walking slowly toward her lodgings. *Well, he will have to wait until I return to speak to me.*

She felt frustrated, anxious, and unsettled. Because of the canopy over the Sultan's dais, she had been unable to see, from her room, whom the Sultan had been speaking to.

Perhaps Tamas wishes to discuss what the Sultan said to him. I wonder if he would tell me why he gave the powder to the Sufi, and how they know one another. Perhaps, if he is truly alone, I should just kill him. But, if Ibrahim has accepted Tamas into his service, such a suspicious death would invite too much interest. I must not encourage Ibrahim's distrust any further. I suppose Tamas must live.

She found herself oddly relieved upon deciding this. Her anger from the night before had abated, leaving her with only confusion and sour regret. *I can hope that Tamas will forget the Mahadevi. Or perhaps someday, when he is ready, I will take him to Her. Or perhaps he will just return home, as he said he might. Since the Mahadevi will not guide me, I must leave all in her hands.*

It was annoying to have the silent, sullen Pramlocha along. Aditi did not want one who was likely serving as ears for Ibrahim listening to her conversation with Tamas. *Ai, she is as bad as Krodha. If only I could be rid of her. But there is no more* rasa mahadevi *and Krodha may well have warned her about that trick.*

They came to the door of the hall where the Goans were lodged, and Pramlocha stood aside, her *shal* draped low over her face.

Aditi discerned from the girl's posture that she was not happy. "Are you afraid, Pramlocha?"

"No," the girl said too quickly.

"There is no shame in it, if you are. I have lived in Goa and I know how barbaric these westerners are. They are, in particular, very rude to women. I don't doubt that one of them will grab you and force himself upon you as soon as we enter. I hope you are prepared."

Pramlocha cast a furtive, frightened glance at the door and her lips tightened.

"Ah, you were not told this might be part of your service? Ai, Ibrahim can be so callous sometimes. He does not understand the sorrows of women. Poor thing. Your family wishes you to marry well, I am sure, and that will be so difficult if you are sullied. Especially by westerners."

The girl sighed and squeezed her hands together tightly.

"It is so unfair. I doubt you would even understand anything I say to the Goans. Truly, His Majesty has misused you."

The girl looked up sharply at Aditi. "You are not afraid."

"As I have said, I have lived in Goa and know their ways. Besides, I am old. Nearly twenty-eight, and I have never married. No one will care if westerners touch me."

"I . . . I have been ordered not to leave your side."

"No one need ever know that you have. We can do this—you simply go to the side garden over there. If you stand behind the laurel tree, the Goans will not see you. I will tell you all that I have said to the Goans, if that will console you. I will come to you as soon as I am finished. Why should you have to suffer for a little gossip? Is my plan not more agreeable?"

Pramlocha still seemed suspicious, but also relieved. "You

will not shame me by running off? You will come right over to me when done?"

"Have I not promised it? Go, hide quickly, before the Goans see you."

The girl drew her *shal* over her lower face and walked swiftly away to the garden.

Aditi allowed herself a little smile of victory as she rapped upon the Goans' door.

"*Venite,*" a man said distantly from within.

Aditi blinked, surprised, and opened the door herself. The large chamber was empty, save for some bits of clothing and armor near the walls. At the far end, seated between two candles on a rug, was the priest of the Orlem Gor. He smiled as Aditi stepped in, but there was no pleasure in his eyes.

All her instincts shouted that she should flee at once, yet Aditi could not tell from what danger. She slowly walked forward, hand on the hilt of the knife in her skirt. She did not see any of the Goan soldiers, yet she sensed they were nearby. *Perhaps I was too hasty in sending Pramlocha away.*

The priest stood as she approached, and held out his hands to her. "Domina Aditi," he said in Latin, "how pleased I am that you accepted my invitation. Please sit with me. I have looked forward to speaking with you for some time."

So. It was he who sent the note and not Tamas, thought Aditi. *This priest's face is a mask and his eyes have no* jiva *in them.* In Aditi's experience, there were those who accepted resurrection as a great gift from the goddess, as Gandharva did. Or those who simply thought themselves lucky and persevered in their life as before. But there were some who thought their new life was stolen from the gods, that they had disrupted some divine plan, or that they were unworthy.

The priest of the Orlem Gor must be one who hates his returned life. Aditi pitied him, but also feared him. A man who believed himself to be a thief of heaven would think no earthly crime beneath him.

Aditi did not touch the priest's hands, but she knelt at the farthest edge of the carpet. She did not speak.

"I must commend you on your cleverness, Domina," the priest went on. "We of the Santa Casa had been searching for you for a long time, to no avail. And, I confess, you had me quite fooled in your role as Domina Agnihotra. Though why you have had the kindness to lead us this far upon our journey, I cannot guess. Something about Magister Chinnery, I should imagine."

Aditi opened her mouth to ask where Tamas was, but caught herself. She shut her lips again and simply stared at the priest.

"You must admit, however, Domina, that the Santa Casa has prevailed, in the end, over your scheming. Your cabal exists no more. Domine Resgate confessed and poor Magister De Cartago," the priest clicked his tongue. "Despite the best of our care, he died unrepentant."

Aditi balled her hands into fists but remained silent. *What does he think I will say? Does he expect me to argue? To boast? To accuse him of murder? Perhaps westerners are inclined to spew torrents of words like the monsoon rains, but I will not.*

"Alas, I see some demon has caught hold of your tongue. Perhaps you do not feel safe here. But that is foolish. We are far from the Santa Casa, deep in the midst of your country. Perhaps you have believed the lies that are told about my work. It might surprise you to know that I took a vow, as all do who join the Santa Casa, that we are not to kill. You need not fear death at my hands."

Ah, but it is so easy to cause death indirectly, is it not? Truly this man thinks me a fool.

The priest paused and rubbed his chin. "Perhaps you do not see the opportunity fate is presenting you, Domina. You wish to bring others to the knowledge and acceptance of your goddess. Here I am, seeking this divine power. You could do us the kindness of giving us guidance, and bringing us to this

Mahadevi whose name is strength. I am not without influence in the Santa Casa, you know. If I become convinced of her divinity, I could spread word of her throughout the greatest kingdom in Europe. But, then, perhaps this has been your intention all along and I simply have not seen it."

Oh, yes, it would please me to bring you before the Mahadevi, for you would not survive the experience. But it has never been my intention to subject Her to your madness.

The priest sighed heavily and began to pour a milky liquid from a ewer into a cup. "I cannot fathom the reason for this silence. I know you understand me. There is clearly no need for us to be enemies now. If you are worried for your golden-haired lover, he is still with the Sultan. I expect he will be returning soon. Here, let us share a drink of peace, and discuss how we might be of aid to one another." The priest placed the cup on the rug in front of her.

Out of curiosity, Aditi picked up the cup and slowly raised it toward her lips. The priest watched intently. Aditi sniffed at the liquid and recognized the sour smell of datura. *He truly does think me a fool. He hoped to drug and interrogate me. We are not so far from the Orlem Gor after all.* Glaring at the priest, Aditi slowly set the cup down again.

The priest scowled. "I regret that you have chosen not to accept my offering of peace." He clapped his hands once, and Aditi heard men rushing toward her. She jumped to her feet and whirled, knife at the ready. But there were four of them with long swords. One of the soldiers batted at her knife with his blade and sent it flying.

Aditi began to scream for help in Marathi, but someone grabbed her from behind and clapped a hand over her mouth. Each of her arms were caught by a soldier, so roughly that her bracelets fell jangling to the floor. She struggled a little, to get the feel for the strength of her captors, and knew she would not be able to overpower them.

"Let us begin again," said the priest, walking up beside

her. "I have said that the Santa Casa does not kill. But we can make life . . . quite unpleasant. We find pain focuses the mind very well and makes priorities clear. It brings me sorrow that you have forced me to this extremity, Domina. As you see, you would have been better off becoming my ally, not my enemy."

Aditi looked at the swordsman on her right and rolled her eyes as if in fear of the blade he aimed at her neck.

The soldier smiled and poked the sword closer. In Portuguese, he said, "She seems frightened enough now, Padre. I wager you'll get all you want from her."

The priest gazed back at Aditi with what appeared to be cool calculation. "No. Anything she said to us now would be lies, told to avoid torment. She must experience the pain before we can be convinced she is telling the truth."

"But what if the Sultan finds out, Padre?"

"What of it? We will simply say she tried to murder one of us. She drew a knife on us, did she not? The Sultan is eager to have us gone. I do not think he will force a trial over the harm done to a dancing girl who is a pagan zealot and a spy."

The priest stepped closer and stared into Aditi's eyes. "Perhaps, Domina, you believe when Magister Chinnery arrives, he will in some way rescue you. I would put that thought from your mind. His arms are not near their full strength, and can easily be disabled again. And if you will tell me nothing, perhaps the sight of you in danger will loosen his tongue, and he will be forthcoming where you are not. I have found his secrecy tiresome and I am glad that I at last have a lever with which to pry his lips free."

Aditi calmed herself to gather her strength. *So. Here is my punishment at last for what Krodha called my hubris. If I do not succumb to their torments, I will be used to make Tamas tell all he knows. While I do not think that is much, I will not allow these western pigs to shame me, or Tamas, or to take pleasure in our agony. Perhaps this is the Mahadevi's final test of my courage. Well. I shall no longer blunder from mistake to mistake. The time has come for sacrifice. Tamas, may you find your true dharma. Great Mother, forgive me and, if I am worthy, admit me to your Paradise.*

Aditi slumped as if in despair. She felt the men holding her relax ever so slightly. It was all she needed. She bit the hand over her mouth hard. As the soldier yelled and snatched his hand away, Aditi lurched as hard as she could sideways, thrusting her neck onto the swordsman's blade.

In surprise, the swordsman jerked the weapon back, which only made the wound deeper. Blood flowed freely down her neck and chest. It hurt, but not as badly as Aditi had expected. She managed, as she staggered forward, to tilt her head the other way, so as to open the wound further. For one brief moment, she caught the priest's horrified gaze and rewarded him with a cold smile. Then nausea and darkness overcame her and she fell to the floor.

Pramlocha walked faster and faster away from the western-ers' quarters, wringing her hands. *What will I do? I am certain it was Sri Aditi who screamed. But who should I tell? And how can I tell it without revealing that I was not with her? I should never have let her leave her rooms. I should not have let her trick me. But did she not merely get what she deserved? No, that is not just. Ah—*

She spotted the blind musician, Gandharva, further down the corridor. Pramlocha had flirted with him at music festivals, and he always seemed friendly and knowledgeable. She ran to him. "Good morning, good Gandharva. It is I, Pram-locha, whom you have spoken with before."

It seemed that the sound of her voice smoothed the frown that had creased his brow and he smiled. "Ah, the honey-scented one. I remember you. But your voice trembles. Is something the matter?"

How perceptive he is! "Indeed, Sri Gandharva, I fear there is trouble. Do you know of a woman named Aditi?"

His frown returned. "I do, my dear. In fact, I have come in search of her. Do you know where she might be found?"

"I . . . In my foolishness, I let her go to visit the Goans, and did not accompany her into their quarters. I have heard a scream and I fear she has come to harm."

The blind man sucked in his breath and his hands tightened on the *vina* slung over his shoulder. "Take me there."

Pramlocha took his arm and began to guide him. "I feel so foolish. I did not know whom to tell—"

"Because you fear punishment? Do not concern yourself, child. I will not bring blame upon you. Did Aditi send you away herself?"

Pramlocha nodded. "She told me how horrible the Goans were. But she said she knew their ways."

"So you see, she was only looking after your safety. There is no blame in this. Can we not go a little faster? I am more resilient than you think."

"Forgive me, I—Gandharva, there are men coming." She gripped his arm tightly. "It sounds like the Goans!"

"I hear them. Do you see them?"

"Not yet. They are approaching from another corridor."

"Is there someplace nearby where we can hide?

Pramlocha looked around and saw a low wall decorated with ornate tiles. "Yes, over here. You must step high, over this wall." She guided his legs, first one, then the other. Out of the corner of her eye, she saw the first Goan enter the corridor. "Duck! Quickly!" she whispered. She pushed down on Gandharva's back and crouched behind him.

"Can you see what they are doing?" asked Gandharva. "Can you watch them without being seen yourself?"

Pramlocha swallowed hard. "I will try." She peered over the top of the wall just as four men carrying a bulging rolled-up rug ran by. She could not understand their nervous mutterings, but she was certain she heard the name Aditi. She felt a tugging at her skirt.

"What are they doing?" Gandharva demanded in a loud whisper.

"Shh." Pramlocha peeked out again and saw the men enter a side-garden where there was a stand of thick, tall bamboo. "They are carrying something rolled up in a rug. Now they are hiding the rug behind some bamboo. They are in a hurry and are afraid of being seen." One Goan looked her way and Pramlocha ducked down again.

Footsteps came closer, and the muttering voices, but they ran past again, without stopping. Pramlocha sighed with relief. She leaned against Gandharva's shoulder and began to cry.

The musician sat up and put his arms around her. "Peace, now, my lovely, do not weep."

"But she is . . . it is my fault!"

"We do not know what has happened, yet. She may not be harmed. It may just be that the Goans are stealing a rug."

"I saw her toes sticking out one end."

"Ah. Well, that is different then."

"What will we do, Gandharva? If she is dead and my part in this is learned, I will be sent home and my parents will beat me for shaming them. Or . . . or I might even be executed!"

"Not necessarily, my sweet. Go to where Sri Aditi was lodged and wait there for news from me. If anyone asks, tell them I led Aditi away from you, and that you do not know where she is. Let any blame fall on my shoulders, for I am close to the Sultan and he will listen to me."

"You are so very kind, Gandharva. But what will you do? What of Sri Aditi?"

"It is better you do not know, my sweet. But suffice to say that if Sri Aditi is dead, there will be justice. The Mahadevi will not look kindly upon the one who has killed her daughter."

XVIII

TOPAZ: This stone is oft of a golden color, or a smoke brown. Worn in an amulet about the neck, it will bring reason amidst lunacie, show the presence of poison, and break enchantments. It is in the provenance of St. Matthew and is a stone of righteousness. Among the Hindoo, topaz is said to be cold and sour, yet bestows youth and forfends thirst. If worn upon the left hand, the topaz will banish sorrow, allow one to evade evil, and enhance courage and wit....

Thomas followed the Sultan as they wandered through the corridors of the *Gagan Mahal,* wishing he could escape the potentate's expansive hospitality. The Sultan was proudly pointing out his treasures; a room of enormous, colorful rugs woven from the finest wool; another room whose walls were covered with tiny paintings—portraits of Ibrahim and other nobles of his family; a chamber displaying only musical instruments, drums, flutes, and stringed monstrosities. There was a room full of great urns of Chinese porcelain— each large enough to hold a man; another room filled with folding screens that showed scenes carved in jade and chalcedony, enhanced with gold and silver foil. Many rooms had walls of delicate wood and inlaid stone latticework, parts of which (at the touch of a certain stone) would slide aside to allow passage to another chamber. One room was entirely faced with tile on which had been painted arabesques so intricate that it made the head spin to gaze upon its walls and ceiling.

It was a dazzling fairyland labyrinth, whose walls and doors might be both visible and invisible. As though some proper cantation, some gesture, a few steps in any direction might lead to another world entire. *If only I knew the key of what led to where. But is't not what every man desires, to know beforetimes which step leads to present joy or future regret?*

"A shame you cannot accept the employment with His Majesty," said Joaquim in his ear. "You could live in all this splendor. Think of the dancing girls you could have had, eh? But, then, my brother *soldados* and I would have had to kill you out of envy."

"How terrible that would have been of me," said Thomas, "to bring you to commit a deadly sin."

Timóteo stared at them, alarmed.

"It is only the joke, little brother," protested Joaquim.

Thomas wondered if the Sultan knew he had been lying in his translation of the Greek on the palm leaf. Pride, or fear of embarrassment, had stayed his tongue from the truth. *Another sin. Methinks I shall be guilty of the lot ere this voyage be done.* What he had, in fact, read was:

"To She who is Strength, your daughter begs your aid, to know your will, whom to assist and whom to destroy of those who seek you. Give sign, for love has made her as blind as I."

Aditi has somewhat to do with this message, 'tis clear. It must be that I am the love who has blinded her to her duty. Thomas was of two minds about this revelation. At first his heart had swelled with joy to know she loved him. And yet, he was concerned, for he had no idea what he might do with her. *Through her love, she may bring me a great gift, lead me to the source of the resurrection powder, or Philosopher's Stone or whatever it may be. And this may someday bring me wealth and fame. But what then? Do I take her home to England? She would be as out of place there as I am here.*

Throughout the tour, the Sultan was asking gently probing questions of Thomas's family, his country, the reasons he had come to Bijapur. Thomas answered that his home was a small, simple island which had nowhere near the wealth and beauty he had seen in Bijapur, and that he had come only for trade. The Sultan did not seem fully satisfied with his answers.

Perchance he thinks me a spy and fears invasion. Yet I know not how to put his fears to rest.

Eventually, the Sultan asked a question that made Timóteo frown as he translated. "His Majesty wishes to know how you are associated with a Domina Aditi. That is the dancing woman you talked to last night, yes?"

Ah. "Tell His Majesty that she traveled with us from Goa as part of our caravan-master's cohort, and I spoke with her only a few times." *And that much is truth.*

"She did?" said Timóteo. "I never saw her there."

"Er, because she closely attended the Lady Agnihotra and was in the palanquin much of the time."

Joaquim looked askance and raised a brow, but said nothing as Timóteo translated.

"His Majesty asks if the lady liked Goa."

A puzzling question. "I think she did not, and that is why she was leaving it. It can be a dangerous place for foreigners."

The Sultan nodded, stroking his beard.

A boy in bright blue jacket and turban ran up and bowed deeply to all of them. He spoke rapidly to the Sultan, pointing toward the central atrium. Ibrahim's eyes widened and he clapped his hands like a child presented with a delightful new toy.

"His Majesty asks us to excuse him, but some musicians have arrived from Bengal and he says he must hear them at once. He says if we follow this corridor straight, then turn right, we will return to our quarters."

Joaquim and Thomas bowed in European fashion to the Sultan as he departed. Thomas sighed as he stood straight again, feeling relieved.

As they proceeded down the arched corridor, Joaquim said, "You have surprised me, Tomás. I had feared you might do something foolish and embarrass us all by taking refuge behind the skirts of the Sultan, but you did not."

"Of course he did not," said Timóteo, a stubborn set to his jaw. "Did he not heal the Padre and help us continue here? He would not let you cowards abandon the quest and return to Goa—"

"Careful, little brother," said Joaquim with a dark smile. "It is a good thing you are a child and a monk, or I would do more than cuff you for your insult. It is not wise to call a *soldado* a coward, especially when it is true. I and my brethren do not stand for such words."

"Besides, Timóteo," said Thomas, placing his hand on the boy's shoulder, "I am unworthy of such fulsome praise. But where are your brethren, Joaquim?" said Thomas, looking ahead. "Usually they are lounging around the garden, but I do not see them."

"No doubt the Padre called them in to lecture, or perhaps they found food somewhere. That is the most wondrous thing about this place, Tomás. They never let us go hungry."

As soon as they entered the main room of their quarters, Thomas sensed something amiss. The *soldados* had piled their gear near the far end of the chamber, and the rug that had been there was missing. A smell of blood hung heavily in the air. Two *soldados* were busily scrubbing the floor with their shirts and one of them was wrapping a red-stained bandage on his arm. Padre Gonsção was wandering among them with a dazed expression.

"Padre, what has happened?" said Thomas.

"Ehm? Ah. Carlos here was cleaning his sword and he accidentally cut himself. It bled terribly, but does not seem to be a dangerous wound."

Thomas walked toward the *soldado*. "Let me look at it. Perhaps I or Timóteo can be of help."

"No!" Padre Gonsção stepped into Thomas's way. "We have cleaned and wrapped it and I am praying for his recovery. No more can be reasonably done. I will not allow you to apply your poisonous salves and harm him further."

"But Padre . . ." said Timóteo.

"I have said no and my mind will not change."

"As you wish," said Thomas, frowning. *Aught is not right.* He stepped back, past the men scrubbing the floor. They cast him only furtive glances. *Such a great amount of blood—if all that came from the benighted Carlos, he should not be standing upright.* Thomas backed into the *soldados'* pile of gear, nearly tripping over it. As he caught his balance, he noted a glimmer of silver and green beside a discarded helmet.

He reached down and picked up a bracelet in the shape of a serpent biting its tail. Thomas's stomach went cold. "Has the Domina Aditi been here? This is hers, I am certain of it."

The Padre abruptly turned away. "Some dancing girl was here, looking for you. I suppose it may have been the one you called Aditi. But she has departed. She would not speak to me and left no message."

"Indeed?" said Thomas, staring at the Padre. "How long ago did she depart?"

"Not long. I do not know. Forgive me, I have been distracted by other matters."

Fearing the worst, Thomas persisted, "In which direction did she depart?"

"I do not remember. I did not notice. Don't you have better things to think about than dalliance with a dancing girl, Magister?"

"At this moment," Thomas said softly, "I think not. I think what she may have to tell me is very important." Thomas turned and walked swiftly out the door.

He heard the clatter of boots on stone behind him and glanced back. The four *soldados* followed, trying to catch up to him. *Aha. They do not want me to find her. Or learn what they have done to her. Well. Perhaps I may put His Majesty's tour to good use.*

Thomas hastened his step until he came to a side corridor. He turned there and took off at a dead run. He heard shouts behind him. "*Alto! Pare!*" It was like so many of his dreams of being pursued, although this time it was not frenzied women but desperate men. *Have my dreams all aimed at this moment? 'Tis passing strange, if so.*

As he turned another colonnaded corridor, he encountered a group of serving women in vermillion saris, none of whom were Aditi. He ran around them and continued on, hearing their shrieks as the *soldados* ran into them and pushed them aside.

Thomas took another turn and saw he was at the room with the painted screens. He slipped in among them, stepping as silently as possible. At first, the *soldados* ran past. But as he got to the other end of the chamber, he heard them enter.

He waited until they were up to the first row of screens. Thomas gave a mighty shove to the screen right beside him, and they fell, with a loud clack, clack, clack, one row upon another until the first ones struck the *soldados*. As the Goans cursed and shouted, Thomas turned to the latticed wall behind him. To his good fortune, it was one of those with a sliding panel, and after some moments he found the triggering stone.

He slid the panel and slipped through as the *soldados* began to clamber over the fallen screens. Thomas shut the panel firmly and ran off again, though not as urgently as before.

Taking one turn after another, he still could not be certain he had shaken his pursuers. He found the chamber with the Chinese porcelain urns and saw his chance. Choosing one toward the center of the room, he lifted the lid and stepped into it. He crouched down, setting the lid back in place behind him.

It was not comfortable, crouching in the near-dark, holding still as a statue so as not to tip the urn over. But Thomas forced himself to be patient. *I have endured the strappado of the Santa Casa. Surely I can endure this.*

He heard argument nearby—the *soldados* had come this way after all. But there were other voices, speaking the native languages, shouting over the Portuguese. Soon the voices diminished, departing. *Ah. Mayhap the Sultan's servants have discovered the damage in the screen room and now drive the* soldados *back to our quarters. Praise God, may it be so.*

Thomas waited a few long, silent minutes more before he lifted the lid and peered out. He was alone in the room. He stepped carefully out of the urn, replaced the lid, and returned back into the corridor. It was empty, save for two people just entering the corridor from the north: a young girl in a green skirt and shawl who was leading a blind man by the elbow.

The musician . . . I have seen him. He played yesternight as Aditi danced. He sat beside the Sultan this morning. ". . . love has made as blind as I. . . ." Thomas remembered the palm leaf message. *Could it be? Is he Aditi's confederate?*

"Wait!" Thomas shouted after them in Greek. "Stop, please!"

The blind man stopped and turned part way. The girl looked back at Thomas and whispered a question to the musician. The blind man patted her hand and spoke. The girl reluctantly left his side and continued down the corridor by herself.

"Thank you. I must speak with you," Thomas said, breathless, as he ran up to the blind musician.

The musician tilted his head. "Who is it who speaks the ancient Hellenica?"

"I am Thomas Chinnery, of England. I arrived with the Goans."

"Ah. Tamaschinri. Of the yellow-hair. You spoke with Despos Ibrahim this morning. An honor to meet you." He bowed. "I am called Gandharva, and I am a travelling musician and storyteller by trade."

"Yes, I remember. You sat beside the Sultan. Have you, by chance, seen Aditi—the blue-eyed woman who danced as you played at our quarters last night?"

Gandharva smiled. "It has been many years since I have seen anyone, my young friend."

"No, no, your pardon. I meant only—"

"Do I have news of her? Yes. You know," he stepped closer, "she had spoken to me of you. She once told me that she felt your lives were joined, somehow. I am beginning to believe she was right."

Wherefore does he prattle so? "Please, tell me where she is, and if I might speak with her. I fear my travelling companions may have done her harm."

Gandharva nodded once. "Harm indeed. Possibly very great harm."

Thomas balled his fists. "Then, please, can you tell me where to find her? Has she been taken to a healer? I have knowledge of healing herbs—perhaps I can help her."

The musician stepped even nearer, such that Thomas could smell his anise-scented breath. "It will take a very great effort to help her, Tamaschinri. But perhaps you are the one to do it. Perhaps the Mahadevi has intended it so."

Aye, he is a believer in the goddess too. He must be the one who sent the note the Sultan showed me. Remembering the phrase used by Aditi and De Cartago, Thomas said, "Her name is strength."

The musician nodded. "So it is. Aditi once told me she hoped you would find the path to the Mahadevi."

"Please. Where is she?"

"You will find her in a side garden that has a tall, thick stand of bamboo. I have just come from there. Some of your Goans left a rug with someone wrapped in it hidden within the bamboo. From what they were saying, I have reason to believe it was Aditi in the rug."

"Wrapped in a rug?" His chest filled with a cold ache as if he were impaled with a spear of ice.

"Nai. I fear she no longer lives."

Thomas stepped back, and turned to run. "I will find her."

"Wait!" said Gandharva. "Let me come with you. I must know if it is she as well, and what was done to her."

With Gandharva's help, Thomas had no difficulty finding the side garden with the tall stand of bamboo. Checking to see that no one watched, he pressed in among the thick, reedy trunks, Gandharva close behind him. Some of the bamboo twigs had been broken or bent, showing where others had gone before. The rug was in the middle of the thicket, with some dirt thrown hastily over it. "Here it is."

"Is it she?" Gandharva said as he crouched down to hide himself.

Thomas pulled away the top of the rug far enough to see her sightless blue eyes and the bloody gouge in her neck. He sighed. "Nai. It is she." *Alas, Aditi. You led us to Bijapur for my sake. How poorly I have repaid you for your aid. I had no wish to lead you to your doom.*

Gandharva sighed as well and his head drooped to his knees.

Thomas reached in and gently shut her eyelids. "Do you know, Gandharva, who may have done this?"

"No. The men I overheard did not reveal it."

"Why did you not call out an alarum, or report it to the Sultan's guard?"

Gandharva rubbed his face. "To protect another who is blameless. Court life is full of peril, my friend, and the sword of justice can cut down the innocent as well as the guilty."

"So I have heard. But I think I know who the guilty one is." *The Padre. How he glared at her when he heard Aditi's name. The Santa Casa must have its vengeance, even at this remove. And I have some blame in it, for pointing her out in my drunkenness. What horrible mischance, to have raised the Padre with the resurrection powder only for him to destroy the one leading us toward it.*

A ray of hope struck Thomas suddenly. "You are a follower of the Mahadevi, Gandharva. Is it possible . . . do you know of the powder called—"

"The blood of the goddess? Had I any, I would have used it upon her as soon as I could. It is by sad circumstance that I do not."

"Ah. Wait! The Sufi Masum has some. I gave the last of it to him when I met him in the serai."

"The last of it? How much was there?"

"Only enough to coat the inside of a small pouch."

Gandharva shook his head. "That is enough to poison, but not to resurrect. You need this much," he indicated the first joint of his index finger, "to return a man his life."

"Alas. I gave more than that to the Padre. Had I known, I would not have wasted so much. But do you know of any other person who might have some?"

"Only the ultimate source, Herself."

Thomas stared at the blind musician. "You know the source of the *rasa mahadevi?*"

"Indeed, Tamaschinri. But it is some distance, and I am poorly equipped to go there by myself."

Thomas grasped Gandharva's shoulders, ignoring the pain this brought to his own. "Perhaps I can help you! Is it possible that we might carry her body there and revive her?"

"Yes and no, my friend. The hidden city of the Mahadevi is some days travel. By that time, Aditi will be in very poor condition. She would suffer greatly, and perhaps would not be whole, if revived then. She would not thank you for returning her to such a life."

"Is there no closer source? No other way to revive her?"

"No, but . . ." the musician tilted his head as if hearing a distant sound. Then he smiled. "Perhaps the source may be brought closer to us."

"I do not understand." Thomas felt his head begin to spin. *Dear God, may I not be dealing with a madman or a scoundrel. But if he truly knows the source—* "The joined caravans of the Goans and the Mughuls are to depart soon. Can a supply of the powder be delivered before then?"

"No. It will take a few days. Aditi must somehow travel with your caravan. The one carrying the *rasa mahadevi* must meet us halfway."

"Yes," said Thomas, "that is a good plan. But how can we smuggle her body along?"

"You must request a wagon of entertainers to accompany your expedition. It is not unusual here, and the Sultan would honor it."

"But the Padre would never make such a request. And I have no wish to speak to him or for him."

"You suspect it is this priest of the Orlem Gor who has killed Aditi?"

"I do."

"That is worth knowing. But if he will not request it, then the Mirza must. I can tell you where the Mughuls are lodged. Your fellow traveler Lakart is there with them, I understand."

"Good, then he might translate for me. Gandharva, if you can help me with this, I will be forever in your debt."

Gandharva nodded. "Do not speak of debt just yet, Sri

Tamaschinri. After all, you will be helping Aditi find justice, and me to go home."

How very annoying this is, thought the Mirza Akbarshah as he faced the westerner Lakart over his fifth cup of clove tea. *We talk around and around each other, neither of us wishing to divulge too much, yet trying to glean all we can from the other.* The Mirza had never heard of S'qatland, where Lakart claimed to have come from. At least, from somewhere, the man had learned passable Persian. *And at least he is not so temperamental as I have heard Goans can be.*

But the man kept glancing eastward, toward another part of the *Gagan Mahal,* as if his true concerns lay elsewhere.

"His thoughts are like caged leopards," Masum said softly to the Mirza in Urdu. "What would he say if they were freed?"

"Eh?" said Lakart, snapping to attention again. "What is it your man says? I did not quite understand him."

"We have noticed that you seem to be . . . distracted. Masum is simply curious as to what is begging your attention."

"Ah. You are right, Highness," Lakart said with a rueful smile. "I am concerned for the well-being of the young Englishman, Thomas. You see, I have sworn an oath to his father to watch over him, and see that he completes his journey. I have not done well by this oath in the past, and I fear I am letting my duty slip too far again."

The Mirza nodded. "It is not unknown among my people to select a guardian for a beloved child. Is he a first-born son?"

"He is. His father has . . . important plans for him."

"The first son is a family's most valuable treasure. This is a weighty obligation."

The westerner stared at the floor. "It is indeed."

The Mirza paused, trying to gauge the mood of his guest. "You need not fear any harm will come to him from our hands. If he is peaceful and respectful, we will treat him with all courtesy."

Lakart glanced up from beneath black brows. "It is not you or your men whom I fear, Highness."

Ah. There is dissension among the Goans. This may prove very useful. Leaning forward, the Mirza said, "If you feel your charge may be threatened, that he possesses something that may be stolen or misused, I could be persuaded to offer protection. My men can easily fend off five ill-trained Goan soldiers."

The westerner paused himself, seeming to weigh the offer against some unknown factor. "Should that become necessary, Highness, I may accept your offer. As of now, my fears may be but shadows cast by a flickering lamp."

"And so I hope they are. I hope it would not offend you to be aided by those who are not Christian. Assuming that is what you are. Please consider the door of my tent open to you whenever you should need it."

Lakart sat back a little, a veil of reticence falling over his features. "I do not discuss my faith with others. But rest assured, it would not offend me to seek your tent if need be."

Stranger and stranger yet. Might he be a Parsi, and therefore have reason to fear both Christian and Muslim? Or a Jew? I shall remember, but not press this matter for now. There came a knock at the latticed door. A servant bowed at the entrance. "Sri Tamaschinri seeks one called Andru Lakart here."

"Ah!" said Lakart. "There is the very charge I spoke of. If you will please pardon me." He stood and bowed and went over to the door.

"An odd man," murmured the Mirza.

"A djinni rides him," said Masum.

"Truly? Can you tell which descendent of Shaitan it is?"

Masum shook his head. "As I have said, I am no *sheykh.*

But it is not the Goan priest or soldiers he fears. That one fears himself."

Thomas could not keep from turning his head one way, then another, to be sure none of the Padre's men had found him. *It must be they are kept close to our quarters because of the damage they have done. 'Tis to my vantage, if so.*

He sighed with relief as Lockheart emerged from the Mirza's quarters. "Ah, Andrew, you are here!"

"You have found me. What, have you no other nurse-maids with ye? The good Padre becomes lax in his duties."

"I have evaded them," Thomas said softly, "and the Sultan's men now keep them in quarters for having marred His Majesty's possessions."

Lockheart paused and raised a brow. "And are you now one of the Sultan's men?"

Thomas shook his head. "My place is not here, nor is there any useful purpose I might serve him. And now Dame Fortune drives me on with a bloody whip."

"Indeed? Say on. Whose blood bedecks the lash?"

"Aditi. Aditi is dead."

Lockheart sucked in his breath through his teeth. "How was this done?"

"She was slain. I know not by whom, but I fear it was the Padre or one of his men."

"The Padre? After all those vaunted words of how the Santa Casa does not kill? I can scarce credit it, lad."

"I would not have thought it myself—and yet he is a man of strong faith and philosophy, and I am learning that when a man's philosophy o'errides good sense, he may do all manner of evil."

"Or all manner of good, lad. For when man strives to be greater than beast, he may all too well succeed for good and ill. But surely you have more proof than his philosophy to lay blame on the Padre."

"I do. When I returned to our quarters from speaking with the Sultan, the Padre's behavior was most strange, and there was much blood on the floor. The soldiers, as well, did not behave as themselves. I found Aditi's body in a nearby stand of bamboo, her throat cruelly cut."

"Strange indeed, though it proves naught. A pity you have used all my *pulvis mirificus*, or you would be able to learn the truth from the misused lady herself."

"Aye, I had thought on that. But there is another way."

Lockheart paused, staring at him. "Someone in Bijapur has more of the powder? You've found another source?"

"Not here, and none but the ultimate source itself. Even had I accepted the Sultan's employ, I would feel now honor-bound to resign it and continue with our journey."

A slow grin spread across Lockheart's face. "It is Fate, as I have said. The people of this land, Hindu and Muslim alike, put great stock in omens, you know. When the hand of the Divine points the way, woe betide the man who does not follow it. 'Twould seem that hand has us both by the scruff o'the neck and drags us onward. Though it seem unkind, yet I might rejoice at Aditi's demise, sith it hardens your resolve. What's the plan, then? Shall we take her corse, the two of us, and slip away into the night, leaving the murthering Padre and all none the wiser?"

Thomas shook his head. "We'd ne'er escape unseen through the city gates. And the two of us could not fight off a band of armed pursuers. I do not know the land well hereabout, and we might well fall prey to ignorant brigands—"

"Enough, lad. I take your meaning. What, then, are we to do?"

"We must continue on as if nought untoward had occurred. We will pretend no knowledge of Aditi's death and permit the two caravans to continue on together, as the Sultan has intended. Thus we will be protected by the Mirza's army from threats without and within."

"Ah, I see. And then some days hence we will disappear from their company, eh?"

Thomas paused. "We must see what circumstances are and then take what opportunity presents itself." *And I know not if I will make you a part of that plan.*

Lockheart chuckled. "You are chary, lad. I cannot blame you."

"One thing more. I must ask the Mirza to include among the supplies that he requests from the Sultan a cartload of entertainers to accompany the caravan."

"Entertainers, lad?"

"That is how Aditi will be smuggled along with us. 'Tis most important. The Padre would never make such a request and the Sultan will not find it surprising from the Mirza. Would you make the request to the Mirza for me?"

Lockheart stepped back and extended his arm toward the latticed door. "Enter and make his acquaintance yourself, and I will translate, and give all the guidance you need."

XIX

VIOLET: This small herb has toothed or round leaves, and brings forth flowers of purple or yellow in summer. It is also called Heart's-Ease, and is given to those who mourn with a broken heart. It is said the violet droops because it grew beneath the shadow of Christ's Cross. The ancients believed the flowers were once dancing girls whom Venus beat purple out of jealousy. The dried flowers cure fits and ailments of the liver. A poultice made from the leaves soothes swellings and itchings of the skin. The ancients used wreaths of violet to bring peaceful slumber and keep nightmares and anger at bay. It is wise to carry violet leaves when passing graves, for it will protect one from the unquiet dead....

Sultan Ibrahim 'Adilshah sat sourly in *durbar*, watching the late-afternoon sunbeams crawl across the patterned rug. His ministers droned like jungle insects, augmenting the stifling heat that the feathered fans wafted by his servants did nothing to abate. He had long ago ceased to listen.

The door at the far end of the chamber opened and Ibrahim sat up, hoping for some timely interruption. Gandharva entered slowly and bowed.

"That is enough! Leave us." Ibrahim snapped at the droning minister. He then glared at the other nobles present to indicate his order included them as well.

"But Majesty . . . the allocation of buildings for the *khanaqhs*—"

"Can wait another day."

"Is your reputation not tarnished enough, Majesty," growled Alim Hassan, "that you continue to prefer the company of musicians to the proper care of your kingdom? Beware for Allah is the Seer of All—"

"In which case, the All-Knowing understands why I must speak with this man, and in private! He brings vital information I must hear. Begone, all of you, until I summon you again."

Grumbling among themselves, the ministers and *ulama* gathered their robes and stood, casting suspicious scowls at Gandharva as they slowly made their way out a side door.

Ibrahim nodded at the servants too, who were only young boys, and they happily dropped their fans and ran out after the men. *No doubt they enjoyed the* durbar *even less than I.* As the last one shut the door behind him, Ibrahim turned toward Gandharva, who waited patiently at the far end of the hall.

"You may come forward, Gandharva. Mind the pillows; my ministers were not tidy."

"I thank Your Majesty, though you need not be concerned for me." Walking cautiously, Gandharva felt his way through the maze of pillows until he sat at Ibrahim's feet. "You do me honor to dismiss your court to hear my meager request, Majesty."

"Do not fool yourself, Gandharva. I was pleased for any excuse to end court." Ibrahim picked up one of the discarded fans and waved it briskly, but the cooling it brought to his face was frustratingly slight.

"Then I am honored to have brought Your Majesty ease."

"Are you? I have hopes that you can do so for, of late, you have not."

"Please tell me how I may have offended Your Majesty."

"You have not brought Aditi to speak with me, as I requested."

"Ah, but that is why I have come, Majesty. I have searched the palace and only just learned that she has departed."

"Departed? Where has she gone?"

"As to that, I cannot say, Majesty."

Ibrahim restrained himself from swatting the musician with his fan out of exasperation. "Who told you she had left?"

"One of the palace servants. It was confirmed by the westerner Tamaschinri."

"Aha. So she is aiding the Goans?"

"Majesty, I can tell you in all honesty that, at this time, she is aiding no one. In fact, now that she has left, I will tell you that she had no plans that were not in keeping with your own. During the brief time I spoke with her last night, she seemed . . . confused. The Mahadevi had sent her no message, no sign as to what she should do regarding the newcomers."

Perhaps because the prayer in Greek never reached the Mahadevi?

Gandharva went on. "There was only one of our visitors whom she was taking careful regard of."

"The yellow-hair."

"Yes."

"Do you know why? What is the value of that strange young man? The Goans were chasing him around the palace earlier today, and damaged eleven of my Chinese screens in the process. I hope the gems and silver on that bible they gave me will make up the cost."

"The loss of your treasures is most unfortunate, Majesty. But I believe the only value Tamaschinri had to Aditi was that bestowed by Kṛṣṇa Himself."

"She loves him?" Ibrahim blew air out his lips. "I hardly think so. There is not room in a zealot's heart for love of any but the Divine."

"Sometimes, Majesty, the desires of the human soul overpower the will of the Divine."

"Hm. If true, this alters my view of her. I am now thinking that perhaps I should retain the yellow-hair on some pretense, to prevent him from going on that expedition. Keeping him near might give me something with which to tip the scales if I must bargain with her."

"No, Majesty! Keeping him here would not be wise."

"Oh? Why say you this?"

"The Goans will not leave without him. They suspect he has vital knowledge that will lead them to their goal. And if the Mirza and his men catch wind that you are hampering their quest . . ."

"Yes, yes, it will not go well with the Padshah Emperor. But what, then, should I do with him?"

"My advice, Majesty, is to do nothing different than you have already planned. Do not doubt your own wisdom."

"But if the yellow-hair leads either party to the hidden city, might not this incur the Mahadevi's wrath?"

Gandharva shook his head. "He does not, in truth, have the knowledge they believe he does. He cannot lead them to the Mahadevi. And the Mughuls and the Goans cannot cooperate for very long. Trust your vision, Majesty. Better to have their expeditions depart to destroy themselves out in the wilderness than to endanger Bijapur by keeping them near."

"Hm. You speak persuasively, Gandharva, as always." *I only wish I knew what game you are playing, and what my part in it is.*

"There is one thing more, Majesty. The Mughuls will be requesting that you supply them with a cart of entertainers."

"Dancers and the like? That is no surprise. My general did report that the Mirza's men were fit but suffered from a lack of diversion."

"Just so. Fill his request, Majesty. And among the entertainers . . . send me."

"You? Why?"

"To be your ears, Majesty, and to ensure all goes as you would wish."

"But you yourself are aware of your . . . limitations."

"People often discount the crippled, thinking them too weak or too trustworthy, or nonexistent. This can be an advantage."

"Hmpf." Ibrahim stood and went to the nearest window, hoping for a stray breeze. "At times I wonder, Gandharva, whom is it you truly serve. The Mahadevi or me?"

"There is no conflict in serving you both, Majesty. Your goals are one."

"Are they?"

"Think on it, Majesty. For what reason would the Mahadevi wish to weaken your kingdom and bring the scourge of Akbar's might closer to Her doors, or the rapacious hordes of the westerners? She can only want a strong Bijapur to be Her bulwark against the flood of the outer world."

Ibrahim gazed out over the glistening domes, the minarets, the walls, and the tall palms of Bijapur. "I have devoted my life, Gandharva, to making this a place of peace and beauty."

"So you have, and with great success. Bijapur is widely proclaimed the most splendid city in the Deccan. Surely the Mahadevi has no wish for its destruction. If need be, I will speak its praises long and loud in the ear of the Mahadevi Herself. I will be your advocate to Her. I will not give any useful knowledge to the Mirza or the Padre. If anything, I will do what I can to lead them astray. Send me."

Ibrahim turned. *There is a mystery here that I have no knowledge of. Am I safer with you near, or far from my court?* "I have often thought that there is more truth in the singing of the *vina*'s strings than in the words of a thousand wise men. And your playing is like none other I have ever heard. I will miss you, Gandharva."

The blind man smiled and bowed. "May I prove myself worthy of your wisdom, Majesty."

Timóteo sat in a corner, fidgeting. *It is unfair. Something terrible has happened, I know it! But they tell me nothing because they think I am just a child.*

Padre Gonsção had told the four *soldados* to chase after Tomás, but then had knelt huddled before his crucifix in prayer and would not respond to Timóteo's questions. The Padre's face did not hold the serene quality of one communing with God; rather it was strained and frowning, as if uncertain that God was listening.

Joaquim professed bafflement when asked about the behavior of his compadres and, for once, Timóteo believed him.

When the other *soldados* returned from the chase, escorted by displeased palace guards and without Tomás, it was worse. Oh, they had always treated Timóteo with affable disdain, or teased him and tried to shock him. But now they avoided him altogether, busied themselves with cleaning their belongings, whispered among themselves, and turned away if Timóteo tried to ask them anything.

It was no consolation that they would not tell Joaquim either. *They act like guilty children. Do they not know that God forgives all if they open their hearts?* It was foolishness. The guards stood outside their door now, to keep them in, and Tomás still had not returned.

How can everyone pretend to me that nothing is wrong? The injured *soldado*, Carlos, still would not even let Timóteo tend to his wound, when there were three perfectly good herbs in the side garden for helping him heal.

Tomás thinks the lady called Aditi has been hurt. Maybe she cut Carlos for some reason, and the others won't talk about it because it injures their pride. Everyone wants to keep me innocent of the knowledge of sin. But if I am to become a priest someday, mustn't I understand sin too? Madre Maria, help me. I feel so alone.

The far doors opened and the guards escorted Tomás and Brother Andrew through, shutting the doors behind them.

"Padre!" Timóteo cried as he leapt up. "Tomás has returned!"

But the Padre only looked up and stared at Tomás, and did not greet him.

Timóteo ran to the *inglês* and almost embraced him. "Tomás, I am glad you came back. Is everything all right?"

The *inglês* responded with an awkward smile, but there was pain in his eyes. "All is as well as can be, little brother."

Brother Andrew put his hand on Tomás's shoulder. "He was merely lost, but now he is found."

"So," said Joaquim, "the rabbit returns to the den of foxes, and in the company of a wolf."

"Did you find your dancing lady?" asked Timóteo.

All the room seemed to turn silent, waiting.

Tomás looked down. "No. Apparently she has departed."

All in the room seemed to breathe again. Timóteo shook Tomás's sleeve. "Do not be sad, Tomás. Perhaps you will see her again someday, yes?"

The *inglês* smiled a little. "Yes, Timóteo. Perhaps I will."

Brother Andrew went to the Padre and began to tell him what he had learned from the Mirza. Timóteo walked at Tomás's side as he went to his bedroll, hoping that the *inglês* might confide in him. "Tomás, something strange and terrible has happened, but no one will tell me what it is."

"Did they tell you about the damage to the Sultan's Chinese screens?"

"Yes, I translated when the Sultan's guards talked to the Padre. But there is something else, no?"

Tomás sighed and sat down, leaning against the wall. He paused before saying, "We are all . . . unsettled because of the necessity of joining our expedition to the Mirza's. When

I saw the soldiers chasing me, I decided to have sport with them and ran to elude them. But I tired of the chase and became lost in the palace until Brother Andrew found me and guided me back."

He lies, Timóteo thought coldly. *Even he lies to me, who I thought was my friend. After I have shared so much of what I know with him. After I saved his soul in the Santa Casa.* "What about the blood, Tomás? What about Carlos's wound?"

"What does the Padre say about them?"

"He will not tell me!"

Tomás looked away. "Little brother, do not concern yourself with these things. Soon we will be gone from this nightmare, and we will have new dangers to face. Return to your prayers, if you would be helpful. That is probably the best thing you can do for us all."

Timóteo felt anger welling up in him. For the first time in a long while, he wanted to smash something. *Even you. You hide the truth from me. So. I can keep secrets too, Tomás. Secrets I would have shared with you. Just wait, Tomás. Wait until we find this goddess monster we are seeking and she turns her hideous gaze upon you and you turn to stone. I have read the records in the Santa Casa, and I know. The Padre does not believe me. He thinks I have listened too much to the old tales my grandfather told me. Maybe one of the muçulmanos will listen. But I will be spared because I have a mirror and I will not see the snakes on the monster's head. And I will speak to her and tell her of the glory of God while the rest of you have crumbled to dust at her feet. And her soul will be saved while the rest of you are screaming in the fiery pits of Hell!*

Thomas watched Timóteo stomp away with a twinge of sorrow. *Forgive me, little brother, but it is best you not know. Stay innocent while you can.* He found his bedroll and lay down upon it, feeling the afternoon heat sap the strength from his bones. Too little sleep the night before and too much excitement in the day took its toll, and Thomas drifted off in slumber.

And found himself standing in a field filled with foul-smelling vapors and Thomas could not see but a few yards around him. Fumaroles belched nearby, but all the rest of the visible landscape was lifeless dirt and stones. The air was heavy and seemed to cling to his skin. Sweat dripped from his brow.

Is this my nightmare come again? he wondered, and he waited to hear the cries of the huntresses. All was silent, but for a distant burble and hiss.

Something moved within the steam and smoke. A female figure, clothed in pale mist, strolled past, just barely visible.

"Aditi?" Much as he had followed her through the jungle outside Goa, Thomas followed the figure through the acrid steam, taking the path she chose.

Suddenly she vanished and the fog cleared before him, revealing a cave entrance in a cliff. With the certainty one has in dreams, Thomas knew he must enter, and he did so.

He found himself in a large, rocky chamber. A fissure ran along one side, from which more vapors arose, but these had the scent of incense and burning leaves. In the center of the cavern, the woman sat on a chair of ancient design. Thomas could not see her face clearly—sometimes the mists around her seemed like angels' wings, sometimes they coiled about her body like serpents, sometimes they formed a dark, concealing hood and cloak.

"I have a message for you," the woman said.

"I am listening," dream-Thomas said.

The woman extended her arm and a brazier appeared before her.

Flames shot up from its bronze bowl, for a moment engulfing her hand. Then they subsided, and she was holding a piece of glowing parchment. She gazed on it and read, "Beware, son of light and darkness. You have not escaped your fate. Your life is pledged to another, and it will be taken. Treasure life. Prepare for death."

The figure faded and the cavern became utterly dark. In the air above him he could hear the fluttering of bat wings. Their high-pitched cries slowly became words. "Murderer! Murderer! You cannot escape! Murderer!"

A claw dug into his shoulder and he felt hot breath on his face. He cried out and, with great shudder, Thomas shook himself awake.

Lockheart was looking down at him, his hand on Thomas's shoulder. "Your pardon, lad, but the Sultan's guards have come. We are no longer welcome guests and we are to be lodged in the caravanserai again this night. He has sped up the pace and our expedition leaves on the morrow. Gather your things."

"So," said Jaimal, "when do we kill them?"

"My Lord!" protested Masum.

"Peace, the two of you," said the Mirza Ali Akbarshah. "They may have knowledge we have need of, and therefore it is in our interests to treat the Goans well. If they cause us trouble, or appear to be trying to interfere with our expedition, then we will see."

"Is not the request for a wagon of entertainers proof that they are trying to interfere?" said Jaimal. "Or at least wish to embarrass us?"

"But," said Masum, "if the immortal queen we seek does treasure music and dance, as Tamas told us, then we would be endangering our mission if we cannot offer such a gift to her."

"Oh, so you believe the westerner's lies?" said Jaimal.

"It is easy to believe," said Masum, "that a woman of great age and learning would value beauty in the arts."

"How fortunate for us, then, to have a poet such as you with us."

"Enough!" said the Mirza. "I accept that the westerners seem strange to us, but we will have much time in which to observe whether they intend good or ill."

"But why did the yellow-haired one request that we allow the monk boy to ride in your *howdah?*" said Jaimal. "Is that not presumptuous?"

"No, no," said Masum, "as I have said, the boy was fascinated by the elephant when we were in the serai. I saw him watching it and petting it. Tamas is doing the boy a kindness."

"Beware, my lord Mirza, that this boy monk does not annoy you by trying to convert you."

"If he does," said the Mirza, "then Masum may do his best to convert the boy to the Faith. It may provide interesting diversion for the long journey. But have you considered it another way, that the boy has been offered to us as a hostage?"

Jaimal frowned. "Why would they willingly do such a thing?"

"I can think of several reasons. The man Lakart knows something of our ways and may have done so as a sign of trust and good faith. But we have also observed that there is disagreement among the westerners, and Lakart and Tamas may be hoping to ensure the Goans' cooperation with us. But, enough. Someone approaches."

A knock came at the door, and then a gaudily dressed serving boy in a striped *jama* and plumed turban entered and bowed solemnly.

"What is it?" said the Mirza.

"Most noble lords," intoned the boy, "the Sultan has decided that your quest is of such importance that he will delay you no further. You are to leave the palace and return to where your forces are encamped tonight and depart upon your journey tomorrow morning."

"Tomorrow!" said Jaimal.

The Mirza held up his hand to silence his lieutenant. "Continue," he said to the servant.

The boy blinked a moment, then added, "All provisions as can be gathered by that time will be put at your disposal. The wagon of entertainers will be provided as you requested."

"Very interesting," said the Mirza, "as I have not yet requested it."

The boy blinked again. "Uh, the Sultan is wise and prescient in all things and has foreseen your request."

"Or someone else has made it for us," muttered Jaimal.

The Mirza ignored this. "Very well. Tell His Majesty that we are grateful for his generosity, and that whatever provisions he can provide will be welcome. The Shahinshah Akbar shall be made aware of the Adilshah's great hospitality."

The boy bowed again, the plumes on his turban sweeping the floor. "I shall tell him, my Lords. Guides will be sent to you shortly to escort you."

"You have our thanks." The Mirza tossed a silver coin to the boy. The servant caught it and, with a huge grin, bowed once more and ran out the door.

"Was that wise?" said Jaimal.

"Kindness," said Masum, "can be the key to more locks than suspicion and hard-heartedness."

"Kindness," said Jaimal, "can be a symptom of empty-headedness. I almost think, O *murid* of the flapping tongue, that you are looking forward to our journey with the westerners."

"I am," said Masum with a smile. "For love of the Divine can only grow as one learns more of its creations."

"Even if those creations deny the True Faith?"

"Even those, for truth shines all the greater amidst error, and only amidst darkness can one approach the light."

"Even if that light is but a candle flame and the queen we seek only a witch of folk tale?"

"To seek the Wise Queen, *Bilqis*, is to seek the beauteous light, the Eternal Sophia. This quest can never be foolish, for it is only by seeking her that one may someday contemplate the Face of God."

"I regret," said the Mirza, "that I must interrupt your philosophic argument, but we have work to do. It would be best to reach the camp before the evening prayer." In truth, however, the Mirza cut short the discussion because it disturbed him. *What if the purpose of our journey is spiritual, not material? Will I be capable of recognizing it, of accepting revelation when it comes? Will I be worthy? I think I would prefer our goal turn out to be a long-lived, wealthy crone living in a cave, then to find spiritual treasure that I cannot possibly grasp.*

Thomas could not sleep in the room in the serai. He did not wish to return to disquieting dreams with baleful oracles. As quiet as he could, so as not to disturb Timóteo or Padre Gonsção, he got up from his bedroll and went out the door.

He wandered along the upper-story balcony with vague thoughts of finding a suitable place to piss. Then he saw, at the top of the squat watchtower at the southwest corner of the serai, a man standing with arms upstretched toward the crescent moon. It seemed as though he would catch the silver arc within his arms as it descended.

At first, Thomas thought it might be a Mohammedan prayer-caller, but no. The man was chanting too softly, and in a language that was not Arabic, but sounded more . . . Greek.

It is Andrew! What can he be doing at this hour? Glad he had not put on shoes, Thomas padded to the tower arch and silently ascended the ladder. *Where are the guardsmen who should be here? Why is all so still?*

At the top, Thomas crept off the ladder. Whatever prayers Lockheart was uttering, they were silent now. The moonlight glinted off of two cups sitting on a white cloth on the top of the crenellated wall. Between the cups lay an oak leaf. *One cup contains wine, the other grains of wheat. How do I know this?*

Memories assailed him: of lying on a white table as a boy, flanked by two such cups; of wandering through a forest surrounded by women dressed in bedsheets accompanied by lean hounds who whined and licked his hands. His father had worn a robe of a dark red, and a tall hat, and had carried a dagger.

Thomas took another step forward and a board creaked. Lockheart whirled, arms cocked ready to deal a blow.

"Andrew?"

The Scotsman sighed and lowered his fists. "By Jove, Tom, you affrighted me. You should not have crept up so."

"You follow the rites of my father's house, I see."

Lockheart nodded once. "Now do you believe your sire sent me?"

"I do. But these rites have lain buried in my memory for many years and I scarcely know them. What do they mean, Andrew? Will you tell me?"

Lockheart paused and rubbed his bearded chin. "Mayhap. Mayhap 'tis time. There is little harm in't now. Your father and I, and others, follow old ways, lad. Ways long fought by Mother Church. Ways older than Christ and the Devil."

Thomas almost smiled. "Hah. You are pagans."

Lockheart shrugged. "Call it so, if you wish."

"And you worship the moon."

"The moon is but a symbol of the Immortal Huntress, the Healer, Diana or Artemis, who brings life to all plants and creatures upon the earth."

"Ah," Thomas sighed. "No wonder you are fast set upon our quest. You seek no Philosopher's Stone. You believe the Mahadevi is your goddess."

"I know not yet what we will find at the end of our journey, lad. It may be only some mineral, or animal's blood that has the property of giving life to the dead. Though I do confess, I find the prospect tantalizing that we may find, as you put it, my goddess. And yours, lad. For you were pledged to her as a child."

Thomas felt his skin prickle. "I was told in a dream that my life belonged to another. But why did my father never tell me this?"

"It is dangerous in your land to worship as we do, and children are never close keepers of secrets. He wished to keep you safe from harm, until the time was right."

"So it is intended that I must convert once more, from Christian to papist, from papist to pagan?"

" 'Tis not needed, lad. You are Hers and She will have you, no matter whose wine and wafer you taste."

Why does the world not fall askew, or my head spin round? Surely my soul knows not where to turn or to whose paradise it is destined. Or perhaps I had the misfortune to be born amidst madmen and I should credit them not. Thomas walked to the tower wall overlooking the dark courtyard of the serai and leaned against the cold stone. "I know not whom to believe, Andrew. I am not convinced it should be you."

" 'Tis no matter. Give it time. The truth will show itself. Our destinies are co-joined and set upon Olympic stone. You have seen how surely we are guided to our path."

"Mayhap. I shall await your proof, then. You know the Padre intends to destroy whatever we find."

"So he says, lad. But I think he will find his prey greater than any arrows he can loose against it. Methinks 'twill not be destroyed but the destroyer."

"Will it? The Padre has proved himself a capable killer already. I'd not dismiss him yet. Wherefore is it dark? Where are the guards?"

"Bribed to spend an hour or two indoors."

"You had the coin to bribe them?"

"Not I alone. Behold the courtyard below."

In the shadows, by the serai gate, Thomas saw men moving, leading horses. Moonlight glinted off their morion helmets and metal breastplates.

"The Goan soldiers," said Thomas. "Where are they going?"

As the great gate opened wide enough to let them through one man at a time, Lockheart said, "Running for home, lad. Two of their number have died of the fever. The rest think the Padre has gone mad and will have none of his quest. No doubt the tale told of the death of your lady-love only made matters the worse."

Thomas tried to count them, but could not see clearly enough. "Should we wake the Padre?"

"And trouble his blessed sleep when he can do naught to stop them? No, let him wake to the sorry news in the morn when he is better rested. This is to our advantage, Tom. The fewer men to watch us, the freer we shall be."

"But we shall have no protection from the Mughuls."

"Twelve men against five hundred would have been little protection, lad. We are better off with the Mughuls' aid, and we have already begun the bonds of friendship with 'em."

"Then let us hope those bonds do not break."

"I shall see to it, never fear."

But fear you I must, until I know you better, Andrew. I must hope to bring Aditi to the resurrection powder in the company of a mad Inquisitor, a blind Hindu musician, a possibly mad Scots pagan, a boy monk, and an army of five hundred Mohammedans. thought Thomas. *I should hope I am the chosen of a kind and puissant goddess. For I shall need all the divine aid I can compass.*

XX

🍃 ORANGE: This fruit tree has bark of a dun color and thorns
that grown amidst its buds. It bears white flowers of a sweet
fragrance. It may be thought a gift of the east, for knowledge of
it was brought north from the Crusades. The dried skin of the
fruit cures ailments of the stomach and lungs. An infusion from
the flowers makes a fine tonic, yet oil from the pressed petals
brings stupor. In the East, the orange is a symbol of good
fortune to come, and enduring love. Yet witches are said to use
the fruit for vengeance–by declaring it their intended victim's
heart, they stick the fruit with pins and hide it in a dark place to
bring about sickness and death. Stuck with cloves instead of
pins, the fruit brings a pleasant odor to air that might otherwise
be foul....

The rising sun was a vermillion orb, dimly seen through the
morning mist. Padre Antonio Gonsção walked among the
Mughul troops in a daze, feeling as though he had been transported to some fantastical, dangerous land. Graceful horses,
jingling bells on their harness, appeared suddenly beside
him as if the man leading them were a sorcerer, materializ-
ing them out of the vapors. Now and then a great grey behemoth, an elephant, would loom out of the fog above him.
Turbaned men, their footsteps unheard, called to one another in their musical language.

The news that the *soldados* had abandoned him in the
night had brought only a gnats-weight of care. Almost as

though he had expected it. Gonsção found he was rather glad
to be rid of their raucous, arrogant company. *Let them take their
chances back in Goa, with a displeased Sadrinho to answer to. My
way is clear and I shall not swerve from it.*

Familiar voices approached and five riders appeared out
of the mist; Brother Andrew, Magister Chinnery, and to the
Padre's amazement, three *soldados:* Joaquim, Carlos, and
Estevão.

"Hola!" Gonsção called out to them. "What is this? You
have not all deserted me in my madness?"

Joaquim shrugged. "The *sargento* would not have me with
him. And these two will hang if they show their face in Goa:
Carlos for smuggling, Estevão for murder. If you will have
such sinners with you Padre, we are yours."

"If Our Lord could meet his doom in the company of sinners, how can I not? I am glad you have stayed. Have any of
you seen Brother Timóteo?"

They stopped their horses beside him. "We saw him running that way," Brother Andrew pointed behind him. "He
was chasing the elephants, looking very happy."

Gonsção slid his hands into his sleeves, feeling the morning chill. "I pray he does not come to harm. He is still young
and thinks of all this as an adventure."

"What harm do you fear he will find?" said Magister
Chinnery. "Physical or spiritual?"

Gonsção studied the young man's face and was disquieted by what he saw there. *There is accusation behind those eyes.
Does he know what happened to the woman Aditi? Or merely suspect? Why should I be concerned? She did not die at my hands. I
may say so in all honesty.* "Both, Magister, as should we all."

"Elephants are creatures of God," said the young *inglês.*
"What has a boy to fear spiritually from them?"

Gonsção frowned. *How can I explain the contamination of
the spirit by foreign things to this . . . foreigner?* "Hindus worship them."

"That is their error. But there is a great difference between worship and admiration. Timóteo's interest can surely be no worse than, say, admiring a camel for the first time."

Gonsção smiled without humor. "Perhaps you should consider taking up the cloth Brother Andrew has discarded, Magister Chinnery. You are beginning to argue like a Jesuit."

"There it is, Tomás," said Joaquim, pointing toward the edge of the milling Mughul forces.

Gonsção turned and saw in the distance a gaily painted cart pulled by two oxen. "What is that monstrosity?"

"It is the entertainers' wagon," said Brother Andrew. "A gift from the Sultan. Every proper Mughul army has them, I am told. Be at ease, Padre. With pleasing diversion, the Mohammedans might brood less upon our irritating presence."

"You are pragmatic as always, Brother Andrew. But I fear you may again be making a virtue of sin. Why were you seeking this wagon?"

"Perhaps the good Senhor hopes to find his dancer ladylove there, eh?" said Joaquim.

"Hope never dies," said the young *inglês*.

"It would be best if you were to forget her and put your mind to other things," said Gonsção. "Women are creatures of weakness, and to dwell upon them only traps the soul in a deepening mire."

"Ah," said Brother Andrew, "was your mother not such a swamp, then, Padre? For you once dwelt within her, but you seem to have escaped mud-free."

Gonsção scowled as the others laughed. "I would have you remember that we have a journey filled with peril ahead of us. I would be reassured to know you are thinking upon this, instead of frivolity. Look around you at this tide of men, steel, and animals in which we are set adrift. We must take care that we are not swept to our deaths by it."

"But you need not see it so," said Brother Andrew. "It need not be a tide, or a rolling boulder that crushes all in its path. Look upon this vast array as a fluid thing, Padre, like the shifting sands in a desert or water in a basin. It can flow anywhere. Our party may be the gentle breeze that scatters the sand, or the hand that tilts the basin and spills the water. Our very weakness may be our strength. Think upon that, Padre, and thereby banish fear."

The false monk seems in a buoyant mood. Perhaps I should not have sent him to sound out the Mughuls. Who knows what deals he has made. Ah, well. It shall be as God wills. "You speak convincingly, Brother, and I will remember this. However, the Mughul Mirza will be asking me if we know which way this river of men should flow, and I must have some answer for him."

"Tell him south and west," said Magister Chinnery. "That will do for now. We must not tell them too much at the start, nor whom among us bears the knowledge of our path."

And that, so far, is similar to what I gleaned from the sorcerer De Cartago's map. He is not, as yet, attempting to lead us astray. "That is sensible," said Gonsção. "Now, I had best go in search of Timóteo before he wanders too far. Carlos, Estevão, will you accompany me?"

The *soldados* walked their horses over to Gonsção. He nodded once to Brother Andrew and Magister Chinnery before striding off, relieved to be out of the young *inglês*'s company. *I must not lose control of these men, and the expedition. Yet Magister Chinnery now views me with suspicion, and the* soldados *watch me for signs of madness. Dear Lord, guide me. This will be a difficult task.*

Thomas, Lockheart, and Joaquim rode up to the entertainers' cart, to be greeted by the giggles of young women in bright-colored skirts and mantles, sitting on its roof.

"If this is a mire of sin," said Joaquim, "I think I should like to drown here."

Thomas smiled and called out, "Is Gandharva here?"

"They won't understand you, Tomás."

But the girls happily pounded on the sides of the cart, shouting, "Gandharva! Gandharva!"

The doors of the oxcart opened and the musician emerged.

"There he is!" said Thomas. "Gandharva, it is I, Tamas."

The blind man grinned and in musical Latin replied, "Would the young Magister like to hear a song?"

"This Hindu speaks Latin?" said Joaquim.

"He is a man of many talents," said Lockheart.

"Yes. Sing for me a song of my beloved," said Thomas.

"As you wish," said Gandharva, placing one gourd of his *vina* over his shoulder and setting the other in his lap. As he strummed in buzzing, droning chords, he sang in Greek:

> *"Your lady lies in deepest slumber,*
> *swathed in honey, sweet as she,*
> *for so was the hero brave Iskandr,*
> *spared from rot and death's debris.*

> *"So she waits in golden splendor,*
> *In this cart her casket rests,*
> *'til her mother's care will mend her,*
> *And breath fill her honeyed breasts.*

> *"Do not mourn, oh brave young lover,*
> *Nor give your sweet one tearful glance,*
> *Before long you will discover,*
> *She's risen up again to dance."*

"Does the song please the young Magister?" said Gandharva when he finished.

"Indeed, it pleases me greatly. You have done well."

The blind man bowed over his instrument. "It is my pleasure to serve."

Lockheart looked at Thomas with admiration. "It was better planned than I expected."

"What is this nonsense?" said Joaquim. "It must be you play the joke upon me. This man sings in strange language and plays a lute whose strings are too loose. How can you praise him?"

"Perhaps it is as the Padre fears," said Thomas, "and I have come to have a taste for native things."

"May I never acquire such a taste," said Joaquim. "For if I do, it is proof I have gone mad. Then again," he gazed up at the girls on the roof of the carriage, "there are better and worse forms of madness."

"Ermão Andrew! Senhor Chinnery!" Carlos rode up to them and spoke to Lockheart in Portuguese some moments.

"It would seem," said Lockheart, "that Timóteo has gotten himself in some manner of trouble. The Padre requests that you and I come to give assistance."

I wonder if it concerns the Mirza's elephant, thought Thomas. *Timóteo still would not speak with me this morning. I had hoped a chance to ride the behemoth might soothe his anger.*

"Let me come with you," said Joaquim. "I would like to see what trouble the pious little brother has gotten himself into. Surely that will be better entertainment than the wailings of this sightless creature."

They rode to what was becoming the head of the river of men and animals, and found Timóteo standing beside the very elephant and howdah they had seen in the serai. The Mirza stood beside Timóteo, towering over him, his hand on the boy's shoulder.

Padre Gonsção strode over to Lockheart as he dismounted. "I am glad you have come. I am unable to make myself understood to the Mirza, nor he to me. And while Timóteo can speak a little, in this instance I would prefer a more adult translator."

Thomas watched Timóteo, whose mood seemed utterly

changed from before. The boy was wide-eyed, nearly dancing from foot to foot in eagerness.

Lockheart bowed and spoke with the Mirza a moment,
then said, "Why, Padre, it is nothing more than an invitation.
The Mirza is offering to let Timóteo ride with him on his elephant."

"Please, Padre!" said Timóteo. "Oh, please, may I?"

The Padre's expression of concern did not change. "I can
see that. But I have no wish to let the boy be in the control
of the Mughuls. I cannot permit such a thing."

"Padre," said Lockheart sternly, "we must travel in peace
with these men, and that means accepting their hospitality
with grace. It is great honor the Mirza offers him."

"Hospitality! Honor! This man means to keep Timóteo
with him as a hostage!"

Lockheart nodded. "That is in keeping with tradition
among these people. The Mirza has no intention of harming
the boy. It is a way of ensuring peace between our two parties."

"Please, Padre!" Timóteo clasped his hands together,
imploring.

Thomas leaned forward on his horse until he was near the
Padre's ear. "Do I not remember that once there was a boy
who would have done anything to ride a camel? And how sad
the boy felt when he could not? You said yourself this will
be a long and treacherous journey. Why not let Timóteo take
what joy he can and thereby also have smooth relation with
the Mirza?"

The Padre glared at him. "You will harp again upon that
string?"

"If it sounds a note that catches your ear, I will play it loud
and often, Padre."

"Hmpf. How very like a Jesuit. As you will have it, then.
Timóteo may ride on the elephant with the Mirza. But I will
hold you personally responsible, should any harm come to
the boy."

Lockheart smiled and translated the Padre's agreement to the Mirza. The Mughul general smiled in turn and bowed to the Padre.

Timóteo jumped into the air with joy. "Thank you, Padre! Oh, thank you! Glory be to God! You will come ride the elephant too sometime, yes?"

"Perhaps someday, Timóteo, but not now."

Timóteo glanced at Thomas and gave him a reluctant grin.

"Well," Thomas murmured to Lockheart, "I nearly think I am forgiven."

"Cuidado, Timóteo," said the Padre softly.

"Sim, Padre, claro," said Timóteo.

A man seated behind the head of the elephant reached back and let down a rope ladder from the pavilion. He held the ladder steady as Timóteo climbed it, agile as a monkey. Thomas found himself feeling envious. *At least one of us shall find some pleasure on this journey.*

The Mirza spoke again to Lockheart for a minute.

"His Highness," translated Lockheart, "now offers us one of his party to ride with us and share knowledge and fellowship."

"Does he?" growled the Padre. "And which heretic does the Mughul prince choose to be our companion?"

"I will ask him," said Lockheart. He spoke to the Mirza.

The Mirza nodded, some amusement behind his eyes. He called out to the crowd of Mughuls gathered around, "Masum!"

The slightly unkempt Sufi in white tunic and turban emerged from the crowd and came forward.

"Madre Maria, no," breathed the Padre.

Thomas could not help grinning. "It seems I will have another chance to learn the local herblore."

"The Mirza honors us again," said Lockheart. "He offers his Sufi advisor to ride with us. Sufis are highly prized by Muslim noblemen as skillful philosophers and moral guides."

"His Highness honors us too much," grumbled the Padre.

The Sufi turned toward Thomas and spoke to him, bowing.

Thomas bowed back in his saddle. "What says he, Andrew?"

"He has an odd manner of speech, but methinks he says that he is pleased to accompany the Divine Gift. I know not what he means by this."

"Either that I am a gift from the gods or that I am a goat meant for sacrifice, 'twould seem."

Lockheart gave him a sharp glance.

" 'Twas but a jest, Andrew. I meant no offense to your faith."

"Certes. But one should take care how one jests, Tom."

"Do not translate it, then." *How strange his 'haviour turns upon a phrase.*

A white dove flew overhead, its wings bright in the morning sunlight. Some of the Mughuls exclaimed and pointed to it as it flew south and east.

"The Mohammedans are saying the bird is a good omen," said Lockheart as he remounted his horse. "It is a sign of favor from Allah, particularly as it flies in the direction we will travel."

"It is also a sign of the Holy Spirit," said the Padre. "And of peace."

"See," said Thomas, smiling. "Even Heaven approves of our arrangements this morn. Surely that must reassure you, Padre." *Who am I to tell them it is Gandharva's message bird? Fly, most well-favored creature, fly home to the hidden citadel of the Mahadevi. My hopes ride upon thy wings. Speak sweetly to thy goddess, Queen of Life and Death, whose name is Strength. Say Her daughter needs Her, bring forth her powder of life, and thereby bring an end to my unhappy journey.*

AUTHOR'S NOTE

Bijapur in the late sixteenth century was a crossroads of faiths and cultures of central and Northern India. Even though it had yet to be conquered by Emperor Akbar, it was similar in many ways to the larger Mughul Empire in its emphasis upon the synchretic coexistence of faiths, and blending of architectural and other art forms.

The two historical figures I have used in this volume of BLOOD OF THE GODDESS are Chand Bibi, the Sultana of Ahmadnagar, and Ibrahim 'Adilshah II, her nephew, the Sultan of Bijapur. Chand Bibi was one of the few historically documented warrior queens of India, renowned for her strategic skill, as well as her ability to survive numerous assassination attempts (historically attributed to her ambitious sons). Although Prince Murad, who harassed her kingdom, died from his alcoholism in 1599, Ahmadnagar did not withstand the might of Akbar's empire much longer, and fell in 1600, despite being stoutly defended by Chand Bibi. Alas, her skill in personal survival could not last forever as well and in April of 1600 she at last was felled by assassination.

The great Emperor Akbar, for all his wisdom and power, was not immune to family politics either, and died in 1605, poisoned by his son Salim.

Ibrahim 'Adilshah II was, as described in *Bijapur*, a lover of the arts, particularly music. The story of his daughter being returned to life by a pagan yogi is from the historical accounts (another of the kinds of coincidence between research and story that makes historical fiction such a pleasure to write), and is given as the reason Ibrahim dallied with paganism despite the heavy Islamic influence in Bijapur.

The description of the journey from Bicholim to Bijapur is based upon "The Travels of Abbe Carré," a French cleric who made the trip in 1672—the only near-contemporary account I could find of that road.

Although English colonies did not take root in India until later, individual Englishmen such as Ralph Fitch, Peter Mundy, and Sir Thomas Roe, visited India during the late sixteenth, early seventeenth century, mostly for purposes of trade. Many details from their travel diaries have been used in *Bijapur*, particularly descriptions of food, drink, and local plants.

Over the course of writing this work, I have learned that India is a lifetime study—several lifetimes, in fact, given that it is a continent with millennia of history, over three million square miles in area, a great variety of cultures, religions, and over seven hundred languages. And yet the author must give up the research and sit down to write at some point. Therefore, any errors that have crept into the text are solely mine, due to insufficient time and research.

Again, I'd like to thank Denny Lien of the Edwin O. Wilson Library at the University of Minnesota for all his assistance years ago in assembling research materials for me; as well as my former writer's group, The Scribblies (Steven Brust, Emma Bull, Pamela Dean, and Will Shetterly) for their critique on the first incarnation of this work; my husband, John Barnes, for his patience; and all the innumerable others who added snippets of historical and cultural detail that add such richness to a work of this sort.